The Totally Awesome Mega Writers Club

The Second Compendium

A Collection of Stories

The Totally Awesome Mega Writers Club is a club of new and previously unpublished authors. None of the proceeds of this book will be used to fund terrorism, ecological destruction, hate fuelled political demonstrations or purchases of fast food. No particular political allegiance is favoured or implied favourably by any aspect of this book.

Please tell your friends to buy our book? Thank you.
All proceeds go towards to funding the monthly club meetings, which keeps us off the streets and away from starting trouble!

A note from our Glorious Leader, 'Head Honcho'.

OK, folks, just settle down and we'll get under way.

you've all got the handout as e-book or hard copy so I'd just like to make a few points before you start.

We aren't expecting any police raids today although you never know. With the contents of these stories there's obviously grounds for Suss – especially with Isis in there

This compendium is tighter than the first, and numbered despite the rearguard action of our anarchist cadre.

Sidney is for our younger fans, including the young-at-heart, but I am sure its based on fact.

If you are allergic to trolls or, indeed, cats,

ghosts or ungrateful offspring, please keep your anti-histamine to hand. The management cannot be held responsible for random enjoyment. George, don't do that!

Throughout the journey you will find coffee breaks for your convenience. Please be aware that there is no convenience anywhere in the book. There are also quaint, meandering poems through which you are invited to wander.

So, now you can just get on with it – and no talking at the back.

Table of Contents

And now for something amazingly rural

By Sally ann Nixon

They had a pig race this afternoon. Up on the Castle fields. It was a lovely day, warm with a bit of breeze and a lot of Welsh ice cream. You could bet on your pig - £1 a stake and there was a great cheer when a dozen trailers, full of snorting porkers arrived, with bright ribbons tied around their necks. We picked up our race cards and made for the ox roast. Normally town functions include a pig roast but we expect they were being tactful.

Clutching a warm beer and an unidentifiable cut of beef, we strolled down to the race track, the field full of stalls selling all things piggy. Figurines, garden ornaments, knitted Miss Piggys, piggy cushions, you name it.

There was a crowd at the track and betting on

the pigs was frantic. The pigs in question, very clean, neat and a bit bemused were being marshaled to the starting point, behind a barrier. We placed a bet on Violet, with a ribbon to match around her neck, a large, strong looking brindled pig with hairy knees and air of confidence. Never mind that her ribbon was such a pretty colour. I put my money and my trust in her.

A man in a vest and shorts, wellies and a large cloth cap clumped halfway up the field to the finishing line and waved a large bag of apples and vegetables. The pigs suddenly became alert and we thought that Violet seemed particularly interested. Small children began to jump up and down, a whistle blew, the barrier lifted and they were off - six squealing, elbowing, trampling porkers, all intent on getting to the mound of food first. Violet briefly took the lead, then became distracted by a sweet wrapper on the ground. But she quickly lost interest and galloped gamely on. Dogs yelped and barked, a couple of Jack Russells attempted to join in the melee, only to be dragged to safety by their owners as the trotters thundered by.

Still elbowing and squealing with excitement the pigs homed in on the veggie pile. And stopped dead, champing down the peelings, apples and carrots as fast as they could. Violet came in second, despite her short lapse of concentration. We felt pleased with our small winnings and our faith in her was justified.

The winner, a pink pig who looked more crackling than brain was awarded a red rosette and was paraded around the field by her owner, to be patted and congratulated. We thought Violet looked pleased to be spared such a fate.

The Llandovery silver band struck up a stirring

tune and marched off in procession behind the winning pig. Violet was last seen dozing peacefully in the straw in her trailer, her ribbon gone and a few fresh carrots under her nose.

With the second race not due for half an hour, we wandered off to the beer tent for yet more warm beer. The day began to cloud over. This is Wales after all. But rain held off. The next two races were just as exciting. One pig tried to escape into the crowd in the direction of a Pastie stall and in the third race our favoured pig refused to hurry at all. Instead she ambled after the others seeming to relish the smiles and laughter of the crowd , thanking them for their goodwill and encouragement but really it was sooo warm darling...

It was all over by 4 o'clock. The pigs were back in their trailers and the stalls were coming down A few drops of rain began to fall. Wales was asserting herself but at least she had smiled upon the pigs.

ISIS and Nut

By Margaret Ingram

The garden was quiet at the break of day. The gentle easing of dark night into grey and black shading was moving slowly into the acquisition of colour as Isis strutted slowly past the laurel tree and fountain, over the low wall into the herbs and under the spreading leaves of the Sage bush in the centre. Isis lay full-length under its fragrant shade, head turned slightly towards the south west. Beyond the villa walls imperial Rome was waking. Sleep came easily and it was full day when Isis opened her eyes again. She was still in shade but the rest of the bed was bright. The voice of Grassius Majorus had woken her. The softer tones of Lola Capriuna floated over her, but she listened carefully because there was the tone she knew meant an argument was in full swing. Grassius had a habit of throwing things and kicking cats when he lost arguments with the mistress. Which he normally did. His deep sounds came again. There was a break then Lola laughed and then he did too. Safe to come out.

Isis stretched and slithered out from her soft couch. The people were over by the fountain, so she strutted across the earth, leapt up onto the wall and paraded along it, jumping down at the far end to reach the shadow under the fountain basin. Lola stood behind Grassius facing Isis and the fountain so Isis rubbed against Grassius' leg and purred. He jumped and then bent down and picked her up, cradling her and stroking. "Good morning beautiful Isis" he almost purred. Lola reached out and stroked her ear and bid her good morning as well. So she mewed back at them, and then started to purr. Cradled in his arms she was taken to the outdoor dining area and he put her

14

on the couch as he arranged himself to eat breakfast. Lola lay down beside him and offered him a titbit of fish then reached over to offer Isis a piece too. Thus the breakfast went along with Isis getting the best from both of her people. Around the villa the rest of the city was starting its daily hubbub. Some of the noise, heavily filtered by the walls and plants, filtered through to the garden but was so normal none of the individuals breaking their fast registered it.

Eventually she had had enough and decided to find a cool spot until she was hungry again. She stood, stretched, and wandered away, circling the other dining couch and heading indoors. The atrium was cool in the mornings and Isis could keep a watch on comings and goings, bestowing her blessing on anyone who stroked her. The door porter sat in his alcove by the front door and opened it as Grassius's clients arrived. They all made a point of stroking her as they passed. Her presence was a sign that all was well. They came alone or in small groups and filed through to the waiting corridor outside Grassius' library where they sat quietly or stood waiting to greet their patron. Over the years the number had grown as his status had increased and now he was a major trader in skins and hides his clients were many and varied. He had given some excellent sables to the emperor's wife a couple of months ago and that had cemented his status. For a middle ranker, an equestrian, he was pretty well set up.

Eventually, when all the business of the day had been negotiated, Grassius and his tail of hangers-on walked out of the house. They were going to the baths and then on to the Emporium but Isis not only did not know this, she did not care. She was awake now and considering her next meal when the door was kicked and then opened again. This time it was a woman who entered and she not only did not stroke Isis, she ignored her completely as she walked quickly through. The door porter closed the door and ran after her, calling something out, but the new woman did not slow down. She went straight through into the garden while Isis sat up and preened herself, waiting to find out whether this happening presaged food in the mistress's rooms.

Isis was just getting round to her tail when the woman came out with the mistress following. They were talking quietly and then Isis heard them giggle which jogged something and made the woman's name float into her mind. Numilla! The human of Sekhmet. The mistress called for her stola, wrapped it around herself when the maid brought it and linked arms with Numilla as they left. Isis saw them climb into a litter before the slave shut the front door. So the cook was probably the best source of food. Isis rose and stretched and sauntered into the kitchen, rubbed around the cook's legs and got a plate of meat shreds for her trouble.

*

On the other side of the Viminal Hill, Nut was washing herself in a shady corner of the terrace along the east side of the house. She had just eaten a very plump little bird that had had the misfortune to fall from its nest. The last few feathers were stirring in the breeze which blessed the garden in the hottest months. She might wander into the courtyard in a few moments to lie in the sun and warm her bones. She licked one paw carefully while she considered this. It really seemed a good idea as she knew her young human would soon be out playing after her lessons. Nut liked the youngster because she was very clever. Some way or another she seemed to read Nut's wants most of the time. Nut stood and made obeisance to the sun, stretching her back and legs and making her tail shake briskly. Then she paraded across the terrace and down the steps into the garden proper. She heard the classroom door open and her human's feet come skipping towards the open air. She decided to run to the human since that seemed to get her extra cuddles.

The human scooped Nut up and laughed and snuggled her face into Nut's hair almost like a cat herself. Nut purred appropriately. The girl put her down and said something while stroking Nut's cheek. Nut realised the human was interrogating her so exuded hunger. It worked. Off they went towards the kitchen and both were given bowls of seafood, one of Nuts favourites. The girl also got some bread which Nut knew would attract birds. Mm she thought.

Afters! Then remembered that the girl didn't like Nut catching the birds. Well, Nut could still have fun chasing them while not actually catching them, which was a good way to make the girl laugh and love as she should do.

In the garden they played and ate for a while. Nut was beginning to need a cat nap when Drusilla, the mistress of the house breezed in and like a strong wind disarranged everything. The girl was swept up in the woman's wake and, another two women, who wore lots of jangly jewellery, was taken into the house and up to the top floor. The mistress's friends were often in the house and Nut did not mind either of them much, since they often petted her and each had one of Nut's pounce in their homes. Nut knew that the roof would be so hot. Humans were very strange creatures to want to brave the sun and heat of the top of the building. She found herself a quiet shadow and sat waiting. As she had hoped a bird, one that had been eating the girl's bread, came bobbing along. Nut stalked, vibrated appropriately and pounced. Afters!

On the roof Drusilla Longina quizzed her grand daughter on the lessons she had had that morning and then let her go to play with the toys in the sand pit in one corner of the roof. Drusilla's sister, Apollonia Capriuna, known as Lola, had listened to the questioning and now sat back to condemn the programme the child's mother Flora Maxinia had set up. They were happy to find fault with everything their elder brother's wife did, but Drusilla had an ulterior motive in her campaign. Her best friend had recently been divorced by her husband and needed a new marriage. Drusilla wanted the woman to marry her brother and had to get rid of Flora for that, which would not be easy as Flora had given the family two sons and a daughter. This had given Flora a place of high regard in the family, which Drusilla had never had.

*

Looking back over the last few days Grassius could not help feeling proud of himself. He had made some fine deals recently and been worried that he was becoming too visible to the palace freedmen. He paid his dues to two of the palace clerks who controlled trade in furs and skins and made occasional gifts to the city praetors and to a whole bunch of senators, as everyone did to make sure their business thrived. The chance to make a gift to the emperor or his wife didn't usually come his way but Marcellus Domitius, the most important freedman he dealt with, had organised the ticket for the poetry reading and then introduced Grassius to the empress. He had the cloak ready and she had been delighted with it. Grassius knew it was fine quality but had made sure it was unique, shades of palest to darkest grey in a leaf pattern. He had been gratified that she had recognised its beauty, had seen it in her eyes, had heard it in the little intake of breath. Now, as he luxuriated at the baths, surrounded by his clients he relaxed. He was sure the link to the empress would keep anyone from trying to stop him trading or trying to take over his business. Another two years as profitable as the last one and he would retire, leaving his eldest son in charge. Pacius was quite good at the job, and his wife, Melissina, was as good a businesswoman as his own Lola. He must talk this over with Lola this evening.   He watched the bath house cat wander past, tail in the air, stepping over or around any puddles. It was known to swim, sometimes from choice and sometimes when bathers kicked it into the pools. He wondered idly if other cats could swim.

The cat, whose name was Bast, caught the edge of his thought and purred to himself. The human owned a cat who could not only swim but who, should she choose to, could fly through the air. Of course that was not difficult for a goddess. Bast himself, not quite as accomplished as Isis, could move from one place to another without being anywhere in between. Of course he didn't do it very often, since it left his fur full of static which itched. He sauntered on, through the archway into the cool plunge pool room.

He wandered along until he could leap up a tree, onto the lowest branch. He climbed the trunk until he could walk alone the branch which reached over the 12 foot high wall between the pool yard and the alley behind the baths. From the top of the wall he leaped across to the roof of the house on the other side of the alley. From roof to roof, wall to wall, he jinked and leaped his way down the hill and finally ended on the roof of the house where Isis lived.

*

As he started towards the Emporium Grassius saw his old friend Maxillus leaving the baths just ahead and turning south like him. He strode out to catch up and greeted Maxillus. They spoke of trade and walked along together. Maxillus seemed distracted and finally Grassius asked if everything was alright. Maxillus stopped and looked around. They were near a wine shop and he suggested a drink in there. Grassius, intrigued by this unusual behaviour from his long-time friend agreed readily and after they were seated and served asked again. "My wife," said Maxillus, "is a bitch and, frankly I'm fed up with her and her family. I've got a nice young woman from a good home who is interested in marrying me, and she has a good dowry. Rosalba Roscius is just twenty, sweet and well behaved. Drusilla, as you know is forty, bossy and ... well I'm fed up spending money of the boys left, right and centre. First they want this then that. Not one of the three of them has any interest in the business, or the cursus. I wouldn't mind if they had ambitions to be senators or farmers or something but they try this then that and all the time it's me who pays. It wasn't so bad until I met Rosalba. The daft thing is I was looking for a wife for the oldest lad which is how I met her. He doesn't deserve a sweet young girl like her." Maxillus sat back and looked into his wine cup. Grassius didn't know what to say. He actually loved his wife, Lola, and quite liked Drusilla. She was quite bossy but that didn't worry him. But then he wasn't married to her. On the other hand, Lola was quite bossy but could have some good ideas and also didn't interfere too much. He asked Maxillus what he planned to do and Maxillus shook his head. "I'm going to divorce Drusilla, but I don't think it will be pleasant."

Grassius thought about it and couldn't help but agree. In fact he thought it would be downright dangerous. Drusilla and the boys, who were all over twenty and quite active, muscular lads, were close enough to gang up against Maxillus. A new wife might produce a new heir who could put them all aside. Grassius couldn't think of anything to say which was positive so he took a gulp of the wine. The wine shop's cat sat and watched them. She was interested in both of them since they had an air about them which indicated contact with important cats. She smelled the aura of Bast on the fatter ones thoughts. The other one had the smell of a sacrifice, an aura of Bes. Interesting. She strolled away to let Horus know. Neither man noticed her.

Bettia was boiling over with anger. She stood in the atrium and clenched and unclenched her fists while bouncing slightly on the balls of her feet. Her maid, Miriam, watched from the arch into the dining room. In this mood her normally decent mistress could lash out. She was close enough to answer any order and far enough distant to avoid any pain. The house cat sauntered into the atrium , sat down and started cleaning her paws. Anuket had heard the exchange between Bettia and her brother-in-law and was interested in the outcome. The man had left now and Bettia was radiating anger so vividly that Anuket's hair was standing on end along her spine.

Eventually Bettia stopped bouncing and started thinking more rationally. Vidius had just told her he was bringing some friends back to dinner that night. His friends were drunken bores who would molest the servants and probably vomit over her furniture. Her husband, Milo, would drink too much with them, all the while being snubbed and belittled by his brother and the friends even though he was the host providing the wine and food. Tomorrow Milo would feel ill and Vidius would mock him. She despised Vidius and was coming to lump Milo in with him. They had been happy before Vidius came to live with them. From the legions, serving in Africa and then in Gaul he had suddenly left, with no real explanation, about two years before his term had finished. Some scandal had been hidden by his friends in the legion but it had left Vidius penniless and so Milo and Bettia had got him as an unwanted guest. Milo had suggested he might like to stay on the family farm in the

Apennines but he had rudely told Milo what he could do with the farm, the mountains and his suggestion. Milo had said nothing.

It was twelve weeks since he had arrived and in that time Bettia had come to loath Vidius, his voice, his smell and most of all his attitude of superiority. As a course, selfish and arrogant, typical Roman male he couldn't be bettered. She was a kind person and usually got on well with most people. Vidius treated her worse then she treated her slaves and she often ended up shouting at him. Unfortunately, that just made him laugh. It was going to be unfortunate for him if she had her way. Anuket caught the thought and purred. Human sacrifice was imminent. She stood, stretched and padded over to Bettia, rubbing against her legs and purring. Mirriam stepped forward and Bettia turned towards her. "Get me some tea, girl, in the garden." and stormed off.

Sitting sipping bergamot tea Bettia sorted out her staff and organised the dinner. She sent a message to her husband warning him of the change in plans and asking him to bring two of his business slaves to help out with the extra work. She sat back and thought about the whole mess. Anuket was asleep under her chair while she sorted dinner out but woke and emerged to sit at her feet as she relaxed. Bettia found her thoughts turning to permanently removing Vidius. Could they pay him to go? She didn't think of anything which would tempt him away from Rome. Even a place of his own in the city wouldn't prevent his leechlike grip on Milo and their income. She wished he would choke on his own vomit one night after stuffing himself and drinking his normal overload. The idea was pleasant, rolling through her mind like a play. If only she could organise it without any risk of getting caught.

That would be the final insult from Vidius, to lose everything for killing him. Anyway Milo would never agree. Bettia rose and walked purposefully into her bedroom. She changed into her second finest dress and got Mirria to redo her hair in a high and intricate fashion. She took Mirria with her as she left in the household's litter for the Gardens of Agrippa.

Anuket rose and stalked out of the garden and through the scullery to the back door. She hurried to her mother's house and settled down with Isis in a warm patch of garden. They were happy that the plan was taking hold. Later Bast called in and they stroked and preened each other as the news was exchanged.

*

Marcus Africanis Plautus marched into the dining room and plonked himself down on his couch. The slaves jumped to fetch his wine and food while the rest of the family hurried to arrange themselves around the tables. His wife had died, some said of misery, nine years before. He housed his two sons and the wife of the eldest, Brutus Ampilus, and their three children. His daughter-in-law, Agila, was responsible for running the household for him. She did it well, and was thrifty and hardworking but he didn't give her any respect; perfection by her was merely the minimum he expected and anything less was the cause of vicious condemnation. He had been known to hit her husband for her failures. He dare not hit her since she was the daughter of a senator and he had never achieved that rank. Brutus had hit her afterwards, and then apologised and cried. Her husband was not a cruel man but his father drove him into a corner. A lot of their time and energy was spent protecting the children. Plautus had a dog which he used to intimidate the slaves and the children. It had tried to upset the house cat, Agila's Heket, known as Hekky, but a quick flash of claws and a leap onto its back had made the dog very aware of its place in the house. Hekky was lauded for her bravery and success in putting the dog, and thus the master, in his place. Plautus hated Hekky but never managed to get anywhere in his sly attempts to kick her, banish her or get his own back. He had ordered her got rid of but had to rescind the order within a week when the house had become overrun with mice and bats and even spiders. He forbade her to enter his rooms even now. Hekky had stayed with Bast for the duration of her exile and rarely stayed in the same space as Plautus now. She did dump live mice in his office from time to time via the window, which Plautus believed was too high to reach and waited for him to find their teeth marks on nibbled scrolls and droppings in his columbarium. He blamed her but she always cleared them out rapidly when he let her into his rooms.

Bettia arrived as the morning break was beginning. Agila gave her a hug and they sat under the shade of the terrace to drink their peppermint tea. They swapped pleasantries until the staff were out of the way and then swapped spite-filled accounts of the morning.

*

On another part of the hill in a road of quiet opulence there was a walled house where Lola and Namilla, the old friend who had collected her from her home, arrived in a cloud of giggles and innuendo. Their hostess was annoyed that they were obviously so close. She led them through the house to the garden and sat them under the shade of the central pine. Nobody could overhear or creep up on them there. Nut watched as her main human brought the other members of her pounce.

They all took a glass of bergamot tea and nibbled the sweet pastries set out for them. Drusilla, very stiff in her role of hostess, listened as they tried to explain their amusement but her straight face and pursed lips quickly calmed them down and they lapsed into a guilty silence. When she had ensured they would listen carefully she started to discuss their plan. They had started out several days ago with a tipsy joke about killing each other's least favourite person. Lola wanted to strangle her mother-in-law while Namilla's sister-in-law needed smothering. Drusilla wanted to kill her husband and didn't really care how it happened as long as she wasn't caught. Lola had been the one to have the idea that had solved their problems. "We wouldn't get caught if we did each other's murders" she had giggled. That had sobered Drusilla up and she had thought about it for a couple of days. Finally she had spoken to Lola, the more sensible of the two others. Lola had been convinced but worried about Namilla's ability to keep her mouth shut. Drusilla was more worried about Namilla having a hold over them, because she knew Namilla had blackmailed her husband into divorcing his first wife and marrying her. The fact that Lola didn't know about that incident made Drusilla very aware of how tight –lipped Namilla could be. Lola again came up with a plan.

"Bet we're not the only ones who need a death to improve their life." She had mused one afternoon. "Bettia for example has that awful brother-in-law living with them and I have heard her wishing him dead."

Drusilla didn't know this Bettia so asked Lola to introduce them. After a few meetings

Drusilla agreed that Bettia was another potential member of the club. She had also thought about her brother's sister-in law, Agila, who was stuck under a tyrannical father-in-law's roof. She wasn't totally convinced the husband would be any better after his father dropped off the twig, but thought it was worth finding out.

This meeting of the three original friends had been arranged to organise a simple swop of targets to ensure each had an unassailable alibi when their soon-to-be-mourned person died. Lola had Bettia's token and Drusilla had Agila's. They had agreed to keep the knowledge of who did what to a minimum. Each of the 5 had produced a token which she could identify. The five tokens were put in a bag and each took one of them out, making sure it was not their own. Each token contained a description of the target and a brief timetable of where the target would be and when over the next ten days. They hid the tokens from each other and, slipping their sandals back on, set out to the gardens of Agrippa to meet the other two accidently upon purpose.

Bettia was sitting on a bench by the statue of Augustus and took her token neatly, making it unclear whether she was involved or not if anyone had been watching. Only the gods watched and they knew everything anyway. Agila chatted and hugged for a couple of minutes and then deftly took the bag with the last token and walked away. Drusilla took her leave of the other two and Namilla and Lola walked up the hill to Namilla's house, where, saying she needed to walk, Lola parted company and wandered alone down the hill towards her home. She arrived dusty and very tired. That evening she complained of fatigue and went early to bed, with Isis snuggling up to her. The next day she stayed in bed and, though she assured Grassilus she was alright, was unable to eat at mealtimes and very weak and tired. Namilla called the next day and only stayed a few minutes. When she got home she had a really bad cough. By that evening two of the conspirators were sick in bed and being left alone most of the time. Bettia had left Rome and was staying about five miles out of town with her cousin. The cousin was old and daft and would swear Bettia was with her all the time.

Drusilla went about her normal routine which included an afternoon nap which no one was allowed to disturb unless the house was burning around her ears. Agila spent hours with friends at the baths, the one place her father in law could not chase her. She used different baths and met various friends who would remember her but not exactly which day she had been there.

The days slipped by and two women and three men died in fairly normal circumstances. One older woman slipped in her atrium and broke her neck, another, younger woman chocked on a piece of must cake. There were a series of knife attacks on the hill and in one of these an unmarried man was killed as he returned to his brother's house, where he had been living for nearly two years. Agila's father in law died of a heart attack at the house of his mistress and Drusilla's husband was the only one in the family who died after they all ate some mushrooms one night. Drusilla was heartbroken! Her son, Titus Majorus, took great care of her and her daughter-in-law, Anthea, was a good housekeeper so Drusilla could sit back and relax. The mistress was evicted from her apartment and Titus let it to a very

41

respectable teacher of Rhetoric and his wife. The wife, Calpurnia Maccibus, was an amateur fortune teller and soon became firm friends with Drusilla.

The five women settled into their improved circumstances and took to regularly meeting for afternoon chats. Agila positively blossomed after the death of her father-in-law. Her husband was a good head of the family and started to make the family richer. Even her mother-in-law cheered up and stopped picking faults with her. Agila was even allowed to get a pet cat, one of the litter Isis produced as the year drew towards its end. She called the kitten Sekhmet and bought a new basket for her.

Bettia had a little trouble with her husband, who began to allow his brother's friends to arrive and drink to their dead benefactor. Milo was a gentle-hearted man and didn't know how to stop them. Indeed he rather enjoyed the fact that his brother was so fondly remembered. Bettia stopped it one evening when she had got Milo to attend the poetry reading given by a client of Titus Majorus. She suddenly had to stay home with a terrible head ache. She had sent the friends of Vidius an invitation and they duly turned up. They were seated and drinks were given out. The slaves didn't know where their master was, so sorry, have another drink, have some olives, some stuffed onions. When the men were fairly well lubricated Bettia marched in and told them she had put something nasty in the wine. The next time they showed their faces here she would kill them, even if they took nothing to drink or eat. From behind her stepped a vision of hell, a woman dressed as Hecate. Behind her was a midget god, Set, who started to dance around, chanting. Suddenly the visitors were surrounded by hundreds of spitting, angry cats.

One of the drunks, less sanguine than the others, perhaps the most gullible, leaped to his feet. A large black tomcat jumped onto his back and another, this one grey tabby, climbed up his leg and bit his hand as the ex -soldier tried to knock him off. Set kept up his chant and Hecate joined in with an ululating, nerve-jangling song. The cats jumped for the other guests, who now ran and stumbled for the atrium and front door. If they tried to turn or slow the cats leapt and boiled over them, all spitting and clawing. The superstitious man was the first out of the door but, a few steps down the avenue he turned and, shaking a fist, yelled that he would see what Milo had to say. Bast was among the cats and followed him home. That night the man fell heavily asleep and Bast considered killing him then and there. Realising his actions could rebound on Bettia he held his wrath, waiting patiently until the man awoke the following afternoon. Heading for the baths with a bad hangover the old soldier was unlucky enough to be hit in the head by a falling flowerpot. The poor woman on the fifth floor balcony swore she was nowhere near it when the pot fell. She was well liked in the neighbourhood so several of the other women swore they had seen her and seen the man being hit. She was not blamed for his death. Bast was pleased.

The mother of Grassius Majorus was a small, neat body who bustled around with a smile touching her lips and a household which ran like the Tiber itself, never stopping and never making too many waves. Like the Tiber, as well, it set the tempo for the life around her. All her acquaintances followed her patterns and agreed with her attitudes or very quickly dropped out of the social life they needed to survive otherwise meaningless and empty lives. Veminia Plautia ran a house where the slaves were very good at anything they did. They cleaned to perfection, cooked and sewed exactly how the mistress wanted and rarely stopped work from dawn until bedtime, making hand work if nothing else, except at the three short meal breaks she allowed them. These trifles were given to her friends and family by Veminia on odd occasions. Her own body servant, Della, was a marvellous needlewoman who turned little weaves and offcuts into embroidered herb sachets which pleased anyone who had to walk through Rome. Holding the sachet near your nose was a sovereign protection against the pong of people and their households. Like all tyrants Verminia never had to raise her voice with her family. The mere thought of her disapproval was enough to terrify each of them. Lola was quick to learn her place and spent a great deal of time placating her husband's mother. However much she did, however, Lola never forgot that she was unable to override any decision taken by Verminia or her husband with Verminia's approval. The summer trip to the country was part of this. Everyone squashed into the country villa for the height of the summer and it was a yearly ordeal for Lola. They had just come back to Rome, which was why Grassius and Lola had been on the edge of another row that morning. Over the years she had learnt to use her sense of humour to avoid confrontation. This morning she had laughed aside her request, but she knew where her enemy lay. Verminia had arranged a tutor for the children and now she was organising their training in the business. Lola was very angry, but not surprised. She wished the stiff-necked old hag were dead. Isis heard the thought and wrapped it around herself. Stiff necks could break. Another human sacrifice would be warm and sustaining.

Daisy's shiny button

By Margaret McNerlin

There among the litter that lay around the demolition site, no one, not even the magpie, had noticed this bright shiny object, it lay there by some daisies, dejected and unloved, until Daisy found it. She had been walking about, feeling dejected, she also felt unloved, just like the button. She picked it up and put it in her pocket, her special pocket, where she placed things that she wanted to keep safe. There it lay until one day she felt its shiny surface as she put her hands into her pocket. Where did it come from? Who did it belong to? It started to make her imagination wondering who it had belonged to.

Did it belong to a lady, who unlike her, was so rich, it didn't matter to her, that she had lost it or perhaps she had mourned the loss of it. What had this lovely button come off? It could have been off a beautiful gown, she thought, as the tears slipped down her cheek, thinking how she would have loved to have own as dress such as this.

Daisy continued on her way, looking for objects she could sell, which is one way she could bring in some money, for her Mother. It could have been a different way of life for Daisy, had she not have been abandoned at birth, by her young birth-Mother.

Luckily for Daisy, it had been a warm night that she had been found in the cardboard box, by a clump of daisies, hence her name. The Gypsy who found her was a kindly lady, who took great care of her, until she was old enough to help with different jobs. For some unknown reason she called her button, Daisy didn't mind, but there had been times she had wondered, what her life would have been like had she not been abandoned by her real Mother. She would often dream "What if" dreams. Sometimes she would have been a princess who had been kidnapped, then at other times her Mother could have been a circus acrobat who had been sold to another circus, but then she would wake up and think of the lady, who had rescued her, who had loved and cared for her, it was then that she had wondered about how she came to be a Gypsy, who was she, and where she had come from, for she didn't seem to have any other family.

That is when Daisy felt the similarity to her, and that special shiny button in her pocket. She in turn had been like the bright shiny button, the Gypsy had picked her up, when she found her lost in a field, and had taken great care of her wondering like Daisy, where she had come from. Until the time that both found out the answer to their question, they would both love and care for the bright shiny button they had found by the clump of daisies in the field.

The Black and White Picture

By Jayne Hecate

The sweat stood out on his brow, pin pricks of moisture that told a story of their own. His eyes, narrowed, his stare was intent, as intent as the blade in his hand. When a man holds a blade like this, he is going to use it, the intention was written in the air around him, but his eyes told a different truth, behind the intention was fear. Fear born in feelings of a youth spent sat alone, on a couch built for three. It was the fear to connect, the fear of being alone among a throng of people. His hand tightened on the knife, the angles of the black plastic handle biting into his soft fingers. He took a breath, pushing the fear to the bottom of his stomach, pushing away the spiteful condescending voice in his head that told him exactly how worthless he was. Where had that critical and angry voice come from? It was the voice of a man that had gone away and never returned.

He had been six years old when his father left, leaving behind a wife with a bruised heart and black eyes that matched the shape of his fists. The man did not even turn back to say good bye. The door slammed shut one last time, leaving behind the hole that he had once painfully filled in his boy's life. Thirty years later, that slamming door still haunted the boy, who had finally grown into a man, afraid of his weakness, terrified of his own strength; fearful that he would follow the missing father who had acted out his violence destroying those too weak to stop him, using his physical bulk to pound his demands into those around him, the man who was in every way the classic bully, hiding his fear through tyranny.

The knife felt alien, it was designed with a

purpose, the blade edge so fine, it cut the air when moved. The plastic handle was cheap; the moulded plastic hollow inside, held together by the appearance of strong rivets, but in truth, all that held the two plastic halves onto the tang, was cheap brown glue. The sharp metal edges slid out of the handle by less than the width of a fine baby hair, enough to make the handle feel painful in an over tight grip, but not enough to cause harm. The fake rivets were given the look of being hammered, but hammered plastic that looked fake. He looked at the handle, the blade extending from his hand like a steel insult, it was itself a fake, a cheap Chinese knock off of an expensive chef's knife. If the knife were capable of thoughtful self-awareness enough to know that it was a fake, it would have recognised the same truth about the man who wielded it, the failure of a man who had his fist closed around the handle.

He had read somewhere, that once the first cut was made, the rest simply followed. But where to cut first? Where could he make that decisive incision that would guide him to the next and the next? How could he demonstrate his love if he could not even make the first cut?

He had met her at school, the girl with the blonde ponytail, the girl who danced the ballet, the girl who sang the school song with the grace and passion of a symphony. If she had ever noticed him, she had hidden it. He was at her first performance, a school play in which she danced the Swan, her lace and frills rising into the air as she spun. He had not understood the feelings that he had felt, but he knew the message from his father. Women were to be owned, dominated, not respected.

He went to college; on his first day she arrived in his class, her face as uncertain as his, the huge campus intimidated them both, but she was more honest about it. When she found her people, she found herself and set the woman within her free. He found a crowd of his own, the ones who hid in the dark, the ones who shunned the sports and the powerful bodies. He stayed away from the masculine, the toxic maleness that made men critical of themselves and more critical of the women around them. He felt the sting and the stink of it, the sick reminder of the father who had beaten his mother until her face bled, until her arms wore the bruises of a victim too broken to fight back.

He saw the dancer dance again, she was older, no more a teenager, she was woman, mature and strong. Her dance a powerful story of its own that sang of gentleness, of resilience, of the joy in pure movement. He watched from the side, a rapture inside of him. Her movements spoke the words that he could never utter and then her eyes found his in a moment and she smiled, actually smiled at him.

The knife trembled slightly in his fingers, the tip raised up and he stared at the end, his intention flowing through the steel and out of the end in the limp premature ejaculate of failure. He heard the voice again, the toxic voice of repression, shouting him down for his weakness. All it took was that one first cut and then it would flow from him, his art expressed in the movements of the blade, but would she smile then? Would she stare at him knowing him to the be the faker that he felt inside? Her hand reached out, she ached with compassion, her eyes tired, her body exhausted after the dance.

They made the cut. His broken soul had healed. Her face wore a smile, her kiss a loving kindness. The toxic masculinity had been purged from his soul. The dancer, had blushed and then said yes, together they shared love, together they cut the wedding cake.

A Trip to a Coffee Shop

By Jan Housby

Lying in the hospital bed, I clutched the tiny gold key hanging from the charm bracelet my Grandma had given to me on my seventh birthday. She had told me it had magical powers and that it could open doors to places that only I could go. I refused to take it off when I went to bed that night, and indeed it stayed on my wrist until I was 13 years old, when I decided I was too old for fairy tales. But for every night I wore the bracelet, I was taken in my dreams to an exquisite place only I could enter – I can still remember the amazement I felt when I woke in the morning.

I hadn't been to this place since I was a child, but I had never forgotten it. And now, eighty years on, lying here in a hospital bed awaiting a general anaesthetic, I once again clutched tightly that beautiful, ornate little key between my thumb and finger. My Grand-daughter Anya had found it in my bedroom at home and had brought it in for me, at my request. I knew there was a fair chance I wouldn't be coming round from this operation. My last will and testament was complete; it was just that I wanted to experience this magical place if this was to be my last time here.

"Mrs Franks, I'm going to place this mask over your face. Just breathe in normally, and start counting back from ten with me".

The anaesthetist's voice was as clear as a bell, and I began the count-back with her. "Ten, nine, eight", this was never going to work, I was as conscious as the day I was born. "seven, six….", and that was it, I was gone, into the most blissful world.

In front of me was a red brick wall – no

windows, no doors. It went on and up forever, no beginning and no end. There were no windows and no doors. However, as I focussed and looked down at the ground, there was a tiny wooden front door, painted a shiny royal blue. Without doing or thinking anything at all, I became as small as the door. There was no way to see what was the other side of the door, but I knew. I had longed to see this place again. It had been nearly eighty years since the last time I was here. I placed the key in the lock, turned it and watched as the door swung open by itself. "Welcome back", said a jovial, male voice, although the voice was not attached to any body. It just floated in the air like a merry tune. "Do come in, this is your place, and yours alone. It is so nice to see you again".

I stepped across the threshold and immediately felt that I had come home at last, after a lifetime of lurching from one trauma to another. There had been landmarks of great joy in that life, but it had been an uphill journey. Now I was finally home, I could let it all go, both the good and the bad, and just be. I took a breath and looked around me. All was exactly as I'd left it. I smiled and remembered. In the ordinary, everyday world I'd found coffee shops the most dull places on earth as a child, and I failed to understand why my Mother insisted on dragging me in to them. I suspect it was more to do with her and my sister-in-law needing the 'facilities' following their visit to a previous coffee shop in the day. This was different though. On frosted shelves around the walls were Victorian decorated plates stacked high with every variety of cakes and biscuits. They were every colour imaginable, laden with sweets and dusted with gold powder.

As I gazed in awe and wonderment, the ground

shifted beneath me. I wobbled and for a moment thought I would fall. The grass had woken up, and as it stretched it had caused ripples beneath my feet. "Thou'd better sit thyself down, lass", the grass said. "Thank you", I said. A pink mallow chair appeared behind me and I stumbled backwards into it, sinking into the warm, lush, velvety cushion. It enveloped every bone in my body and smelt of pure strawberries. I pulled a bit off and ate it. Divine!

My attention was suddenly drawn back to the grass under my feet. "Am I not squashing you?", I enquired meekly. The reply was somewhat muffled admittedly, but the reply was a resounding, "No!!! I get far worse than you sitting on me!". I giggled. The grass, suddenly deep in thought, spoke out loud. "Actually it's nice and dark being beneath your shadow, I think at long last I can get some sleep. Before I do, would you like to eat a bit of me? I'm quite tasty, an invigorating lime jelly flavour."

"Thank you", I said, "it'd be rude not to", but before I could even place a strand in my mouth the grass was snoring.

As the mallow chair wrapped me gently in its warm folds whilst chocolate rabbits hopped around my feet, the sun of pure gold warmed my body and spoke to me gently. "Luna my child, it is time for you to decide if it is right for you to finally come back to us". In the distance I could hear the annoying beep, beep of a machine plus some frantic voices. I thought about it momentarily. As the beep turned into one long continuous sound, I said, "Yes, it is time", and smiled. The beep drifted off into the distance. The sun smiled. I was home.

Postscript: the reader might wonder what became of the gold key on the charm bracelet. After Mrs Franks had passed on, her Granddaughter Anya wore it every night. And every night in her dreams, Anya met with Mrs Franks, the grass, the mallow chair and the sun, and they laughed, ate and danced until dawn. Then Anya had to return to the real world. But she knew that one day it would be her turn to return home too. And the cycle would repeat eternally.

Puss Cat

By Geraldine Paige

Puss Cat Puss Cat where you be at?

I be in the kitchen waiting for food.

Puss Cat Puss Cat where you be at?

I be next door hoping for more.

Puss Cat Puss Cat where you be at?

I be at the dog that's sat on the mat.

Puss Cat Puss Cat where you be at?

I be at cat flap and am stuck in the door.

Puss Cat Puss Cat where you be at?

I be on diet, co's I be so fat.

Puss Cat Puss Cat where you be at?

I be on your lap having a nap.

Puss Cat Puss Cat where you be at?

I be at the cat mint that grows in the park.

Puss Cat Puss Cat where you be at?

I be curled up in your best hat.

Puss Cat Puss Cat where you be at?

I've opened the fridge door and your food is on the floor.

Puss Cat Puss Cat where you be at?

I've be gone next door to see young Tom.

Night Night

Pricking in my Thumbs

By Sally Ann Nixon

It was about twenty years ago - a grey, cool night.

My son and I walked down the common lane.

Not late, but dark, the trees swayed overhead.

Each night we went in sun, or snow or rain.

We walked our three dogs and it didn't vex us,

Wind, dark, the changing seasons but tonight

Something was different. A small hand touched mine.

"Can we go back now Mum?" He gulped in fright.

"I don't like it." So we retraced our steps.

The wind picked up, the clouds obscured the stars.

Nothing there really. But a feeling stalking.

We picked up speed, were glad to see the cars

On the main road ahead. We hurried on.

The dogs scurried behind sensing our fear.

We reached our door, light, warmth and safety gained.

"What was that Mum?" He's holding back some tears.

Twenty years on, I walk the twisting track.

Three different dogs, now by myself , alone.

I do it every night, come rain or shine.

In case I slip, I clutch my mobile phone.

Tonight is different, cold but close and still.

The stream chatters and there up above

A ring glows round the moon. A bad moon rising.

No small hand clings to mine in fear and love.

A voice sounds in my ear. "Can we go back now?"

I shiver. "Yes, oh yes, of course we can".

The pricking in my thumbs is stronger still.

I need the light, the warmth, a glass of wine.

Breaking Curfew

by Margaret Ingram

The sound of seven bicycles passing over the crossroads reminded him of reptiles, snakes perhaps, or large lizards. The tyres hissed and the Doppler Effect exaggerated his fear. He pressed back into the shadows although, as he watched the riders, he saw they were intent on their route – cycling in the darkened streets was hazardous and they were moving fast. Their eyes were fixed on the roadway ahead to make sure they avoided all the potholes, drains and tram tracks that would tip them over. They wanted silence for their night-time jaunt because they were breaking curfew as much as he was. The Italian authorities weren't too strict about it but it was still better not to be caught.

He waited in the foul smelling archway, breathing through his mouth and trying to ignore the smell of stale urine. The seven cyclists passed out of sight and hearing and he counted slowly to 87, shook his head and smiled. He looked out along the street; saw it was empty and walked uphill again, trying to look like someone who should be where he was and also someone who was totally unthreatening. The street was empty but there were probably eyes watching him – or at least it was better to assume that one was being watched and to try always to appear uninteresting and unimportant. He'd learnt that lesson many years ago in Turin, when his father had been beaten by the Blackshirts for being in a hurry when they decided to stop him and question him. Although his father had been polite he had made the mistake of saying he couldn't be stopped, he had to go. He had spent the next week in hospital and several months recovering completely from the beating. They had left his father, unconscious and bleeding in the gutter and had walked away laughing. They hadn't bothered to arrest him because it was just a bit of fun for them, not real policing. He reached the corner of Rue St. Joseph and slowly eased himself round it until he could see the square of the crossroad was empty. Even then he walked slowly around the edge, not across the open ground. He moved easily from one shadow to another until he reached the church on the west side of the square. The night was quiet but his footsteps didn't break the silence. Softly he could hear a radio somewhere playing a French chanson and somewhere nearer there was a quiet mumble of conversation. The only other sounds he could hear were the soughing of the breeze in the trees scattered throughout the old town. He took one last quick look around the dark crossroad then opened the church door and slipped through the gap.

He stood still while his eyes adjusted to the gloom in the church. The lamps flickering in front of each alter and a few scattered candles broke the interior into several distinct pools of comparative light and dark. He breathed in the musty cold incense-scented air and relaxed his shoulders. Then he walked quietly up the aisle, consciously did not genuflect, and turned into the sacristy. He quietly closed the door and said 'I am come as you asked. Why here, why now?'

A lamp slowly grew brighter and the man sitting by it came into the circle of light. He was fat, wearing a priest's cassock and smiling. 'My friend, the safety of my own body, yours and those of your friends all depend on your discretion. There are murderers I will give you and you will advance, my conscience will be clear and defenceless people will survive. Is that worth your effort?' The priest gestured to a chair pulled into the table and then to a group of glasses and an open bottle on the table beside him.

Max ignored the gestures and shrugged slightly. He looked away from the priest for a moment, turning his eyes towards the ceiling. He walked further into the room and leant against the armoire, crossed his arms then looked back at the man. 'Why me, why here, why now?'

'Because you know the Italian Commandant, you are working with Liz who in turn acts at the Victorine Studios. Most of all, because I trust you. The information I have came to me from the confessional. I can never name the man who told me of these murders. I have thought this through and can't let the murders go on.'

'For God's sake, Henri,' Max burst out 'we are in the middle of a war that will last for years and kill millions. You are telling me you can't live with a few more deaths? This is mad.'

'I cannot stop the war. I cannot stop the millions of deaths. I can pray for an end to the war,' Henri stood and leaned towards Max, 'but I have been told of plans to murder some people. I am trying to do something about what I can prevent. I come to you for the same reason. You cannot stop the war but you and your friends can protect some people. Help me and help them and so help yourself.'

'Or I could go home – having broken the curfew one way I will probably survive breaking it to go home – and forget about risking anything for anyone I don't know.'

'What will you be risking? The Italian will be pleased with you, you and your friends will be protected by him and your immortal souls will be slightly safer. Saving lives will be good for you.'

'So why aren't you doing it yourself? You know Marco Comalini. Go to him yourself and he can use the state apparatus to arrest the murderers.'

'Because I can't risk the confessional confidentiality, because Marco won't act on what I can tell him – it's one version of what is going on, second hand and vague – the man didn't give me names or dates or anything. But most important is that the Quaestore's apparatus is involved without him knowing. Some of his staff are happy to kill Jews and Gypsies, all of them are quite happy to get extra money. The people running the murders are using some of the property they steal to bribe their foot-soldiers. Comalini will be killed if he lets on he knows what is happening because they know he will not participate.'

Max scratched his head, looked around and pulled out a chair for himself by the table. He reached across the table, took a glass from the group by the lamp and poured from the bottle standing open near Henri's hand. He took a long drink and swallowed slowly. He looked at the bottle as he realised that this was a decent Cotes du Rhone, and raised an eyebrow at Henri. 'O.K., I'm hooked if you can explain how they can possibly know that.'

'He was moved here because he broke up a similar killing ring in Turin. It is rumoured that Il Duce personally wanted him here to go toe to toe with the Gestapo and the French Milice. Benito himself has a deal of faith in our boy Marco and no love for the Bosche or the Petainists. Marco could end up running the north west of the Italian state at the time Italy goes toe to toe with the Nazis. If that happens we might be safer than if the area is run by self-seeking criminals.' The priest shrugged and smiled at Max. 'Apart from that I like Marco and don't particularly want him killed. He will notice these murders eventually and the minute he moves he will be taken out.'

Max broke in quietly, 'He has noticed them, he has moved and he is quite aware of the danger.' He kept his eyes on Henri as he took another mouthful of the wine.

Henri's eyes widened for a split second and then he nodded. 'Too clever by half, the Questore. So,' and he shifted in the chair, leaning forward slightly and moving his wine glass into the other hand, 'he told you, he wants you to help?' His eagerness told Max that Henri was a good deal more drunk than was obvious. Henri needed to be handled carefully to keep things tight, hidden, and safe.

Henri stared at him and Max nodded. Henri sat back in his chair and gazed into the middle distance. He slowly made the sign of the cross and finished by murmuring 'Mother of God, pray for us.' He focused on Max again and said, 'How do you know? No, I can guess. He came to you and asked for your help.'

'Not quite,' Max smiled and reached for the bottle to refill his glass, 'He has recruited the six of us, Liz and Louis, Leon and Josie, me and my lad, to help him. Just this evening. We didn't believe him. We have been trying to work out what he really wanted. The only thing that rang true was that they found a body at the film studio today. I kept very quiet about knowing Marco and he didn't let on, but I was really pissed off that he had pounced on us. Now, here you are doing the same. What is going on, Henri?'

'I will tell you what I was told. I know nothing of the man except that he is not a regular of mine and that he told me he is a municipal policeman, a vigile. I think he is about 1.85 meters tall, medium build and he favours his left leg, like it was badly broken and not set straight or he has arthritis in his knee. Not a big limp, but a definite 'walk', if you follow him. I have a mirror in the confessional, before you ask, so I can see who is coming into me and who is going out. I don't always use it nowadays, getting lax in my old age, but I was more safety conscious in the old days. Now I mainly watch pretty young women walking away! This one I only watched as he left, God forgive me, and so I can't give you more than that description. One other thing you need to know is that he had on very expensive clothes and shoes – more than anyone in the vigile should have been able to afford even for their wedding. '

'So, a fool or a sheep.'

'Yes, that's what I would think. He doesn't like some of the things he has been involved in and his conscience sent him to me. Or perhaps the Divine Planner,' he looked toward the ceiling and made the sign of the cross, 'has decided that I can do some good and so sent this sheep to me. 'He shook himself and Max watched as he took a sip from his glass. Henri looked at the glass, frowned and shook his head. He put the glass down and smiled up at Max. 'Too much wine always makes me see God's hand. The sheep wanted to unburden himself and didn't want anyone to know so he found a different priest is all there is to this. No divine mystery to worry you, Max.'

'I don't care if it is God, a god, or accident that brought him to you. Just tell me what you know and I will give you the absolution you want.'

'Damn you, Max.' Henri said quietly and bowed his head. Then he looked up, sighed and sat back. 'So, the story I was told. The truth, if I am any judge. This municipal servant, this policeman for the city, told me that for the last few months, about once a week some rich refugee Jew had been identified, kidnapped, tortured for details of his wealth, what he had on him, with him here, what he had in banks here or in Switzerland or anywhere else. Then they killed him. To start, it had been fairly clinical. Usually they just slit his throat. But lately some of the squad had got a thrill out of nasty killings. This was the problem for my good little Catholic confessee. He didn't like the sadism! OK to torture, steal and kill, but please do it nicely! Anyway, he told me that the last one had taken almost a day to die and that they had bundled him up into a canvas sheet and dumped him in the back lot of the film studios. Evidently the studios are regularly used because they are remote and one of the group has keys. He said that two of the big shots in the studio are involved. He thinks they got involved because they need the money, one is a brother-in-law to one of the cops, and also they are keen on the torture. He said the final straw was that the last death was filmed and that they are planning to film the next one.'

'I don't suppose he said when the next one is scheduled for?'

'That's why I wanted you here tonight. It's going ahead now, as we speak.'

'Bloody Hell!' Max jumped up. 'What am I supposed to do about it? You tell me someone is being killed and we are sitting here, drinking a rather good burgundy!' he slammed his fist on the table. 'Shit, Henri. I knew you had gone to pot, but I didn't realise just how bad you were. Didn't it occur to you that telling Marco directly was this poor fucking Jew's only chance of survival? Oh, never mind. I'm going to him and...'

'Wait' Henri jumped up and grabbed Max's sleeve, 'don't make too much noise or you will get Marco, yourself and possibly all of your friends, including me, killed.'

Max stared at him and realised that Henri was right. 'OK,' he said, 'let go of me. I hear you. But I am going to Marco, right now and I am going to try, very discretely and safely, to save the poor bastard. And I tell you this. You are right. I can't stop the war but I can do my best to stop murdering bastards from running my world. I'll keep you out of it. You know nothing, if anyone asks. OK?' Henri nodded. 'Now tell me everything you know.'

'There isn't much more I can tell you. The target has been invited to dinner and a game of chess with one of the group who has pretended to be a Jew and befriended some of them. The group will be waiting for him, the victim, they'll take him somewhere to get the information and then dump him, probably in the harbour.'

'Is that it?' Max demanded. Henri shrugged. 'I couldn't ask for details, could I?'

'Well, it's something at least.'

Max turned and left quickly, hardly realising that as he opened the door Henri had scrabbled to dim the lamp.

Max hurried through the church and stopped by the door, with his hand on the latch. He took two deep breaths and closed his eyes.

He opened the door and listened. Nothing! He swiftly looked around the square then around the rooftops of the square. Nothing!

He stepped into the shadows, took another steadying breath and walked quietly along the buildings and round the first corner into a shadowy alley. He quietly walked through the lanes of the old town until he reached Place Garibaldi. He used the walk to sort out a plan. He thought Marco would be with his mistress, hopefully at home at her apartment by now. He turned uphill and crossed the road to the shadow side. Keeping his eyes and ears open he made his way the half kilometre to the apartment block and broke into the street door. He walked carefully and quietly past the concierge's apartment without rousing her and climbed quietly to the first landing. He reached out to ring the bell then stopped. He got out his pick-lock again and opened the door for himself. He slipped into the hall and was relieved to see the sitting room light still on and hear the radio playing some dance tune. As he stood there, not sure how to proceed he felt a cold metal object push against his neck and heard a quiet voice say, 'Don't move.' He froze and said, quietly, 'Marco, its Max.'

'I can see that. What are you doing?'

'I need to speak with you. It's urgent, dangerous and ... and I didn't know what else to do.'

'You could have knocked.'

'I didn't want the concierge to know I was here.'

'Or me?'

He looked round then at Marco, puzzled. 'Yes, of course you. I came to see you.'

'See me and kill me?'

Marco had stepped back as Max looked round, but the gun was still pointed at Max's head. Marco was not smiling. Max realised that he had behaved like an assassin. He froze, still looking at Marco.

'No.' he said, 'I've just walked here from the old town, through the curfew and I'm not really thinking straight. I need to tell you about a crime, a murder, that's happening now and I need to make sure no one knows or you and I and everyone connected to us will be killed too.' His words came out in a rush but he moved as little as possible. As he finished speaking he felt himself straighten and relax from the ready stance he had had when he stepped in. He relaxed a little more, but tried not to move, though his legs now felt like jelly and he needed to take a deep breath. He stopped his chest from heaving. He made himself stand still though his body was demanding more oxygen. He kept his breathing calm.

Marco stared at him for what seemed like hours, but Max knew was about ten heartbeats. Each beat got louder in his ears. Finally Marco moved, the gun lowered and his left hand rose as he said, 'OK Petal, you can relax. This one is a friend.' He was talking over Max's shoulder. Max looked around and saw Marco's pert little mistress, in nothing but suspender belt, stockings and high heeled shoes, pointing another gun at his body. She was using a double handed stance and her legs were firmly planted, slightly bent. All in all she looked very arousing. Max was quite glad he was too scared for his body to react. Marco must have seen the same thing Max had, because he chuckled and said 'Cara mia, go get some clothes on – not too many. You are just too distracting like that.' She straightened and grinned. She tossed her hair and turned back into the room, saying as she went, 'It's what I love about you, that one track mind. We are to be assassinated and I must dress appropriately not to distract the assassin. '

Marco waved his gun towards the sitting room door and said 'Go in, Max, and let's hear this story.'

Max walked into the lounge and collapsed onto a chair opposite the door. Marco walked over to a cabinet behind the door, turned the radio off and poured two glasses of brandy, handing one to Max and sipping the other. 'Why didn't you phone ahead?'

'Is your phone safe?'

'I'm the head of the Guardia Civile!'

'And? Is your phone secure? Are there microphones in here? I have been told that you are in danger, and you behave as though you expect to be attacked, assassinated. How in the name of all that's Holy did you know I was here?'

Marco smiled and nodded towards a lamp by his right hand. 'I have surveillance and protection everywhere I go. Loise has told my bodyguard all is well, so we won't be disturbed by them. Loise is one of my guards, by the way. I will always thank you for the sight of her a moment ago. When I am too old to perform, that image will brighten my days.' He laughed quietly.

'I thought she was... I mean every one...'

'My mistress? Yes, that too. A woman of exquisite charms. And many skills. Well Max, now you are breathing normally again, what the hell are you doing here?'

'I found out something about the murders tonight. A lot. There is one going on now, probably at the studio. The policia municipale are involved and the studio bosses. Well at least two of them.'

Marco sat down to Max's left and nodded

encouragement. His eyes never left Max's face. Max took a deep breath and sorted frantically through his thoughts to get them into some sort of coherent order. 'A friend, a priest, called me this evening.' Max took a sip of the cognac. 'We have a code that means 'come at once' and he used it. No one listening to the call could have understood. I went to his church and he told me that he had heard a confession. He asked me to tell you and to keep him out of it. I'm telling you about him on the understanding that he never knows I told you this much about him. OK?'

'I won't let Father Henri Thibout know that you betrayed him.'

Max stared at Marco.' How? How could you know?'

'Doesn't matter. I should remind you, though, that I have all the local information and I am a good spymaster. Where I grew up my mother could have taught Machiavelli and the Borgia's a trick or two. By the age of seven I could outwit her about fifty percent of the time. Max, just assume I know more about you and your friends than any of you know about yourselves. Go on.'

'Then you probably already know about the vigile and their racket of kidnapping Jews to torture them for their secret accounts and any bits they brought here.'

'I knew it was happening. I didn't know for certain which faction was doing it. I do know they will kill me and anyone they think is going to stop them. I've lost several good policemen recently around this lot of bastards. I think the Unione Corse is involved. If it is I 'm up to my neck in shit. If it is only the municipales that's good. I can deal with them. Any names?'

'No, but it's happening now, probably at the film studios and one of the municipales has a funny walk. He made confession because he doesn't like the sadistic killing that has just started. He was OK with the kidnapping, torture and killing! What are you going to do? Can you save the one they have now?'

Marco gave Max a strange look, half puzzled and half amused. 'I'll get a group of my lads to do a sweep of the studio because of today's body. If they accidentally catch something well and good. I'll also get someone out to each of the bigwigs for the studios to see who is not at home. That might give us who is involved or at least a short-list. OK?'

Max relaxed and suddenly felt very tired. 'Thanks Marco. I couldn't bear the thought of it happening and I did nothing. I ... I'm sorry it was all a bit melodramatic. I didn't mean to ...'

'Disturb me?' Marco finished for him. 'Of course you did.' He leaned forward and put his hand on Max's leg. 'And we both got to see Loise! That will buy you a great deal of my favour, Max. 'He leaned back in his chair with a contented smile on his face. 'A great deal.' He said again, quietly. Then he seemed to shake himself and looked again at Max. 'Probably best for you to spend the night in custody and be let out tomorrow. No. Better you stay here this night and I'll get you to somewhere neutral in the morning. He looked at Max. Yes, your clothes will do for walking home in the morning. Of course! A brothel'

'Max shrugged. 'A bed for the rest of the night would be welcome, but I must remind you I have never yet had to pay for a woman.'

Marco chuckled. 'A sweet conceit. What is real is that you have never paid money to a prostitute, but my dear chap, you paid with your body for Mme Remissieur, Mme....'

'That was different.' Max said. 'That was business.'

'So you are the whore and now you are defending your honour. Max, you should go to bed before you get totally confused and think you have any influence on what I do. Good night, my friend.'

Max realised that someone was standing in the doorway. He expected Loise but saw it was a man with a gun pointed at him. The man said 'This way, Monsieur.' And waggled the gun. Max looked at Marco, shrugged and got up. The man walked into the room and patted Max down to check for guns. Then he stood back and let Max walk past him and back into the hallway. There was a door to the left and when Max looked enquiringly at him the gunman gestured he should walk through. Max was taken up a short flight of stairs and shown into a small bedroom. The gunman asked him 'Do you need food or drink, sir?' and Max said no but he would like to wash. The gunman pointed to a door beside the head of the bed and said 'En suite, sir.' Max turned away and walked toward the door. He didn't turn back when he heard the room's door close and lock behind him.

Meanwhile, Marco had waited until Max left the room and then phoned his deputy, Nico at the police headquarters. Nico had taken down the orders and asked no questions. Marco finished his drink and went into the bedroom to get dressed.

Loise was on the bed, still wearing only shoes, suspender belt and stockings. Her nipples were erect and she smiled as he came in. He looked at her, said gruffly 'Bloody get dressed.' and walked into his dressing room. He put on his uniform as quickly as he could and was pulling on his boots when she came in fully clothed in navy blue trousers and high-necked jumper.

She still looked desirable and he noticed that her nipples were still erect though their outline was softened by the wool of the jumper. He pulled her tight against his body and she laughed as she realised he was hard. He kissed her and she responded then they broke apart at some unspoken agreement.

'Work to do.' She laughed.

They ran down the stairs to the garage and were driving out towards the film studios, and the body, within minutes.

The adventures of Sidney Sat-Nav

By Geraldine Paige

Sidney finds a new Home

"I've won, I've won" shouted Mrs Morgan from the hallway.

"Won what?" came Peter's voice from the kitchen.

Mrs Morgan came running in holding a piece of paper, "Look, Look".

"Mum, how can I when I am trying to eat my breakfast and you are running around waving a piece of paper?"

"Oh sorry dear, it's just that I am so excited, I have never won anything before, it's a voucher towards a Sat-Nav."

"How did you manage that?"

"It all started the day we went to see Gran's new home and Dad got lost, do you remember?"

"Oh yes, how could anyone forget! We went round and round in circles. Dad almost had steam coming out of his ears, it was awful."

"Well, I was so upset, that the next day I went into town to find one of those car accessory shops, and, as luck would have it, they were having a competition, you had to write a short story saying, why do you want a Sat-Nav?, so, I wrote about our trip to Gran's, and I won first prize. I was thinking that it would be a nice present for Dad on father's day"

"Oh Mum, that's a good idea, it means that if Dad gets lost again, he can blame it on the sat-Nav and not on your map reading."

"Now, now, don't you start, why don't we go into town this Saturday to see if we can buy one? You can bring your friend John if you like?"

"OK, I will ask him and let you know. I must go now, John is coming up the path and if we are late for school again this week Mr Smith our games master, said that we will lose our places in the end of term gymnastics display team, and we have been working so very hard. Bye Mum, see you after school."

Saturday morning arrived to find the Morgan household very quiet, until the silence was broken by Peter running down the stairs, shouting at the top of his voice. "I forgot to tell you Mum, John will be here at 10 o'clock."

Mr Morgan, who was in the kitchen having his breakfast, overheard the remark. "Why is John coming round so early? You normally meet up outside the Town Hall at midday, then go for lunch that seems to last until tea time."

Mrs Morgan came to the rescue, "oh it's OK Dan, John wants Peter to help him choose a birthday present for his girlfriend."

"I didn't know he had one", said Mr Morgan.

"Dad!!!"

"Yes Pete?"

"He made me promise to keep it a secret."

His Dad, giving Peter a knowing wink and tapping the side of his nose said, "It's OK son, mums the word."

"Oh thanks Dad. Really Mum, fancy telling that to Dad."

"Oh Peter don't fuss so, come and have your breakfast, John will be here in about half an hour."

10 O' Clock John arrived, as luck would have it, it was Mr Morgan who let him in. "I say John, what's all this I have been hearing?"

"Hearing about what? Mr Morgan."

"The Girlfriend of course, kept that quiet didn't you, who's the lucky girl, and what's her name?"

"Sorry, but I don't quite understand".

"Come, come now, no need to be shy, tell me all about her?"

A very confused looking John stood in the hallway unable to say a word. Peter overhearing the conversation said "It's alright John, Mum has told Dad that you are going to buy your girlfriend a birthday present, and that we are coming along to help."

"But I haven't!!!" Before he could finish his sentence, Peter interrupted.

"Don't worry, John, Dad will keep it a secret, now let's go. Mum, are you ready?"

When they were outside and safely out of earshot, Mrs Morgan explained that they had made up the story because her husband wanted to know why all three of them were going out so early .

"Oh, now I understand, but if your Dad goes round saying that I have a girlfriend, it will eventually get back to school and you know what will happen then, I will be teased like anything."

"Oh John, stop worrying, dad wouldn't do that, he's cool. Now, race you to the bus stop."

Being a Saturday, town was packed. "OK boys, what shall we do first?"

"Let's have a snack Mum because we will need lots of energy, if we are going to help with the shopping."

"You boys are always hungry."

When the trio had finished their snack Mrs Morgan sent the boys to the car accessory shop in the high street, while she went to buy some wrapping paper and a father's day card.

When the boys found the shop, Peter took a deep breath, marched up to the first assistant they saw and said in a very confident tone, "Please can you direct us to the Sat-Navs?"

"Certainly Sir, if you will please come with me I will show you where they are." The boys were taken to a long aisle with shelves packed with Sat-Navs. "Is there anything else you would like to see?"

"No thanks," said Peter. The assistant turned away and left the boys to look around on their own.

"I say Pete, what sort are we looking for?"

"Search me, they all look the same. I'll stay here until Mum comes. Why don't you go and see if you can find a present, to give to your Dad for father's day?"

"Good idea", said John, "see you in a minute."

As soon as John left, Peter thought that he heard a voice. "Buy me!"

"What?" said Peter

"Not what, I said buy me." came the voice again.

"And who is me?" Asked Peter.

"It's me, Sidney,"

"And who is Sidney?"

"Sidney Sat-Nav of course."

"Oh stop messing about John!"

"It's not John, my name is Sidney and please will you buy me?"

"How can I, when I don't know where you are?" asked Peter. "You could be anywhere."

"I am on the top shelf to your right."

Peter looked to his right with his eyes fixed on the top shelf, walked slowly down the aisle. Just as he started to think that he had been hearing things. There it was right in front of him, a little round face wearing a big grin with deep blue eyes and a mop of black curly hair bouncing around the screen. It made Peter laugh. "But you are not plugged in, so how can you talk? And, why did you choose me?"

"Well, because I only appear to children."

"But what about the other children that must have walked past by you?"

"They all had grown-ups with them, are you on your own. And how can I talk? Well, it all happened when I was delivered to the shop. The bottom of the box I was in, fell open, and everything dropped out, the staff thought that they had picked up all of the Sat-Navs, but I had landed on some rubbish in the gutter, so I was overlooked and left out all night."

"Oh you poor thing. Then what happened?"

"Well as I was laying there, cold and all alone, a thunder storm started and I was struck by a bolt of lightening, which must have given me magical powers. Because the next thing I remember, I was in the shop sitting on this shelf. If you would like proof that only children can see and hear me, go over to the help desk, and say that you have a problem with the price tickets, and please can an assistant come and help you."

Peter just stood there looking at Sidney as if to say, 'is this really happening?'

"Peter, get a move on" shouted Sidney. In no time at all Peter was back with an assistant.

"Now which tickets do you have a problem with?" Peter pointer out two sat-Navs, an ordinary one and of course Sidney, who by now was bouncing around and singing his head off. "No problem at all young man, I will have them scanned."

Peter, trying to keep a straight face said "Thank you." By the time the assistant came back, John had returned with a bog smile on his face, holding some car mats.

"I have written the prices down for you, is there anything else I can help you with?"

"No thank you."

When the assistant was out of earshot, and the boys were on their own. Peter picked up Sidney and said "You were right Sidney."

"What did you say Pete?"

"I am talking to Sidney."

"And who is Sidney?" inquired John.

"It's me." Peter handed Sidney over to John,

but before he could explain anything, Peter's Mum arrived.

"Hello boys. Well, how did you both get on?"

"I've found a good Sat-Nav."

"And I've found some great car mats for my Dad Mrs Morgan."

"Good. Now. What would you both like to do for lunch? We can stay in town ad eat at the local restaurant, go back home and I will make something for you both or buy some sandwiches and eat them in the park?

A chorus of "let's eat in the park went up.

"Mum, you go to the park and find somewhere nice to sit, John and I will treat you to some sandwiches."

"Oh thank you, but before we go, hadn't we better pay for our goods?"

When they had finished paying for their

purchases and were outside, John and Peter made their way to a sandwich bar, while Mary went to the park.

"Peter, now that we are alone, I have something to ask you."

"Ask away."

"What was that all about, you know the Sat-Nav?"

"Oh, you mean Sidney. I bet you thought you were seeing things."

"Well Pete, it had crossed my mind."

"I will explain everything to you at a later date but right now my Mum's waiting for us on the park."

That night, Peter wrapped up Sidney and hid him in the bottom of his wardrobe ready for Father's Day. Sidney had found a new home.

Coffee shop

By Margaret Ingram

The door slid up and I stepped over the lip. The tongue moved gently out of my way.Beyond the rows of shining white tables and chairs was a dark wooden counter with a pale faced man standing in the centre. He was smiling at me. Once he saw my eyes were on him he pointed behind and above him to blackboards covered in writing.

As I walked closer the letters congealed into a list of drinks I had never heard of. I looked at the man and asked for a tea but he frowned and shook his head. I tried chai and he smiled and nodded. Reaching below the counter between us, he brought out a jar and twisted off the lid. The liquid inside immediately started frothing upwards towards the lip. He banged the jar on the counter and the froth stopped. He put a striped drinking straw in and handed it to me. It was the right colour for tea, and I could feel it's heat through the glass. I took a small sip. Ah! That tasted good. Jam doughnut, my favourite.

'Twisted'

By Jan Housby

"Twisted, wasted, twatted",

The song went round and round.

"Drug rings, fights and fascists",

All voices did resound.

"Worming, snaking, crawling",

As the monkey tied them down.

Down and round the twisted went,

On and on, like an intestine fed.

Down and out,

Until they were DEAD!

The Train

By Margaret McNerlin

Oh how they wished they had not made that misjudgment earlier on in their journey. Everything seemed to go haywire by them going to the wrong platform in the first place. But the journey itself had been quite nice, but of course of there always had to have a BUT. The journey had been quite nice, seeing all the lovely views, as the train puffed its way through the countryside, and Jenny had made some lovely sandwiches while Bob had prepared a good flask of tea. In fact he had decided to make another "You never know" he'd said with a wink, Jenny had laughed, "Your a true boy-scout". That is how their day started.

By the time the train got to their station, the night was starting to fall, and they realised there wasn't anyone around, to ask for directions to where they were staying. That is when Bob suggested to go back into the station, as he thought there must be a rest-room. So that is what they did. They made themselves comfortable, as best they could, and decided to finish their sandwiches, but leave the second flask till in the morning.

They didn't think they had been asleep that long when a train pulled up. This surprised them they had been told they had been the last train that night, perhaps they'd not heard rightly. The door burst open and in ran 2 little girls, laughing and giggling. they were so excited for they were going to the sea-side, and so looking forward to it. They were followed in by their Father and Mother, trying their best to calm their daughters down, but not making a good job of it. They were followed in by a little old lady, who was greeted by a tall gentleman, who had been seated in the corner. Jenny looked at Bob, "I never saw him come in, did you? Bob shook his head. Several people followed in but no one seemed to notice Bob & Jenny, dropping back off to sleep. When they next woke up the waiting room was empty except for them so they finished their last flask of tea, before going on their way to the boarding house they had decided on for their stay.

It was a lovely day for the start of their holiday, so they decided to take a stroll along the prom, the weather looked as though it was going to stay sunny for them so they thought they would have a look around the shops, where Bob bought a local paper. They then they took a rest on the first bench they saw, when Bob noticed the headline, "10th year Anniversary" of train-crash, where local shop-keeper and his Mother were killed alongside a young family visiting comprising Mother, Father and two young daughters. Bob froze, then he decided to sit on the newspaper, and discreetly left it when going back to their rooms to continue their holiday. The day they left to go home, Jenny didn't notice Bob checking out the rest-room on the other platform. Had it been a dream?…

The Sacrifice

By Jayne Hecate

"Would she ever know what I have done?"

The question hung in the air, ponderous and dark. Mathews tapped his pencil on the desk, eraser side down so that the noise was a soft hit rather than a hard tap. "No one will ever know what you have done; none of your friends, your family or even your wife."

Again there was silence until Willard spoke. "She will be looked after? And my kid? They will want for nothing?"

Mathews smiled faintly. "They will live comfortably for the rest of your wife's life and your son will have a generous allowance as soon as he reaches twenty one." Willard held his pen over the line, for three heartbeats he hesitated and then almost too quickly signed his name, dated it and gave the final signature on the bottom of the page. "There is one more on the other side too Mr Willard."

Willard flipped the page over and signed again before dropping the pen to the table and leaning back in his chair, a huge weight lifted from his body, his face grim.

"How long do I have? Do I get to see them one last time?"

Mathews gave him a sad smile. "I am afraid that this is it. You can see their on-line presence. People in your position often like to see their memorial before they enter the machine. In the modern age, this includes watching the tributes on social media. No doubt your wife uses popular social media to communicate with her friends and family. She is likely to announce your loss on there."

Willard nodded, he knew for a fact that his wife often spoke to his Canadian cousin via Facebook and they had grown close over the months since he had found his lost relatives. "What will you tell her?"

"That you were killed in an accident, something that will consume your body leaving nothing behind to identify. This is how we cover your loss. We often use office fires, industrial accidents or even natural disasters."

"I see." Willard swallowed the sudden accumulation of spit in his mouth, his mouth seemed excessively wet, like every word he spoke was accompanied by the moist chew of a dribbler. "When will you tell them?"

Mathews settled in his chair and closed the folder into which he had placed Willard's freshly signed form, wrapping the closure with a soft silk thread. "Probably this evening, no need to waste time. The forms are final, we have no desire to drag out this suffering for you, given what you have coming in the next few days."

The office was overly clean, the smell was of cheap pine floor cleaner, zesty furniture polish and the ozone from the old printer, Willard wondered what he would miss, if he was capable of missing anything once he was in the machine. He got up from the chair, wandered across the office to the window and looked out from the great height of the building and across the dirty and polluted city. The yellow streak in the air was the colour of cigarette smoke ruined wall paper. The clouds hung low in the sky, the top of the nearby buildings seemed to disappear into the grey. It was just another miserable day and yet in a strange way, this was likely going to be the last one he would see with his own eyes. Who knew what came next. Mathews placed his hand kindly on Willard's shoulder. "What you have done will never be known by anyone outside of my organisation. We make a promise never to take from the same family again. This sacrifice is yours alone and despite no one ever knowing, the gratitude that we have for you is beyond mere words." He paused, "come, let us begin the process. Infinity waits for no one."

The Police car was moving painfully slow as it crept up the steep hill that made up the street upon which the Willard family home had been built. It was a self build home that Tom Willard and his Wife Sophie had built together. Three storeys of stone and plaster, clever triple glazed windows that looked period aged. The front door was a heavy wooden effect steel security door that had been designed to keep out even the most insistent home invader. The car stopped at the entrance of the Willard's short drive way and the two officers within, both in their late twenties climbed out and approached the door of the house. Before they could press the door bell, Sophie Willard had it already open a small amount. The driver of the car spoke first. "Mrs Sophie Willard?"

"Yes, can I help you?"

"May we come in please Ma'am? we have something that we need to discuss with you?"

Sophie opened the door wide and showed the two women into the living room, one of them sat down on the sofa where Sophie had directed her, the other stood by the mantle over the fake open fire, looking at the family pictures that hung or sat there. The officer sat patiently until Sophie Willard joined her. "Mrs Willard, I am sorry to have to tell you that your husband has been involved in an accident at his place of work this afternoon and he has been killed." Sophie looked at the young woman, her face suddenly felt numb, her mind in a silent chaos. A multitude of words filled her mind, but none of them felt right and she sat there simply unable to speak. The seconds passed and when it became obvious that she was not going to speak the officer continued. "During the resulting fire from a machine shop explosion, many of your husband's colleagues were trapped behind a burning unit. He managed to beat back the flames, but he fell and then the ceiling fell in on him. As of this time the fire is burning out of control, fire crews are working hard to put out the flames, but it is unlikely that your husband's remains will have survived. He did a very brave thing Mrs Willard, he saved six people from certain death."

Willard himself watched the small screen in the darkened room, his wife had sat there blank, her face unreadable and then she had broken. Not in a weak way, or even a needy collapse into overly kind arms, but the strong single tears that had filled her eyes and then once they had gathered enough mass did begin the journey down her cheeks to her chin, where they drooped perilously before dropping the short gap to her dark blue skirt. "Tom is dead? He can't be, I saw him this morning when he left for work. I complained that they had called him in on one of the rare days that we have off together."

Willard turned from the screen, his own eyes heavy with tears. Mathews turned the footage off. "Our operatives are very convincing when they need to be. The small cameras that are part of Police uniform catch every intricate detail you will notice. We have given you the heroic death you requested. Not everyone is comfortable with this part, some have asked for less public ways out. Some have even asked for their death to be recorded as suicide, but these ends tend to leave unhappy family behind."

Willard dabbed at his eyes with the harsh feeling paper towel that Mathews had given him. "What about my son?"

Mathews smiled sadly once again. "We spoke with your son in the office of his university tutor, he is being supported where he is and we have offered him transport so that he can be with your wife. Would you like to see the footage? He is a remarkable young man, but then we expected nothing less, given his father." Willard shook his head and slumped forward in his chair, his head in his hands. Mathews spoke again. "It is imperative Mr Willard that you do not compress these feelings within you, your journey will require that you carry all of that sadness with you."

Willard appeared troubled. "I find it hard to grieve when my wife and my son are still alive and within reach."

"You can feel their pain though, Mr Willard. I can see that in you, Sir, your empathy is one of the reasons you were chosen. Your resilience is the other trait that makes you the perfect candidate for this work."

Willard looked up at the man and smiled, his face tear streaked and his eyes carrying the unbearable sadness of a man who has lost his entire family. "Could you not create someone special for this job, pick some orphan or unwanted child and teach them how to do this job? Why do you need a family man for this?"

Mathews shook his smooth bald head. His grey eyes were firm and appeared much older than his face suggested. "Such a chosen one approach tends to lead to a pious nature in the sacrifice which does not benefit us at all. I will also add that the male gender is also not a requirement. Your predecessor is a woman of African origin, her name is Delilah and she was a mother to six children, wife to a kind and thoughtful husband. We ensured that her family lived a better life in a safe country away from the war zone in which they had lived. All of the children grew up safe, believing that their Mother had sacrificed her life to save them from a brutal murderer."

"Is this the only way?"

"It is, but then I suspect that you know this, given that you read our document and then signed the forms."

"You are sure that this will save them all?"

"Your actions are going to save many billions and who knows, maybe even yourself. Your sacrifice will give rewards to those who loved you."

The days passed, Willard was held in a white room, with no furniture except a small flat box of a bed that was fixed to the wall. His only companion in the room was a large book that he flicked through on the first day as the hours passed in isolation. On his second day alone, once he had consumed the plain breakfast that had appeared on an automated panel that slid from the wall, he picked up the book and began to read the words within the thick old tome, they gave him little comfort and he began to wonder if he had the courage and the strength to do what he had agreed to do. He read the pages diligently, absorbing the information, learning from the parables and myths within. The time slid past slowly, but as it passed, he learned more and more about his role and the job he had agreed to. After a basic lunch of smoked fish and rough bread had appeared from the same panel that had given him breakfast, Willard returned to his bunk and lay down with the book. As he read his eyes grew heavy and it was only after he realised that he had been staring at the same page almost unconsciously that he closed the pages and then lay upon the soft white pillow. The cotton was very high quality and the coolness of the fabric against his face was a comfort that he needed. The feelings of loss for his family had grown to full grief and as he slipped into sleep, his final waking thoughts had been of his wife. The operative behind the camera turned down the lights to allow Willard a restful sleep and after a short while the sleeping man began to dream.

He awoke to soft light and the knowledge that he was not alone. As he shifted his face from the pillow, his eyes met those of Mathews once again. The man smiled kindly as Willard sat up on the soft comfort of the bunk. "This is your last day among us Mr Willard." He smiled once more and then stood up and offered Willard his hand. "I thought that you would like to see something before you enter the machine." Willard took the hand and used it to stand up from the bunk. His sleep had been unusually restful and for the first time in many months if not years, he felt fully rested, almost energised. Mathews led him out of the small room and past the office of the man who had been monitoring Willard. As Willard looked in, he was met with the same sad but genuine smile.

"Are all of you people so damn nice?" Willard had not meant his words to sound so bitter.

Mathews turned mid walk and stopped facing Willard. "Mr Willard. We appreciate the nature of your sacrifice, there is not a person here among us who takes the severity of your duty lightly." He studied Willard's face for a moment as if reaching a decision. "Would you want it otherwise?"

Wilting under the gaze of the pious young man, Willard replied, his voice containing no trace of his former cynicism. "I guess not."

Mathews turned back towards the end of the corridor and led Willard into a darkened room. As Willard entered, the sensor-activated lights had warmed up enough that the glowing orbs were already filling the room with soft light. A small desk stood placed in front of a large screen, the screen itself showed the archaic floating screen saver of days long passed in computer technology and as Mathews sat down at the desk and slid his palm over a shiny black plastic panel in the table top, the screen froze briefly before it turned blue and showed the log-in box. There was no obvious keyboard and Willard wondered how he was going to log in. Yet as he sat down, the screen changed once again and showed a list of files with dull looking names made up of three letters and six numbers. Mathews looked up and spoke quietly. "Before you enter the machine, there are some things that you will probably want to see." Mathews then let his finger hover over the black pad and as he did so, the mouse pointer hovered over the first of the files. Mathews tapped the panel twice and the file opened to show a screen capture of a Mrs Willard's Facebook page. The post was a simple one, the words few, the sentiment almost broke Willard's heart as he read the words of his wife's grief. The replies which had come from her friends were words of comfort, words of kindness, words of admirations for Willard's sacrifice in saving his colleagues.

"Your wife is grieving for you, she has a great deal of support and she knows that you gave your life to save others. She does not know the actual details, but she believes that you saved those men and women who you worked with."

Willard looked at the screen, the words were unbearably sad, the emotions within him were choked and painful. "Surely my friends in work know that it was not me who saved them? They must have seen that?"

Mathews smiled again, this time more certain. "Mr Willard, the human mind can be easily tricked into believing whatever we want it to believe, especially when under such stress. All that they saw was a man who held back the flames with a fire blanket for long enough for the floor to be safe enough for them to pass. When the last one turned back, you had already been crushed by the burning mass above you. We are very experienced in these matters."

Willard nodded, his face an unhealthy grey colour, his mouth viscously dry, his stomach felt like he was going to either cramp or vomit.

"I need to get out of here, I feel ill."

"That is the effect of the suffering that you are beginning to feel Mr Willard. I wish that I could tell you that it will get easier, but we both know that if I did, I would be lying to you and none of us have the desire to deceive you, Sir." Willard shifted in the seat so that he could feel a tiny bit more comfortable. "Would you like to see the newspaper reports of your death Mr Willard? Some people choose to see them, some choose not to. It makes little difference at this point." Willard nodded silently and the screen flashed up a tabloid headline.

"Hero saves workmates from Fire!" The screen flashed again with another headline. "Engineer saves colleagues in fire." Again the screen flashed. "Man aged fifty three saves six lives. Soon to be retired Engineer saves Six!"

"Enough. My ego cannot take any more."

"As you wish. Would you care to see the service held in your honour?"

"Not really, I am an atheist."

"Well, not for much longer Mr Willard. I can assure you that the almighty does exist, also your service was lovely and your wife and son both wept for you."

Willard almost laughed, but the sound choked in his throat. "He was real then?" He paused for a moment, "Jesus, he was a real man?"

Mathews looked like the sort of man who spent his days dealing with naughty boys, his eyes were filled with forgiveness, coming across as always as friendly. "The man known as Jesus Christ was an ordinary man like you Mr Willard, he was just as real as you are; as were the many thousands of men and women who went before him or have followed him and his sacrifice."

Willard shifted uncomfortably in his chair. "How many thousands have done this?"

"It is hard to say, the records are not as complete as we would like. What I can tell you is that Christ was not the first, not by a long way. He was just one of many, but his story got out and we had to make of it what we could." Willard clutched his stomach as a powerful cramp almost overloaded him. His chest constricted, his heart felt like it would burst from his chest and the urge to fall weeping to the floor almost swallowed his whole being. "What you are currently feeling Mr Willard is the accumulation of what we call sin, the conjoined awfulness of our species and now you know why we do this. Your sacrifice will take this sin away from this world and use it to drive away a terrible evil." Mathews placed a kindly hand upon Willard's shoulder. "Your sacrifice makes you an equal to the being known as God and as such you can fight off the despotic maniac who would enslave our planet and use us as a mere pawn in the battle for whatever regime he fights under." Willard writhed in something akin to agony, but rather than a physical pain, his body was responding to an emotional overload. "Come along now Mr Willard, it is clearly time for you to enter the machine." Mathews helped Willard to his feet and led the barely stumbling man out through the door and into the large room that held the machine. A small team of technicians and theologians worked steadily at consoles, monitoring the health of the slight black woman who stood face first in the small doorway that no one could really see through. Whatever it was that made up the light-absorbing blackness, also supported the body of those who made contact with it.

"It is almost time Mr Mathews. She is close to

the end, there only a few seconds of power left in her and then we must swap to the next being." The technician pressed a few control buttons and a small timer appeared on the screen that was fixed to the wall next to the bleak grey metal of the machines cases. The machine itself was a featureless grey box of painted metal. Even under close examination it was impossible to see how it was constructed, not a single rivet head or bolt could be seen on the entire surface and it stood only just larger that the doorway to the darkness that it contained.

As the countdown began the descent through single figures, two technicians approached the well-dressed and ancient looking woman who stood in the doorway. As the counter hit zero, she staggered backwards and fell into their waiting arms, her eyes completely black and her mouth a black hole in her agonised face.

The technicians held her firmly, soothed her with words of kindness and comfort, watching her as she faded away from reality. As she did so, her body turned to powder and she fragmented into a fine dust as Willard watched. He suddenly felt firm hands on his arms and he was pushed forwards towards the blackness, self-preservation made him push back for a second, but a deeper, hugely powerful desire to preserve all forms of life on the Earth hit him in the sternum, harder than anything he had ever felt before. With a new strength in his spine, he willingly stepped forwards into the darkness of the doorway in the machine, his soul consumed by the darkness. The machine whined as it reconfigured for the new form within it and the timer changed from a reading of minus Zero to a new figure of seventeen years, eight months and six days.

Mathews gazed at the numbers for a second or

two before he spoke. "He is rather powerful is he not?"

The technician pressed a few buttons and the screen changed to a new set of figures. "It seems Sir, that once again you chose a good man, the reading shows that his loving thought is that of his wife and child, it is a powerful force sir, he has pushed back the darkness to almost the edge of the universe."

Mathews stepped closer to the readout and barely audibly whispered to himself. "Thank you Mr Willard, you have sacrificed so much to keep us all safe." Another machine alarm suddenly began to bleep loudly, accompanied by a rapidly pulsing amber light on the control panel, dragging Mathews back into the world from his silent prayer. "What is it, what is wrong?"

The technician pressed the control panel

system and flicked through several on screen menus. The read out flashed up and the beeping turned silent although the light pulsed and the figures still flashed on the screen. "It is nothing wrong Sir, it is just that it seems that Mr Willard is actually a little more powerful than we had first anticipated, we have had to back off the power slightly and the result of which is the time has gone up a few more years."

Mathews looked at the figures as they changed. Twenty six years, three months and two days.

"My god, he is the most powerful one that we have had for decades. His sacrifice is even greater than we knew."

Gothic Weather

By Sally Ann Nixon

The weather is Gothic. Sword length icicles hanging from the eaves and heaps of snow covering the yard. Really lethal. Where you don't slip up you trip over some object under a drift.

She survived the night though there was snow on the inside of the window pane and on the window sill. The boiler rumbles and cranks in an effort to keep pace with the freezing temperature in the corridor. She slams the window shut, dislodging a small avalanche onto the bedroom carpet and shivers down to the kitchen, pursued by Bella and the cats. Mab is still angry at her disturbed night and takes a slash at Becks as he passes her. From feuding children, to really difficult teenagers, to spatting cats… Life holds more.

At least the kitchen is warm. There is an imperative rap on the window. That's the Robin and his band of feathered fiends joining the food queue. "Stand back you lot and all of you stop wailing and snuffling. I'm getting it." Outside it starts to snow again. The yard is icy.

The Thing under the wall pokes up a bony finger to test the air then pulls it back quickly. The good thing about being dead is that that you don't feel the cold but you can remember what it is like. The black cat had a game with him in the dawn light. He waggled a finger. Black Cat tried to jump on it. Over and over. He gets on with cats. They understand the why and wherefore of him, unlike the pudgy dog who backs away in alarm. The Thing under the wall likes these sort of days. That woman stays inside. She doesn't start messing about with plants, cleaning old furniture and especially does not put on that machine that dries her clothes, thump, thud, thump, thud. If the Thing under the wall could get a headache, he would but that thudding can still get on his non-existent nerves.

He had watched the storm. He braced the building against the blast, calling encouragement to the oaks and the hazel trees. He watched the rickety fence blow down but that was not his problem. His job was guardian was a guardian's. To keep the barns standing no matter what the elements nurled at them. He summoned his friend, the Loper and together they crouched in the dark, as gleeful spirits of earth and air hurtled by on the gale. Black cat got cold so Thing sent him in. "Cuddle up to that woman, survive the ice."

Danger over, the Loper was gone. The barn and the trees still stand and although the snow is still falling, the Thing relaxes vigilance. He has seen off worse storms than that. He can hear the woman complaining to a friend. "I can't get out, I'm snowed in again." She laughs. "At least we had plenty of warnings this time. The trees are fine though they were groaning away..."

"Truer than you know" thinks the Thing. "I heard them too. Hold fast. Hold fast."

She lugs out the log basket and picks her way to the wood store. Picks her way back and gets some sausages out of the shed. The Thing smiles. After a heavy night of defensive magic and incantation, he looks out at his handiwork and finds it good. And she is going to cook sausages. A good smell, reminding him of the wild boar that he used to hunt along the valley, warming his cold dead bones. Briefly he touches the woman's ankle as she passes by. She doesn't notice. And the snow blankets the land.

The adventures of Sidney Sat-Nav

By Geraldine Paige

<u>Naughty Sidney</u>

"Mum, Why can't I go to the fun fair today?"

"Oh Peter, will you please stop moaning, you know why. I've told you enough times?"

"Yes. I know it's because Dad wants to take photo's of a load of old stones, so he can give a talk about another Ancient Burial site at his History Group next week. How Boring"

"Yes, it might be boring to you, but a lot of people like that sort of thing, and I am only too pleased that your Dad has a hobby."

"But do we have to do it ALL DAY?"

"Yes. We do. He has a lot to do. And by the time he has finished, the fair will have packed up for the day. We can go next weekend."

"But that's no good" shouted Peter, "John and his parents are going away that weekend. Then the following weekend, the fair moves on to another town."

"Please don't shout at me, it's not my fault. Now will you please tell your Dad that I'm going to pack the picnic things into the car?"

Peter wearing the saddest face he could possibly make, made his way into the front room where his father was programming the Sat Nav. "Dad?"

"Yes Pete?"

"Mum has sent me to tell you that the picnic is ready to go into the car."

"Thanks Pete, I'll not be too long. Why are you looking so sad? It's a lovely day and Mum has made one of her special picnics."

"You know why, I told you last night when you said that you were going to that burial place."

"Peter, Peter, really. I do hope that you are not going to sulk all day, just because we will not have enough time to go to the fun fair?"

With a toss of his head and in a 'feeling sorry for himself' tone of voice said "No, it's alright I'll get over it. I'll go and help Mum."

"He really knows how to play the martyr" thought Dan. "Peter, Peter" he called. "Come back."

Peter thinking that his big martyr act had worked and that Dad had given in, rushed back into the room with a big smile on his face. "Yes Dad, what is it?"

"Can you please put the Sat Nav in the car for me, seeing that you are going in that direction?"

Peter's face fell, in fact if it had fallen any further, it would have hit the floor. Peter took the Sat Nav, and started to make his way towards the car. Then he suddenly had a thought. "Sidney," whispered Peter.

"Did you call?"

"Sidney, please can you help me?"

"what's the problem?" Very quickly Peter explained. "OK Peter, leave it with me."

With a triumphant smile upon his face, Peter continued to make his way to the car. Where Mum had just finished packing the picnic. "Mum?"

"Yes Peter?"

"Dad has given me his Sat Nav, where shall I put it?"

"Just lay it carefully on the dashboard. Now, are you ready?"

"Yes."

"In that case, get yourself comfortable in the back seat. I'll tell Dad to get a move on." Before Mary could get to the front door, Dan appeared equipped with notebook and camera. "OK. Are we ready?"

"Yes dear, just waiting for you."

"I'll just finish locking up, wont be long." While Dan was locking the house, Mary got into the front passenger's seat, turned around and said to Peter, "now Peter, no more long faces, this trip means a lot to your Dad."

"Yes Mum, I know, I am sorry I was miserable. But I am alright now."

"Glad to hear it. Now where's Dad?"

"Here he comes Mum."

"Right all locked up now, let's plug in the lovely Sat Nav that my wonderful and thoughtful family bought me. I must say, since I've been using it, I've never been lost again. Thanks gang."

Dan turned on the Sat Nav, then started the car. "Drive two hundred yards, the nturn left at the first junction, then drive two miles."

"Mary, I think that we are going in the wrong direction."

"Dan, are you sure?"

"Well, it's the landscape, it looks different. I am sure I put the right directions in. I'll just have to follow what the Sat Nav says and see what happens." After some time, Dan started to recognise the landscape. "It's OK folks, Sat Nav has taken us a different way, we are almost there. In fact, if my memory serves me well, the burial mound will be at the bottom of this lane" and sure enough, there it was.

"Dan, that was a very odd thing for a Sat Nav to do!!! Take us a different way, even though you put the right directions in."

"Yes Mary you are right, it's as if it has a mind of its own. Oh well, never mind, we are here now and in record time. Peter are you going to come with me or stay with Mum?"

"I'll come with you Dad, you can take the photo's and if you tell me what to write, I can do the notes."

"Good thinking son. So when I give my talk, I can say Peter and I gathered the information." Peter just smiled and nodded his head in agreement. Little did his Dad know that Peter just wanted to finish as soon as possible, in the hope that he just might get to the fair.

"OK boys, I am off for a walk, see you for

lunch at 1PM. You both have watches, so there will be no excuses for lateness."

After walking for a short distance, Mary came across an old green park bench, that was still in good shape and sat down upon it. "Peace and quiet at last. That sun is a bit hot, better put my hat and some cream on." Being surrounded by such calm and beauty, with only the sound of a Skylark, Mary fell asleep.

Back at the burial mound, Dan and Peter were so engrossed in their work that they didn't notice the time until Peter's tummy started to rumble Looking at his watch he noticed the time. "Dad." Shouted Peter.

"What's the matter Son?"

"The time, have you seen the time? Mum will

kill us."

Dan's face turned very pale when he glanced at his watch, "Oh dear, let battle commence."

Arriving at the picnic area. They found a very disorganised Mary frantically trying to put the picnic lunch together. "OK, OK, so I went for a walk and fell asleep on an old park bench. On one's perfect!" said Mary. Dan and Peter thought it best to just sit down and keep quiet.

"Dad?"

"Yes Pete?"

"I'm getting a bit cold, is it alright if I get my jumper from the car?"

"Yes Son, of course, here's the key, you know how to unlock it."

"Thanks Dad." As Peter was sitting in the car, Sidney suddenly appeared.

"How's it going Pete?"

"Oh Sidney, lovely to see you. Well apart from Mum falling asleep, which means we are having a late lunch. All is OK."

"Please don't worry about running a bit late, Sidney has it all in hand. Your Mum's calling, better go."

At last, the Morgan family were sitting in the sun and happily munching their way through the picnic. "Dan, there is still some cold chicken and a few cucumber sandwiches left?"

Dan wiping his mouth with a napkin and patting his tummy said "No thank you Mary, I'm full up, and that was a really lovely lunch."

Peter on the other hand said "May I have the last of the chicken please? It be less weight in the car and it will save you taking it home"

"OK, point taken, you can finish off anything

you like. Dan? Seeing that you had an early start, will and Peter be much longer?"

"No no, we're almost finished. Peter? Got your note book handy?"

"Yes Dad."

"Well let's go."

Mary had just settled down to read her magazine, thinking that she would have a bit of time to herself, after packing up the picnic, then the boys turned up. "I say, you were quick, are you sure that you've remembered everything?"

"Thanks to Pete, yes. Any Chance of a drink? Don't like driving with a dry mouth."

Peter with a big cheeky grin on his face, just like Sidney said "You don't do the talking, the Sat Nav does."

"Yes, you are right there, but I still think that that Sat Nav has a mind of it's own. Better put our post code in, with a bit of luck, we will be home early. And I can a good start on preparing my talk."

Just then Sidney appeared bouncing around the screen, singing "We are off to the fair." Dan started the car. "Drive 100 yards then turn left, drive 400 yards."

"Oh no, here we go again, sorry folks, it's another mystery tour" said Dan.

"Dad, maybe the Sat Nav is taking a short cut. Remember that happened this morning."

"Yes Son, you could be right. I'll just follow and see what happens. It's a nice afternoon for a drive."

Peter seating quietly on the back seat thought to himself "Not long now, before the fun fair comes into view. Good old Sidney. Better start reading my comic and pretend I don't know what's going on."

"Dan, Dan" shouted Mary. "Look, the Fun Fair. We have been taken to the Fun Fair."

"I know, I can see it. But really what is goig on? I know I put the right postcode in, I do know my own home address."

"Now's my chance" thought Peter. Putting on his 'I'm so sweet and innocent' face, said "Why don't we finish the day off by having a few rides, you never know, we might meet John and his parents."

"Yes, let's. Dan what do you think? The fair closes in about four hours so we do have the time."

Dan was not in favour, but seeing that he was outnumbered, gave in. The moment they entered the fair ground, Pater started to make his way towards the announcement tent. "And where do you think that you are going young man?"

"The announcement tent Dad, I want to put out a call for John and his parents."

"Well just slow down a bit and we will all go together, because this fair is a big one and we don't want you getting lost."

"THIS IS A CALL FOR JOHN, FRANK AND JANE SMITH. WILL YOU PLEASE COME TO THE ANNOUNCEMENT TENT WHERE THE MORGAN FAMILY ARE WAITING FOR YOU. THANK YOU."

"Peter, will you please stop pacing up and down, they will be here soon."

"But Mum, what if they didn't hear it?"

"Peter, now that is enough, do as your Mother

says. Sit down." Peter didn't have to sit down, because the Smith family suddenly appeared.

"Peter, Peter. Lovely to see you. I thought you said that you could not make it."

"I've got Sidney to thank for that."

"And who is Sidney?" Asked Dan. Pater had to think quickly.

"It's our name for a wish come true, we call it a Sidney. Now that we are all here, why don't we have a few rides, then finish off the day by having a cuppa in the tea tent?"

And that is exactly what happened. That night before Peter went to sleep he said "Thank you Sidney for a lovely day, but you were a very naughty Sidney."

Relentless Execution

by Margaret Ingram

The strategy builds on our three focus areas, which are profitable growth, relentless execution and business-led collaboration.

Long after the sun had set and the sky had darkened I sat and stared out of the car window. Echoing in my head was the sound of Teglar's words. I understood the profitable growth and the business-led collaboration but wondered exactly what he meant by ruthless execution. Of course he had been taken to mean the obvious by most of our shareholders. One or two had shown their deeper understanding, however. I had seen Jerimondo tighten in his chair and Smerillia had been a strangely pale shade when my eye flicked to her. Most of us were good enough at Texas Hold'em to hide any obvious reaction but little tells had been there. Nickolo had avoided my eye after the meeting started to break up and Teglar had made a point of catching my attention and shaking my hand and patting my upper arm, a sure tell.

And then my decision became clear. I had to make sure the ruthless execution worked for me. I had spent too long building this up to let the other faction beat us now.

I started the car and set it towards the centre. To the mattresses now not then. Having declared war, if only in my head, war was where I must be from now.

Chapter 1

My first actions were to buy a new pay-as-you-go phone and swap out the sim. Then I accessed my bitcoins and transferred funds to the hidden wallet. A new card, obtained a year ago and used occasionally for non-specific stuff was always in my stash. I accessed an internet café and sent the code e-mail to my team from the hidden account. Thank the powers that be that I can remember strings of random numbers and letters.

On the way over the hills and into the centre I had dumped my chips so I was off the radar. I guess that was the real first action but in some way I didn't count such a negative action as the start. For me attack is when I begin. I phoned each of my 3 associates and war began.

So now I had dumped the car in a public place, where it would be returned to the company automatically in the morning. I had moved out of the area, watching for CCTV and avoiding any I noticed. I had changed my appearance regularly as I went, coat on and off and inside out, hat and no hat, scarf and different walks. I could even do the stiff legged hip-hop walk and of course I changed tempo. I walked about two kilometres and entered the shopping centre we had rigged as our safe centre. Slipping into service areas cleared of surveillance and climbing up into the roof space I reached our safe-house. I was not the first there.

Chapter 2
Smerillia

I knew Pol had seen through Teglar so I was already moving when I got the call. I had changed vehicle and jumped onto a PT bus by the time Pol called. I changed look and jumped off illegally at a light, attracting a little attention but needing to cut the string. I dumped my chips and sims as I walked. The night was drawing in and the street lights made the shadows a safe dark web across the city centre. I watched the entrance to our safe-house for a while and then moved in. My last shape change had made me taller and wider and I waddled like a duck up the corridors and stairs, puffing and farting if anyone got near. The artificial farts were stinkers and I easily lost contact and dived into the service area unobserved. My holdings and my proxy votes were important and I had no intention of helping Teglar's friends. Pol and I went way back, so far that we had serious splits in policy but never hampered each other. I wanted Pol at my back in this emergency.

Before I reached the safe house I retrieved my emergency stash and checked it for tampering. No foreign DNA or other traces showed so I was fairly sure it was safe. Fairly would do for now and after this meeting I would dump it and re-tool. I sidled up to the entrance to the safe house in the roof. I was not the first. Nor the second and I found Pol outside, running security on the person inside. I said nothing and waited, Pol may have noticed me but gave no sign. I was now her back-up if the first one there was hostile. Could it be Teglar? Worse would be if it was his minion. Pol took her time and I could feel the sweat on my spine cooling in the forced air currents of the centre's air-con. I took cleansing breaths and readied my weapons, a Taser and a spray. I slipped my face mask into place. Any of the three of us could release a toxic gas at any moment, one more toxic than my methane farts.

I waited and registered the fourth person across from me. He was tall, possibly Jerimondo, but also possibly not. Pol did not react but I guessed she had also registered the arrival. She completed her check and opened the now guarded door, slipped in and confronted the first arrival. Then she came back and gestured as she closed the door. I moved away and knew the other was also retreating. The first was hostile. I must proceed alone.

Chapter 3

Jerimondo

Back in the corridor I watched one move away. Must be Smerillia since Pol had gone in. My route was this side of the door but if we were that compromised I decided to fall back onto the simplistic back-up plan. Simple change of look and into the service area. A van was available behind the bookshop and I took it out into the bustle of the city. I swung round into Smerillia's route and pulled ahead of her. Noticing a follower I opened the door to her and she looked then leapt in. We switched lanes and heights and then dropped the van at the pre-arranged office block, walked through and caught the cab programmed to be there for me. As we settled into the seats she let out a big breath. I waited but she said nothing. We were nearly at the next change point so I changed clothes and stuffed some new clothes into her hands. She changed and we left the cab and slipped into the pub, walked slowly through the crowd into the corridor leading to the loos and exited onto the river landing stage. The boat wasn't there! Shit. A dead end, possibly literally. Then she nudged me and I looked down where she was pointing. Under the stage the boat rocked gently on the tide. We descended the slippery wooden steps and climbed in. the engine was quiet but powerful and we were out and heading under the bridge in the dark of the night. No one followed us onto the landing stage, no boats followed us. We might be home free, but I wasn't banking on anything after the problem at the safe house. We made it to the container ship inside an hour and were well on our way to the open sea before I really relaxed.

I went to the lounge where Smerillia sat. She looked up and smiled wanly. "No word from Pol?"

"None" I confirmed. "let's plan our next few moves."

"Mm. I think no safe house exists any more. I have a mobile escape planned in North Africa."

"This will rendezvous with a yacht in about two hours. That could take you somewhere suitable then take me on. Would that suit?"

"Can you drop me into mainland Europe? I can travel on from anywhere, really."

I felt a strange pang, wanting to stay with her yet knowing we must split as fast as possible. I thought for a moment and said "Honfleur?"

"That will be fine." She smiled again. "Have you got any clothes and luggage I could use?"

I took her down to the private suite I had and she found some clothes and an overnight bag which let her change again. The bloke standing there was obviously not the person who had accompanied me onto the ship. I looked like any Joe and my bald head was probably the best change going.

"So," I heard myself saying, "We are on our own against Teglar." Inane idiot waffling, I knew but somehow I needed it said.

"Yep" she nodded and looked away. "I am going to start up some clones to keep the smokescreen up. Then I'm putting my assets to getting things sorted. No way is Teglar going to be able to enjoy his next few weeks. After that we shall see."

I sat beside her and twisted to look at her. "I

will keep things moving so he can't relax. You will see me wafting around but it won't be me. Look-alikes for me, not clones. Too risky if I get bumped. Especially having dumped our chips."

Smerillia looked at me with her head tilted to one side. "I have markers to protect the clones and me. But I see what you mean."

It was at this opportune moment that my mobile buzzed. Now this was a shock, since it was a new, unlisted pay-as-you-go. I took it out like it was a tarantula I had not expected to find in my pocket and answered. The voice was strained but recognisably Teglar's. "Where are you?"

I almost dropped the bloody thing in shock. "Hi," I said, "Good to hear from you."

There was a deafening silence on the other end. "Jeri," he said, "is that you?"

"Yes, who did you think you were calling?" I said with as light a tone as possible.

"I thought this was Pol. But it's good I got you." There was another short but deafening silence while he shifted gears. "Pol and

Smerillia are nowhere to be found. I have been trying to contact them for a couple of hours now and their numbers aren't answering. Do you know where they are?"

"Yes," I said, grinning at Smerillia, "I'm just heading up to Pol's holiday cottage on Anglesey. I think they are both there. Can I be of any more help?"

"Oh good. Um, yes. Jeri, I want to call a skype conference tomorrow to plan for the new strategy. Can you make it? And can you find out if they can?"

"Yeah, no problemo, Teg. What time and on what site?"

"About 10 and on the normal website? That suit you?" I could hear him grinding his teeth at being called Teg, and I smiled. I hate being Jeri so sucks to you, Teg old boy! "Listen, have you got anything drafted?"

"Well, I do have a few ideas. I'll mail them to you now and maybe we could start there, tomorrow?"

"Great. Till tomorrow." I cut the line, briefed Smerillia and walked onto the deck. I was going to drop the phone overside but thought better of it. The ship was already targeted if we were right about Teglar. We must be or how the hell had he got my number?" I put the phone in a crack between two containers and watched the yacht we were transferring to come alongside. Smerillia also left her new phone in the crack and we jumped ship. The massive bulk dwindled over the horizon as we made the best time away that we could. I was surprised it hadn't blown up while I was talking to him. This was all getting very confusing.

Chapter 4

I dropped Smerillia off at Honfleur three hours later with the tide and wind pushing us along at a fair old lick. She had equipment to make the video conference and set off in a campervan of all things. The yacht headed north and back through the channel towards the Baltic. I was hiding in plain sight.

At 10 the next morning with no e-mailed info from Teglar, I was in a bland corner with the skype working to patch me through to Teglar via the London router with cut-outs before that so he might think I was there or, more likely knew I was hiding. The cut-outs were of my own design and bounced around the web every few seconds, too often to trace and with no pattern. I am good at limbo dancing as well. Smerillia showed up a couple of seconds after me and then, glory of glories, Pol. Calm as a fish she greeted us all and I could read nothing in her performance. Where was she?

Teglar called us to order and started discussing some changes in project priority. Pol cut in after a few sentences. "Teglar, sorry to interrupt, but I really think we need these changes in detail and e-mailed to us. Then we can come to a quick agreement. What we do need to discuss is the board structure going forward. If anything should happen to any of us there could be major disruption given our separate alliances throughout the group. I was thinking about what my removal might mean in lost contacts and opportunities. Rather morbid of me, I know," She paused, and Teglar gave a tell, his eyes narrowing slightly before he smiled. "Pol, your position is irreplaceable as far as trans galaxy trade is concerned, you know that." he said.

She smiled right back at him, "Exactly. I am worried about that for the group. I propose we all cross-train at least two others to replace us for continuity's sake." She sat back. I couldn't believe I had heard right. It was suicide to remove our individual value from the game. Smerillia was quicker than me, though. "What a wonderful idea." She smiled and sat forward, " I would be happy to train any or all of you up in return for widening my pull."

I followed her lead, "What do you think Teg? I'm up for it myself. I have an apprentice or two who could cover me while I train in other areas and they could help out on training you." I didn't wait for Teglar to answer but turned to Pol. "When do you want to start?" I had a role to maintain. I rarely spoke but when I did it was always for action and fast.

Teglar broke in. "I'm sure this needs some thought and planning. If you three want to go ahead I'll give you my decision in a..."

"No." Pol interrupted again. "you and I will start this now, Teglar." She stood and we watched her move away from the camera which then seemed to follow her. A drone! Good thinking Pol. She walked about five steps and opened a door which led into Teglar's office behind his desk. We saw her appear behind him, and he spun to face her palming a needler. She had a shield up and sapped him before I had taken a breath. She stood over him and clicked her fingers. Two men followed her through the door and one injected Teglar. Pol turned to us in Teglar's camera. "I'm bringing him to the station after I download some of his information. I will be sharing everything with you two but we have to keep his faction off balance so be careful. Out." And the screen went dead. So did her drone. I looked at Smerillia, who had a perfect game face on. "The station?" I asked. "I think so," she agreed. We chorused "Out" and cut the links. The question was could I trust Pol? Not much choice.

I gave the pilot new instructions and we headed back to Boris Island and the air shuttle up to the space station. From there who knew where it would lead. Good job I am a gambler.

Chapter 5

Pol

The ambush at the Mall safe house didn't work. I was sure it wouldn't but had to let it happen for verisimilitude. Jerimondo and Smerillia were good and made clear headway in their escape while being careful not to burn any boats. The tell from Jerimondo had shown he was convinced Teglar had hit me. I was pretty sure he had not started to think about the phone. If I kept him moving he wouldn't and that was important.

Using Teglar to connect the two to his kidnapping had been necessary. Now they would head for the station and I could manoeuver them onto their yachts and away to the Alpha centre. There I could explain and we could work out how deeply Teglar had compromised our holdings. Would I tell them that I had smelt his interference like mouse-spoor months ago. He had spent two years making the corp richer and safer and had gotten plenty of support for his plans through successfully taking a few chances. As we drove his drugged body to my shuttle at the airport I watched the M11 scenery and wondered how chancy those opportunities had been. The first had involved a minor mining unit in the Sol asteroid belt which had found rare earths in a patch of the floating rocks. We had gobbled the unit easily. Then a bigger public concession for our catering arm, the first Earth corp to win a bid on Morgainian territory. The Morgs were omnivores, like us and we had researched their needs and cuisine successfully. Earth companies had been selling foodstuffs to them for centuries but now we had a world to supply! Lots of lovely lucre would flow, and it had bolstered our profits nicely so far.

The last gamble had been bigger, and had been almost a year ago. Building and maintaining another station at the Barnard's star crossing had won us prestige across the known galaxy. The speed and efficiency of its construction had nearly bankrupted us but had won plaudits and very quickly revenue had poured in to refill our bank accounts. I hadn't been there yet but Jerimondo had and told of wondrous, Las

Vegas , style. Teglar had used one of Jerimondo's pet architects to design and implement the building. I wondered if that could have weakened Jerimondo's dislike of Teglar? I was betting it hadn't because Jerimondo was a stiff-necked dandy and Teglar was like prickly pear to him, leaving behind tiny spines at every meeting. It would help if Teglar stopped calling him "Jerri". That is if Teglar wanted to reduce the tension. Which I didn't think he did. He'd tried it with Smerillia, calling her "Smerri" but she didn't care. Her real friends called her "Lia" which she liked, and Lia and Pol had had many a night of conquest and pleasure together through our long friendship. The things we knew about each other were myriad and dangerous. Which added a frisson to our occasional fall-outs. The good thing was our spats were always about business and so minor in the real world we both inhabited. We never fought over lovers or friends, which were the important part of life.

I was eventually cleared for take-off and we headed out to the space station. My new yacht was prepped and we would launch in about six hours. My staff told me that Jerimondo and Smerillia were on their way as well. The rendezvous was pre-set at Ursa Minor station, which Smerillia organisation ran. Her income had dropped with the new station at Barnard's Star. Liners had re-routed to the new casinos there from her provision. I wondered at the time if that had been part of Teglar's plan, and now I wondered again. As I crossed the transit lounge to my new yacht I was aware that there were eyes on me. I left that to the security that had picked me up as I docked the shuttle. I would be away clean or I would die.

I got away clean, as you probably guessed since I am writing this. History is written by the victors. So now you are wondering if Teglar was as Machiavellian as I draw him. Of course he was. Had he been a true disciple of my hero he would have been much nicer and much deadlier. Like me.

The journey to Ursa was without incident and Jerimondo and Smerillia arrived soon after me. Smerillia

My nerves were shot to pieces. I'm not good at these violent games. Pol and Jerimondo thrive on them but I would rather be finessing a new lover over cocktails. Anyway, I had got here and no tails or bugs came with me. I organised a routine inspection as cover and we three settled in to plan Teglar's downfall and demise. Pol had been watching him for many years, and I knew he was not her only study. Now she had used her trip to plan a cascade of disaster for him. If he was wise he would call a truce and walk away. If not, he would die, but only after he was ruined. Pol explained each step, which seemed to me to build a pretty good stairway to hell. At the end she leant back in her chair and looked at us. Jerimondo looked at her, then at me. Pol said "What?" and looked puzzled.

Jerimondo looked down the sat back in his chair and took a deep breath. "I like the plan." He looked up at her and sat forward. "It is excellent, elegant, enigmatic. However," he sat back, "I think we should just kill him."

I gasped. Pol sat up straight. Jerimondo leaned forward again and reached across the space between himself and Pol, palm up in a gesture of invitation. "Machiavelli" he said.

Pol looked startled, then frowned down at her feet. I just looked from one to the other. Finally I demanded "Explain, please."

Pol looked up and said "Machiavelli always advised the complete removal of enemies, by killing them and their followers. I just thought…" her voice wound down and petered out to silence. I caught on. This was a critical moment, especially for Teglar. My vote would carry him to possible humiliation or to certain death.

They both looked at me. I hate it when I have to make the choice. Even choosing the coffee shop for a morning's chat was hard for me. What if they didn't serve us well? What if the cakes were nasty? What if there was no parking? What if, what if! I looked around at the comfortable room and then down at my shoes, which were comfortable, red and shiny. Enough procrastination, pretend thought. I had made up my mind hours ago. I am a gambler and I knew what this move would be. All in.

"Kill him." I said.

Talk Coffee

By Geraldine Paige

My foot taps out a rhythm. Down the road, mind the cracks. Down the road, mind the cracks tap tap. One foot down other foot life. Dee Dum Dee Dum. The air is bringing a message to me. Here it comes. Coffee. Coffee. Aroma. Aroma. Drink. Drink for your tum. Follow the sound of the smell. The doors are welcoming me in. In I go. The seat is saying, I am comfortable, comfortable. You are comely, comely. Come sit on me. Waitress takes the order. Brings the coffee and a plate of biscuits. The biscuits just lie there waiting to be eaten. One I think is shaking with fear, so I stay clear. The coffee just sits in the cup, not a word comes up. So I have a stir. The spoon goes, tap tap on the cup like Morse code, it says drink me up for I am getting cold.

Too Much Winter.

By Sally Ann Nixon

Bloody snow and bloody ice,

If I've slipped once, I've slipped up twice.

The trackway's furrowed, hard and dour.

I really will need superpower

To get back home without a fall.

I grope my way along the wall.

The dog's not keen, I'm going back,

If I survive this lethal track!

Cling to the gate, hug on the trees.

Whoops! I'm nearly on my knees.

Get round the bend, a few yards more.

Thank God for gravel. There's the door.

The Bike

by Margaret Ingram

The bicycle was in its usual place. I wasn't in my usual state so of course I fell over it. At least, that's what I worked out had happened the following morning. Pauline confirmed that she had heard a loud noise like someone falling over a bicycle followed by me giggling and singing daisy up the stairs. What could I say? I went to my purse and gave Shelly twenty quid. "Enough?" I asked.

"I'll let you know." And ze turned and left.

Nursing my head and stomach I spent the rest of the day between bed and loo but felt much better by the evening. When Shelley returned and gave me 20 pence change I gave ze a hug. Which made ze squirm, which was my intention. Ze loved that bike and I could understand why. It was a piece of engineering to gladden the heart of any mechanic and Shelley kept it pristine until he went off on one of his club runs. Tomorrow he was planning a 90 mile race around Dorset, Somerset and into a bit of Devon. Pauline and I were his crew. This meant we followed his team in a van and sorted out any problems, like flat tyres and buckled wheels. The worst problem was torn or split shorts but luckily they didn't happen often.

All too soon tomorrow morning came and we loaded the van and set off for Sherborne before the sun was up. Shelley was keyed up and I was pleased to see the big grin on Zes face. Pauline and I were happy, too. The pubs and countryside made a typical race day tiring but in a good way. Its just something we enjoy, partly because it means we can chat and sing to our hearts content.

The bicycle was in its usual place. So was everything else in the flat. Except me. I was standing on the polished wooden floor in my hiking boots. I stood there for about five minutes before my partner noticed, or at least before they admitted they had noticed by looking in my direction.

They looked at my face and slowly looked down as though I was an ugly apparition. I smiled as they got to my feet and went red. Purposefully I scuffed my right foot backwards and forwards. Then I shifted my weight and shuffled my left foot around a little. Not too much. Just enough to mark the floor. The red was fading and I knew the mouth would start flapping any second. Now to finish the process. I turned, took two steps and lifted the bicycle off its stand. With it balanced on my shoulder I walked out of the door and slammed it. Then I ran up the steps to the roadside and leaped onto it and cycled away as fast as I could. The sound of swearing and yelling followed me until I turned the corner.

About twenty minutes later I pulled up at Marie's and chained the bike to the railings. Plodding up her steps I rang the bell and waited. As I heard her coming to the door I looked down at the bike in time to see a young woman cutting the lock and grabbing the bike. I screamed "Nooo." and ran down but of course I was too late. The woman was on the bike and off like a bat out of hell. She looked back over her shoulder as she got to the corner and waved, wobbled but regained her balance and disappeared. Marie had stayed on her doorstep but now she came down. "Come on," she said, "I've got her photo and I know the police are interested. She's knocked off several bikes in the area. My neighbour had his knicked a couple of days ago."

I was frozen to the spot. All I could think about was how this would completely finish the relationship. That bike was more loved than the dog or anything! I had taken it, ridden it through the streets and now got it stolen. There was no possibility of forgiveness. I started to cry. Marie turned back when I didn't follow, saw what was happening and put her arms around me. I sobbed until I could control myself. Then we went into her flat and phoned the police.

After going to the police station to make our statements and give them the photo we went back to Marie's. We talked around the problem and then I found myself telling her everything. My suspicions about my partner's cycling, my sneaking around to see what he got up to and finally seeing the kiss. Marie tried to soothe me but she wasn't very successful as the tale went on. Marie had had her problems with unfaithful partners and wasn't going to sit on the fence. "What are you upset about?" she demanded. "It's his fault. If he hadn't been playing away you wouldn't have touched his bike and then it wouldn't have got stolen." She explained, which at one level was perfectly logical but at another level was deeply flawed. "If I had smashed a cup or two I wouldn't have got into this problem." I said. "I've lost the moral high ground as surely as if I had told him I had been snooping."

"You didn't tell him you'd seen them? What did you tell him?"

"I said everyone knew and someone – no names, no pack drill – someone had told me."

"What did he say?"

"Nothing."

"Nothing?"

"Not a word. He just turned away and went into the kitchen."

"Brute!" she got up and started pacing. I was amazed at her anger. It made me feel uncomfortable because all I had seen had been a kiss. Fairly passionate for him but not exactly the biggest snog in the world. We talked on for ages and I ended up fighting his corner while Marie slagged him off. Then the phone rang and the police told us they had caught the woman, found lots of bikes and would I come down to the station to collect mine? I expected that they would need it for evidence but they were sure my statement and the photo would do.

Fifty minutes later I had the bike back and it was a bit dusty but fine apart from that. I wheeled it along to Marie's and she asked if I was going to stay with her. I had made my mind up when I saw the bike. It was going home as fast as possible. I was going to get this sorted out and move on because I had had enough of the anger and tension. Better a complete break than this fighting. Marie thought that was a good idea and suggested I chuck him out, bike and all. I promised I would think about it.

Cycling back to the flat I was still thinking about how to approach the problem. Should I go in blazing and angry? I could be hurt and sad. I could be very business-like. I still hadn't made a decision when I walked through the door. I nearly dropped the bike when I saw the woman sitting on the sofa. His new ... new what? He stood there and didn't look too comfortable. I stood there and cycled through incredulity and anger to murderous rage before I saw the look on her face. Triumph never looked more assured. I took a deep breath and knew I was not going to be beaten.

"Hello, Sweet." I said. "You'll never guess what has just happened to your bike."

"What?" he walked across and took it from me, the woman forgotten.

"Won't you introduce us?" she said.

He didn't hear her but I walked over and held out my hand. Hi. I'm Karen. Bill's wife."

"Laura." she put her paw into my hand and I gripped and shook it several times. "Lovely to meet you Laura. Bill never brings his secretaries home." I turned back to Bill. I hope you have made Laura welcome, Sweety. Put the bike down and make us both a cup of tea, please."

My voice got through to him. He said "Laura's a project manager, not a secretary."

"Well, she still needs a cup of tea. If she doesn't I do."

He walked into the kitchen without another word. She didn't know what to say or do so I started talking about Bill and his work and she interrupted after a while. "I didn't realise Bill let you ride his bike."

"Why wouldn't he?"

"Because," Bill said, coming back in with a bottle of wine and three glasses, "My bike is more important than any bloody woman." He set the glasses down, opened the bottle and poured two measures. As he was about to pour the third Laura stood up. "Not for me." And she marched out.

"Well?" said Bill, "what happened to my bike?"

"It got stolen, photographed and recovered."

"Really?"

"Honest Injun, pardner!"

He started to laugh. I found myself joining in and we ended sipping our wine while I told him the details.

There was a short period of quiet then he said "I'm very relieved you are here and she isn't. The idea of an affair is much more appealing than the reality. Do all our friends really know?"

"Only Marie, and she will probably dig at you forever now, but she won't tell anyone if I ask her. Why did you do it?"

I kissed her twice. I never did any more than that. I did think about it. She came here today out of the blue. When I saw her in this setting I knew it was going no further. You are the only one I can see here. The only one I would let ride my bike."

Suddenly I knew that everything was right with my world. We both turned and looked at the bike, which was in its usual place.

Step Back

By Jayne Hecate

I watched my life wash away before me, the missteps I had taken, the regrets I made with each bad decision. Four years of my life that were to begin with quite happy, but that was before it all got a bit messy with kids I never wanted and dead ex-partners. It is fair to say that it was then that I lost my way. I was forty two when I met her, her brown eyes had connected with my own baby blues across a packed bar and I think that I fell in love with her right then. No scrap that, if I am being completely honest, I fell in love with the idea of falling in love with her.

We dated for three months before me made it official, just a little dinner out somewhere nice or maybe a trip to the cinema once or twice a week. My mountain bike that prior to her, I rode almost every day, developed a layer of dust instead of the mud that usually collected on it when I went out on the local trails. My weekends changed too, from fun out with the lads to instead being spent with her, doing dull household shopping or attending boring children's birthday parties with her kid. The kid was five when I met him, I want to say that he was fun, but the truth was that I found him rather irritating. I had never wanted kids and there I was being a step father to a kid who had lost his Dad to a car accident. Kids like him tend to put things in basic terms too, there had been this one day I had an afternoon off work and I had thought that me and her could have spent it having it some fun. However, I actually ended being with her when she picked him up from school, where upon he asked me a difficult question. "Rick, are you my new

Daddy now?"

Embarrassed, I did not know what to say, I kind of mumbled a bland sort of admission about me and his Mum and I saw that she watched me with the suddenly hawkish intensity of a predator hunting a dying animal. I really did not want to lose her, I honestly liked her a lot, but really I was not so sure about taking on a dead guy's kid. As we took that long slow walkout of the school, my mind became flooded with future plans. Maybe I could buy the kid a bike and teach him mountain biking? Maybe I could teach him about the other things I loved too and then watch him graduate from my old university? But there were also the darker thoughts and fears. Maybe he would fail me, come to nothing at all or worse still become a junkie and die of an OD? So many possibilities.

His Mum said nothing to me as the boy took

my hand in his own small fingers and we walked back to my car. Her face though was a cardboard mask of unreadable thoughts and doubts. I opened the rear door of my car, a car that had changed so much, gone was the camping kit and the bike tools, replaced by little hand smudges on the rear windows and a booster cushion on the back seat. The expensive cycle carrier that had almost been a permanent fixture on the back, before her arrival, had been removed so that I could carry her shopping and her kid's stuff when he occasionally went of to stay with the dead guy's parents.

After four years, we ended living together just like a real family, although it was not entirely by my choice. Her landlord had died and the house fell to the guy's family who then wanted a quick sale so that they could afford to pay the tax bills for such a large inheritance, which meant that she was looking for a new place to live and fast. My flat was not really that big, just two bedrooms, a kitchen-diner, a bathroom and private parking space. The kid took the smaller bedroom, my bike got moved into the hallway and from there it got shoved around because where ever I put it, it always seemed to be in the way for someone. The layer of dust on the frame was now so thick, I could barely read the graphics. The chain had almost seized with the fine layer of filthy dust that had stuck to it, but worst of all was that I found small childish drawings done in crayon and pen that she seemed to think were nothing worth speaking of.

Four years, from what I was, to what I became. I am not sure that I was happy; I just seemed to float along and accept things. I had become passive in the creation of my own life. When she told me to consider selling my old bike because it just got in the way and I never used it anyway, I took it outside to wash away the dust. I sat outside in the sunshine washing the dust and the drawings from the frame and the misery from my soul, when suddenly I discovered that I was full of rage and regret. Four years wasted being someone who I really did not want to be. I felt for that place in my heart, the sore place at my core and there it was ruby red and full of grief for my lost life. My emotions blazed in that ruby of regret and as it glowed, I knew that I needed a reset. Four years wiped clean in a single backwards step. I felt the fall backwards through time, I saw myself as I had been and I felt the knowledge transfer, from who I had become to who I once was.

Her brown eyes met my own baby blues across a packed bar and I remembered every decision that I was about to make with her. I smiled politely at her and quietly left the bar, the future changed with a sickening jolt and reset clean, I set about it all again, but different, after all I was looking forwards to a bike ride with the lads at the weekend and it was going to be the hardest and most dangerous trail we had ridden as a group. I could feel the excitement already building in my heart.

The Adventures of Sidney Sat-Nav.

By Geraldine Paige

Sidney Saves the Day

"Mary, I am just popping into Town for a few things before we leave for our holiday. Would you like anything?"

"I would love a few magazines to read for the journey, and please don't forget, we need extra spending money."

"Now, would I forget?"

"Yes, you would. I have noticed that sometimes you seem to go off into another world. Please try not to be too long."

* * * * *

"Mum, was that the door closing?"

"Yes Pete. Dad just left for town."

"Oh bother. I wanted some comics to read. John can't come with us this year, and I'll have no one to talk to."

"I know that you are upset about John slipping over and breaking his leg. But accidents do happen. Why don't you start writing a holiday journal, and when we get back you can spend and afternoon together reading it."

"Mum, what a great idea, and I will send him lots of postcards. So he doesn't feel left out. But I haven't got a journal to write in."

"It's OK Pete. I've got a big writing pad that will be perfect for the job."

* * * * *

"The Parking in this town is getting ridiculous, we need another car park." Muttered Dan to himself as he drove around and around, trying to find a parking space. "At last, found one, bit of a squeeze though, never mind it will do. Right. What's next? Get parking ticket, then go shopping." Dan was so wrapped up in his thoughts, that he didn't realise that he had just locked himself out of the car.

Back at the Morgan household, Mary was getting worried. As it turns out, she was not the only one. "Mum. Dad is taking a long time. Why don't you call him on his mobile?"

"I was thinking the same thing." Mary dialled the number, only to find a very upset husband on the other end waiting for a locksmith. Mary trying not to laugh, wished him well, and with a "see you later", put the phone down.

"Mum what's the matter, why are you pulling a funny face?!"

"Right Pete. If I tell you, you must must promise me two things. One is do not mention this to your father. And the second one is do not laugh."

"Scout's Honour Mum."

"Your father is late because he has locked himself out of the car and is waiting for a locksmith." If anyone had been passing the Morgan household just then, they would have thought that the place was inhabited by laughing Hyenas.

By the time Dan arrived home, Peter was already fast asleep in bed, and Mary was making sandwiches for the journey. "Mary I am so sorry for being late, but at least I have remembered everything. And I have also bought some comics for Peter to read, in case he feels a bit lonely. It's the first time he has had a holiday without John and they are such good friends."

* * * * *

Peter looked out of his bedroom window and shouted. "Yippy. It's the first day of the hols, the sun is out and I am going to start my journal." But before he could put pen to paper, he heard "Peter. Are you up yet?"

"Yes Mum. Just starting my journal Mum."

"YOU WHAT YOUNG MAN?" No you are not. You are getting ready. NOW!"

A very disgruntled "Yes Mum, getting ready Mum. Wont be long Mum." came from Peter's bedroom.

"Peter, do I detect a note of sarcasm?"

"Sorry Mum."

* * * * *

"Well that's an improvement, two hours to get

ready."

"And what do you mean by that Dan?"

"Last year it was three hours."

"You are beginning to sound just like your father, he was always timing things."

"When I turn the key in the ignition, we will have started our holiday."

Click… Vroom.

"Now, can I start my journal Mum?"

"Of course Dear."

Apart from a stop, which was spent eating their way through one of Mary's special picnics, the dive to Seaweed Cottage was very straight forward.

"Why do they call it Seaweed Cottage? Just look at the hollyhocks. If I owned the place I would call it Hollyhock Cottage. And why are you both laughing?"

"Mum! You say the same thing every year. Isn't that right, Dad?"

"Yes, son. Now let's get started with the unpacking."

Peter, clutching his journal in one hand and his suitcase in the other, was first out of the car and up to the front door.

"Haven't you forgotten something, son?"

"I don't think so. Journal, suitcase!"

"The key son, the key."

Dan made his way to the front door, turned around and bowed to his family. Then, in a very theatrical manner, said,

"I put my hand into my pocket. Where there is a locket. And in that locket, there is a key, which is for you, me and thee."

Then he opened the door.

"OK gang. Let's get started."

Like a flash, Peter was upstairs and unpacked. Leaving his Dad downstairs, complaining about the weight of his wife's suitcase.

"Really, Mary. You do this to me every year."

"Do what every year?"

"Pack the kitchen sink."

"Now why would I do that? I've got one here. I'm off to the kitchen now to sort out tonight's tea."

Just then Peter came downstairs and announced that he was going for a run along the beach.

"That's a good idea, Pete. Give your legs a stretch, don't forget your watch, don't want you late for tea."

"Don't need one, Mum, My tummy tells me

when it's teatime."

* * * * *

Peter returned from his run to be greeted by one of his favourite smells. Risotto. When everyone had finished eating, Dan said that he was going to plan the outings.

"Right you lot, is there anywhere special that you would like to go? Or would you leave it to me?"

Peter just shrugged his shoulders. Mary nstopped clearing the table, had a short think then said,

"I'll leave it to you. Now I must get the dishes done."

"Dad. Shall I get the Sat Nav for you to program?"

"No. It's ok. I don't really need it this week. I should know how to get around by now. We have been coming here for some time. In fact, come to think of it, the first time we came here you just a baby."

"Yes, that's right. Mum has shown me holiday photos and they were always of here. Why is that Dad?"

"Because it's the perfect holiday place. Lovely neighbours. The beach at the bottom of the front garden. Village shop within walking distance, and peaceful."

"So the Sat Nav is having a holiday as well?"

"Yes you could call it that. But it's only a machine, not a real person."

Peter just smiled to himself as if to say, "If you only knew."

"Dad?"

"Yes son?"

"I' think I've left my jumper in the car, can you

unlock it for me please?"

"No Peter, I am busy trying to work out the week's outings. Here, you have the keys."

"Gosh. Thanks Dad."

Feeling very grown up, clutching his Dad's car keys, Peter made a dignified walk to the front door. But the excitement of seeing Sidney got the better of him and he was out of the cottage and down the path like lightning. Getting himself comfortable in the front seat, he called out,

"Sidney."

Peter waited for a few minutes, then called again,

"Sidney!"

Still nothing, Peter was beginning to worry.

"That's not like Sidney. He's always there. I'll call just one more time, then I must go in.

Sid-----".

But before Peter could finish, a very sleepy,

"All right, all right. I heard you the first time. Can't a chap get some sleep. I hope it's important, because I was having a lovely dream."

"Well it's important to me Sidney. Dad has turned you off for a week, because we are on holiday, and John has broken his leg, so I am a bit lonely."

"Sorry to hear that Peter, but why did your Dad turn me off?"

"Because he knows this part of the country very well."

"But I don't, I want to see as much as possible."

"Well that is the reason why I am here, Dad is making a list of the places that we will be visiting. When I get hold of the list, I will show it to you. So that you can enjoy the scenery. Better get back, see you soon."

Peter tapped on the front room door. "Dad, just to let you know that I've left the car keys on the hall table."

"Thanks Pete. I've finished the list, come and have a look at it."

Peter picked it up, studied it for a moment or two, then said "that's nice Dad. Mum will love that Dad. I think I've left my sandals in the car, must go and have a look. Won't be long."

"Sidney, Sidney, wake up sleepy head, I am back with the list. Quick have a look."

"Thanks Pete. Now we must have a code word."

"Code word, but why? You know when Dad is driving?"

"Yes, but I might be asleep, and also it is a bit of fun."

Peter was thoughtful for a moment or two and then came up with "mind the hedgehog."

* * * * *

Because it was such a lovely evening, Mary and Dan had decided to go for a walk along the beach. "Dan, I'll leave a note for Peter just in case he is not back from the car, before we go."

"He should be back by now, he's only looking for his sandals. But yes, you had better leave a note."

When Peter finally came back, the cottage was empty. "Where on Earth have they gone?" Feeling a little bit rejected, Peter made his way upstairs with the intention of writing in his journal. But before he could open the book he noticed his parents walking along the beach holding hands. "What slush, can't write about that, bet John's parents don't do that sort of thing."

"Peter we are back." Called Mary

"You might have let me know where you were going. I came back and the place was empty."

"But Peter, I did, you must have walked past the note. Just out of interest, how's the journal going?"

"It's OK Mum, but I am not writing about you and Dad holding hands on the beach, because John will think that I have peculiar parents."

Next morning Peter came running into the kitchen where his parents were having breakfast and shouted "Yippy. The sun is out and I am very hungry."

"Peter really, do you have to shout, we are not

deaf. You are having one egg and two slices of toast."

"But Mum, I am a growing boy, I need two eggs and four slices of toast. If I don't by lunch time, I will be dead of starvation."

"Peter, that's enough. You will eat what your Mother gives you. And don't dawdle. Mary, want any help with the picnic?"

"Well yes I do, we need to buy some cans or bottles of soft drinks because I have left the flasks at home."

"No problem. We can get some at the local shop."

While the Morgan family were getting ready for their first outing, three criminals had just escaped from the local prison and were looking for transport.

"Right you lot, into the car, seatbelts on and

yes Mary, I have not forgotten about the drinks."

"Mind the Hedgehog!"

"What hedgehog?"

"Sorry Dad, I thought I saw one, but I was wrong."

"Hi Pete," said Sidney. "Lovely to see you, looking forward to seeing the manor house and gardens. We have a lovely day for it."

"Sorry gang." Said Dan, "I will have to park on the outskirts of the village because the road is a bit too narrow to park in."

Dan was able to park by the hedge, unfortunately, unbeknown to him, the three criminals were hiding on the other side. "Hi Jack, did you see that?"

"See what Doug?"

"That family. They have left their car

unlocked."

"You kidding me? Are you sure?"

"Yes Doug, honest Doug."

"Right then, Dave, you go and start it."

"Why me Doug?"

"Because I am the brains, so move it. Right?"

"Yes Doug."

Dave slowly made his way to the car. "Cor, you will never believe it. He's only left the key in the ignition! OK you lot, let's get in."

Just as the Morgans were leaving the shop with their drinks, Mavis the local shop owner's friend came running in saying "The local radio station had just announced that there are three criminals on the loose. And, if you see them, you must phone the police."

"Thank you Mavis, I better put a notice in the

window."

"How exciting Mum, criminals on the loose. It's just like in the films."

"Peter stop being silly. Mind you it will all look good in your journal."

"Right, let's get going. Mary, have you got everything that you want?"

"Yes, I think so. Peter, will you please stop looking at the comics and get a move on."

* * * * *

"Dan, where's the car? I thought you parked it by the side of that hedge."

"How do you know know that it was that hedge Mary?"

"Because it's the one with oak tree in it."

"Dad, now what?"

"Now what indeed. Better start walking back to the cottage and ring up the local police station. Well, it's a nice day for a walk."

Walking back to the cottage, a group of cyclists stopped to ask them where the nearest shop was. When Dan had finished giving directions, he described his car, and asked if anyone had seen it. Almost everyone said yes, because there were three men in it driving like mad. "If it's any help to you," said a young lady wearing a yellow cycling outfit. "They turned left at the cross roads."

After Dan had thanked them, they parted and went their separate ways.

* * * * *

The attendant at the manor house and garden's car park noticed a car that had been parked for some time, and no one as yet had bought a ticket. He approached the car to investigate just what was going on. All he found were three men just sitting there staring into space saying "the car is haunted, the car is haunted."

"Oh dear, I'd better get some help, they could be ill." But before he could even turn on his radio, to ask for help, a policeman approached saying "this car is stolen, I will deal with it. Please stand aside."

"I wouldn't if I were you, it's not a pretty sight," said the attendant.

"Now now, move along. I've seen it all before."

The attendant just smiled to himself as if to say, "I bet you haven't seen this one."

As it turned out, he hadn't seen anything like it at all in his life. Two ambulances had to be called, one for the criminals, still repeating over and over again, "the car is haunted." The other one for the policeman saying over and over again. "He was right, it was not a pretty sight."

How did the Morgans get their car back? Yes readers, it was Sidney that did it. Let me explain. As you know the criminals stole the car. Sidney could see and hear everything. So he locked the doors and took control. Not knowing that the family had gone back to the cottage, made his way to the manor house and garden's car park, where he waited for the law to come along. The Morgans received a phone call from the local police station, telling them where the car was. And please could they collect it. That night just before Peter fell asleep, he said "thanks Sidney, you saved the day."

Coffeehouse Bluze

By Jayne Hecate

It was the day I started my meds, the grey world swam away from me leaving only colour and sound that merged synasthesially into flavours that made my tongue tingle. Every bus that went past tasted of lemon sherbets, but soaked in piss. It was not pleasant.

I was taking meds because I had tried once again to have a little accident, the first time I had slipped with the bread knife, the second time I had swallowed a box of pain killers, but this time I had tried to stop a train with my legs. People made such a fuss, but I had stopped the train, which proved that it was possible.

The street tasted of bubblegum and washing up

liquid, not overly gross, but it took the edge off of the taste of the sunshine which was pure zinc. I walked along the toffee pavement, each step sounding like a gong played with a soft brush, if I hit the paving slabs in the middle, the sound was clear and smooth, but if I hit one of the many lines or cracks, the sound developed a hiss that reminded me of my old tape trading days before Dolby became a thing. When I reached a drain cover, I wondered what it would sound like if my footsteps tracked along the triangular edges rather than crossing the vast zigzag patterned steel. The colour of the metal tasted of ketchup mixed with how dog food smells, which was surprisingly pleasant. So I stepped onto the metal and the sound was disturbing, a thousand voices whispering one word. I don't know what the word meant, but it sounded ominous and scary. I stepped again; again and again the voices whispered their single ominous word. "Plooog".

The yellow and blue sign of a café tasted of cinnamon with a delicate side flavour of rain soaked stone after a long hot summer, I could not refuse the taste and I was hungry for a drink. Inside the noise was the colour of second class stamps and tasted of damp cotton sheets. The smell of the coffee though was almost overpowering. I sat down and ordered a cup, ignoring the nagging feeling that the colour of bench I was sat on smelt and tasted of chips on the beach. When my coffee arrived, it was in a mint flavoured cup that sounded like tinkling bells made from fine glass. The steam sounded like mornings feel and I let the flavours and sensations wash over me, before reaching into my peach flavoured purse and pulling a dog shit smelling five pound note from the zipped pocket. I signalled to the waitress and asked her to take the offensive smelling note away and showed her my wrist tag that explained it all in rhubarb flavoured colours. She returned with a small collection of coins that smelled of petrol stations and dry soil which I dropped back into the custard interior of my purse, which I put away in my own zippered pocket.

The coffee was strange. The rich colour tasted of the road, the smell gave sparkles of light I could see only if I turned my head sideways and blinked, but the taste was something exquisite. It was like walking on angel feathers and fractured glacial ice, a texture so beautiful it made me weep. My silver tears dripped from my cheek and landed on the table with a thud so loud, I thought that I would be asked to leave. Instead the waitress sat down opposite me and passed me a wallpaper paste flavoured napkin to wipe my eyes with. On her wrist was a watch that I could not stop staring at, the hands gave out the flavour of parsnips as every second ticked by and the taste was foul. Yet I could not turn my eyes away. My tears continued to land on the table top with concrete slams, the touch of her hand on mine was sparkles of light in rain and I shivered with the cold of it.

The waitress knew me, she knew my name which when she spoke it, was balloon red splats of smoke in a pure azure sky. Her name was on her badge and when I read it, it tasted of strawberries and apples, but fizzy and not mixed up. The strap on my wrist was glowing with a flavour of elderberries, I had never tasted elderberry before, but I knew the flavour instinctively, just the same as I knew the flavour of the man from the hospital when he spoke to me. I left my half drank coffee and let him guide me into his chocolate chip muffin flavoured car. When he started the engine the noise was bright sparks of sickly black and orange, which turned sunset red as he sped up. I did not want to go back.

Gravel.

By Sally Ann Nixon

10 tons of gravel here, delivered, spread.

It's covered up the quagmire just outside.

The mud that squelched all over the front yard

And swallowed up Mab cat like rising tide.

Poor cat was right up to her tum in mud.

The terriers waddled, wallowed in accord.

Nothing stayed clean, nothing was safe from
them.

The walls were splattered, sofa, carpets pawed

With thick, black mud - it shone, it quivered,
stank.

The rain made pools and lakes across the yard.

Mud sucked our shoes and lapped around our jeans,

So we fought back with gravel, grey and hard.

It did the trick. The yard's a better place.

No sinking feet and under a bright moon,

I can look out and not expect to see

A creature rising from a Black Lagoon.

Three parts of four

by Margaret Ingram

For three parts of four I gave you a home

my breath for you, my body, blood, bone.

And later the other

Holding you I gave you food, love and song

Telling you stories all night long

And later the other

Wisdom and comfort I gave to you

Strength for the dangers to come

Shelter and peace I gave you

When others did you wrong

My arms and council

Knowledge and shelter

I gave you and later the other

I know you, do you know me?

You mirror my pain, my doubts

Your worth, strength, pride you show me

I know your victories and routs

Look up and out and finally see

How similar we are

For you are like me

I had to deal with another

You have many others to face

Both the other I gave you and

The ones your father put in your place

Perhaps they are worse than the other

So you chose your battle wise woman.

But now look up and out and in the mirror

See your strength, brains and beauty

And know you are better than any other

And that if we could, believe your mother

We would all be like you

Rest in my heart and know

That you are like no other

Spring

By Geraldine Paige

Spring, Spring, I welcome you with a big fat grin.

Spring, Spring, you bring the light showers. That make my face zing.

Spring, Spring, You make everyone sing.

Spring, Spring, where have you been?

Spring, Spring, brings out the lambs that gambol.

Spring, Spring, brings out the people that ramble

Spring, Spring, is the beginning of everything.

Spring, Spring, with your clear fresh air. There is nothing on Earth to compare.

Spring, Spring, you bring the light, that makes the flowers bring delight.

Spring, Spring, you make the hedgerows sing, with a chorus of primroses, daffodils and other things.

Spring, Spring, there is one more thing. You must pave the way to let summer come in.

Observations on a pleasure town:

a mannered and ponsey look at refreshment.

By Margaret Ingram

"There is," he spoke softly, "something very English about this hostelry." He looked at the bar and the people congregated around and behind it. "if the purpose is to make profit by selling refreshment and some small pleasure to travellers, visitors and locals, then this place is the most inept I have seen for a while. However, if you know the locals, the visitors and most of the travellers are from England then its ethos becomes effective." He stood and watched, while the echoes of his thoughts bounced in my ear. I turned and looked at him, then turned to look where he looked. We were in amongst a loose crowd along the bar. I had been in many a crush along a bar where the serving had been fast but had not kept up with demand. This was different. The queue, for that was what we were, was not linear or horizontally pushed against the bar. We hovered, with only a few actually touching the bar, the rest steps back and yet, English to the bone, we knew our place in the queue. Godly wrath would fall on a queue jumper.

Behind the wooden barricade were two of the slowest servers I have ever seen. They never stopped moving but never moved fast. Therefore we of the attending masses waited, watching each of the steps in our preceder's order being carried out with some slow elegant grace. A walk to the far side of the bar for a packet of crisps, a slow pulling of levers to dispense the drinks, a measured tread to find the wine glass and a retreat of gentle elegance to find the wine. An order of fruit juice required a sweet gavotte to find the bottle and shake it, to remove its cap and then to reach for the tumbler, put in ice from the bucket along the bar, retreat the two steps to the mat and to pour half the bottled nectar. The bottle placed gently beside the iced and frosted glass completed the set.

Payment took mainly electronic form and even here the pace was gastropodic, formal and watched by the waiting crowd. "Why the people serving," his quiet, accented voice murmured in my ear, "should be called the waiters is beyond my comprehension. We are the waiters and could, indeed be the supplicants at a stone-hearted master's feet for all the deference these people offer. He raised his hand to silence the answer I had prepared to give. "I know," he turned and smiled at me," but look without preconception and it is both beautiful and masochistic in its perverse opposition to the theoretical situation. Come.

We will find another place to refresh ourselves and there we will consider the English business form."

Later, in a small restaurant on a major road from nowhere much to somewhere else, we discussed the idea of the pub in the now distant town. Here the service was discrete and rapid without the need to rush. There were empty tables now, since it was almost evening, too late for lunch, too early for anything but cream tea. We would eat an all-day breakfast. The irony was amusing and the food good. I wondered why the French, especially around Charlesroi and Lisle had not found this gastronomic fry-up. They had the ingredients, provided you avoided the Americanisation of hash browns and stuck to refried left-over cooked potatoes.

"You were going to explain how that pub survived." I reminded him in my best nudge technique.

"Do I need to explain it to you?"

"Indulge me." I smiled. His ego needed no massage yet fed off my request, I knew.

"Then imagine, if you will, the same type of establishment in any other country." He watched me and so I thought of bars and bar-restaurants I knew in Europe, the Americas and Antipodes, in the north and south of Africa, for they are surely different places, and lastly in Asia, north, south and easternmost. In all of these places, service would have been faster, the waiting less uncomfortable because either we would have been seated to be served or the queue for service would have been shorter or, in the worst case scenario, less hostile to each other. In some long, slow queues I had made friends and swopped stories and shared misery and laughter.

"I accept" I said, "that it is an extreme example of inefficiency. Perhaps that is why so many pubs are closing."

"No. That is why so many still exist." The drinks were ordered which gave me a moment to reflect on his answer. He resumed when we were alone again. "Some other would-be customers left, we were not the only ones."

I nodded and waited as our drinks were served and we ordered our banquet du jour.

Somewhere where the wilderness is still

by Jayne Hecate

The grey sky hung above him with the indefinable heaviness of an old military blanket, the damp cold ground upon which he lay was grassy, not of delicate lawns or even rough playing fields, this was the clumpy, wild countryside. The blue green agricultural grass gone wild, mixed with sedges and the soft fronds of violet tinged mosses. In summer the hills were filled with walkers and mountain bikers. Likewise the winter saw similar although hardier groups still out playing on the rare sunny days. The rocks encrusted with decades of foot prints, wearing through the lichens and bog moss, leaving a shiny smooth trail of pretty destruction. The contours of the ground were broken up by walls and fences or worst of all, open cast mining. Water jets tore into the soft ground, washing out the precious minerals and turning the ponds they created into turquoise pits of toxic sludge. With every new mine, with every worn out pathway, he felt a bit of his soul die until all that was left was despair.

The walk to this haven had taken over six hours, across bog and mire. His boots were cold and the outer layers of fabric sodden with water and mud, but he cared little for the feeling, he had at last arrived at the most beautiful place on Earth and, despite the grey skies and cold air, this place was a paradise of serenity. The small brook was fed by water that ran from the bogs and mires, the saturated ground was sealed, tens of meters below, by the heavy igneous rocks of white and grey melted minerals. Built up over thousands of years, the black acid soil was a sponge for the rain and, when it rained here, the rain poured heavily for hours, bring life from the heavens. The brook itself was as wide as any man could jump, the steep grassy banks made landing treacherous and the occasional muddy footprint showed where some unlucky fool had failed to make the jump cleanly. The damp leafless thorn bushes waved tatters of fabric to show where they had tried to help, reaching out with sharp prickles to stabilise the falling. The brook with its bare rocky bottom was not so kind and many an ankle had been sprained on the slippery algae-coated rocks. The safest way to cross was to plant one foot safely into the stream, allowing the water to flow across the toe box and if the boots were poorly made, through socks and across frozen aching toes directly. The sound of the stream was a constant gentle whisper of water over rock. The fast flow biting into whatever soft sediments had tried to settle between the boulders and cutting against the banks, trying to drag the soil away from the roots that held it together. For as long as the rain fell, the streams that fed the rivers, that led to the ocean, would try to cut ever deeper into the ground over which they climbed, ever downwards towards the swell of the sea.

He took a breath, the cold air tasted of winter, it had the gentle aroma of the rot and vibrancy of the peat, the scent of plant life fighting through the cold and the damp, but most of all it smelled of peace and of freedom and of letting go of all of life's awful artificial stresses. This place of peace, smelled of the lack of mankind, the lack of pollution and the wild musk of the animals that kept the grass cut low with constant grazing and even sleeping. He sucked in every tiny fragment of natural joy, inhaling the intoxication of pleasure that came with being so utterly alone in a place that had such a threatening natural beauty. This was not a place for the meek and the mild. This was a place for those with powerful souls and the will to fight across country to be alone, to feel a billion miles away from the nearest human soul.

Laying next to him on the damp grass was his pack, an expensive backpack designed to climb in vast mountain ranges, with pockets and straps for equipment not needed on this trip. The two tone brown fabric had been chosen for the muted camouflage of the experienced outdoors adventurer and although it was light weight, it was considerably stronger that the thin fabrics made it look. On many occasions he had over filled the bag with climbing ropes and karabiners, strapping the tiny amount of food and drink that he would need for the day onto the outside almost as an after- thought. What had mattered most was the call of the adventure, the ache to be in the wild away from all of those fucking people. The beauty of the mountains was anathema to most people, the assumed risks and unjust terrors kept them away. To the experienced wilderness people, these places provided a comfort that modern streets and houses could never give. The crusty crackle of frost on his sleeping bag, while he slept on winter camp, had often filled his heart with a joy that central heating and thin duvets could never come close to replicating.

He took out the flask, the blue painted metal was aged and chipped, but the vacuum with in its walls held firm against the press of the atmosphere that tried with every second to invade the unnatural space. The hot chocolate within tasted muddy, bland, but of late, everything had tasted bland. Even life itself tasted only of greyness and nothing. His food may have tasted of glue and dust for all the notice that he took, spooning the mass of whatever he had dropped into the pan, from the plate to his lips.

The tablets went down easily, all he had to do was wait for the darkness and a final unending peace, a calm so deep and restful, he would never rise from it.

Demonika and the War in Fairy Land

or

How I learned to stop worrying and love Morris Dancing!

By Jan Housby and Jayne Hecate

This story is set in the Fairy Kingdom, a world that was first visited in the previous club release, The First Compendium.

Although it is not essential to have read the previous story, some extra understanding of some the scenes herein may be found by having done so...

So if you have not yet read Bobney, King of the Fairies, why not put this book down and read that one first?

It will be worth it...

Trust us...

Chapter 1:

The Devil went down to Winscombe

Winscombe was the largest city in the whole of Somerset, which in turn was the largest country on the largest landmass, in the whole of the Fairy Realm. The city ran from the coast, where a busy sea port saw giant ships in giant bottles, carrying giant cargo. There were also mighty dragon boats that were real mighty dragons. The main road to the port was lined in the evening with every kind of lady of the night that a sailor would or could imagine, from granite encrusted trolls, to pretty young elves, all "paying their way through medical school". The carts that flowed through the port during the day, did so at great speed and pulled by numerous types of beast, from beautiful centaurs who owned their own businesses, to multi-legged giant insects held under magical charms. In the evening the same trading carts could be seen traveling far more sedately along the port road, stopping occasionally to negotiate a deal of carnal exuberance with the chosen working girl, working boy or working non gendered being (that had a suitable protuberance or orifice), in exchange for a few of the newly minted coins that had the head of the new King of the Fairies, King Bobney, stamped upon them.

Moving in land, through the streets of

Winscombe, many travelers found themselves at the rough and ready pub known as 'The Rusty Plough'. In the human world, a pub this run down and this full of heavily tattooed drunks, would have been a rough bikers pub, the ample car park would have been crammed full of custom choppers, filth encrusted rat bikes and heavily modified, gleaming streetfighters. Men and women dressed in stinking black leather jeans and patch covered leather jackets would gather to drink, to fight, to date or just sit and drink tea while gazing lovingly at their newly built bike. In the fairy world, it was exactly that kind of crowd who drank there! The ample cart park contained various types of sparkling dragon, stinking demon or racing unicorn, tethered to holding posts, with their owners sat gazing at them lovingly.

Moving away from the pubs the weary traveller would find themselves in the strange and unusual streets of the entertainment area, a part of the city where the gaudy painted shops, glinted with fake gold, bought from dubious alchemists. Lining the walls of these monuments to poor taste were the gambling stations, gaming tables and even the one armed bandits, who would shoot anyone lucky enough to actually win back even a single penny more than they had lost at the games!

The Mayor of the city was a thoroughly ordinary man, who went by the name of Pencil Goldflower. He stood at just a little under six feet tall; he was cursed with a brutal haircut that resembled the pubic thatch of an elderly and over worked goblin prostitute, he had eyes that naturally squinted as if he were always gazing into the sun and his skin that had somehow taken on the grey dull hue of a rendered concrete wall. Goldflower had risen up through the ranks of petty accountants, where he had started his career, to become the leader of the city. No one was entirely sure who had given him his seat in Governance, but if asked, almost everyone, human, fairy or troll, all denied having voted for him. Yet every four years, at the annual election, the vote count found that once again Pencil Gold Flower had well over three quarters of the vote.

No one seemed to mind though, that he barely did his civic duty, although again if asked, no one was quite clear on what it was that Goldflower actually did. Yet if they were pressed, they were all sure that he was worth the enormous salary that he asked for doing it. When it came to the Mayoral Day of respect though, he could be seen marching at the head of the column of city troops, his bright red robes of office, rich in ermine fur (and maybe even a bit of old soiled ferret for good measure) flowing around him as he strode along the cobbled streets. His hands always contained the biggest ring of fake paper flowers, which he laid to rest at the base of the statue that was dedicated to the memory of those brave souls who had died so valiantly and often so pointlessly, in the fairy wars.

With his duty to the statue done, he would meander through the crowds, kissing a few babies for the press, shy away from shaking hands with any of the actual troops and then happily tell everyone that he would proudly see them all next year for the next parade. Once back home and away from the actual populace he found so tiresome, he would scrub his hands with strong soap until they were raw, just to wash away the stench of the foul poor people he had been almost forced to shake hands with and then finally relax in peace and solitude in his private hot spring that had been enclosed in his huge and ugly official residence.

Winscombe was spread even further though, out into the hills and valleys of darkest Somerset. The distant mountain peaks marked the edge of the country and just over their peaks was the exotic nation of Norfcorea, a place of mystery and intrigue, a place of a happy people who worshipped their great leader, King Jong Ill. King Jong Ill was said, with the kindest of intentions, to resemble a fat short teddy bear. Many had joked that the kings eyes resembled coat buttons, behind his thick drink bottle glasses, his delicate nose was small and a small mole on the end made it look like the tip was black. The king wore his hair shaved around his ears in the most peculiar fashion and he always wore a tight little jacket, that buttoned right up to his throat.

Being born into a Royal household, Prince Jong Una had been a studious and careful young man, he had spent his youthful years reading the many books that his father the King had kept around the palace, books that the king had brought in specially from the human world. The result of this was that when the old King died, Prince Jong Una knew an awful lot of recipes for fabulous food, but absolutely nothing at all about effectively ruling his people in the old ways of the Norfcorean kingdom. The result of which was a few years of chaos, until at last he set upon the idea that would save the Kingdom from economic collapse.

King Jong Una had turned the whole of Norfcorea into a huge exotic food takeaway. His many kitchens produced meals that would be delivered by magical beings, all across the fairy world, always arriving just mere seconds after the food had got just that tiny little bit too cold to actually enjoy. The business was a huge success and it turned Norfcorea from a bankrupt shit hole into the sort of place tourists could go to for years, just to enjoy the sort of exotic food that they could cook at home, but could never really be arsed to do so. With the money pouring in, the Kingdom of Norfcorea became rich once again and as the people prospered, they put aside their vicious weapons, their petty arguments and instead set about extracting as much money as they could from what ever foolish person would rather call them for hugely expensive food, rather than cook their own. This is the story of how Norfcorea became great again.

* * * * *

Demonika Trumpett stepped from the ship and stood on the flag stones that lined the dock, her high heeled shoes shone in the gloomy early morning sunshine, with all of their patent glory, the needle thin metal tipped heels clicked as she strode along the dock, her left hand held a single small case, made from ancient and scuffed brown leather. The handle though was shaped from hand carved ebony, into a two headed dragon that held the loops of the case in each of its mouths. She was dressed smartly, but plainly, in part to disguise who she truly was and partly because Winscombe was not a particularly fashionable city. Her long grey silk skirt covered her thin spindly legs. A matching long grey jacket covered a cerise satin blouse, meaning that only the occasional flash of colour escaped from within. Her hair was the jet black of volcanic glass (a colour that matched her shoes perfectly in highlight and tint), it shone like polished coal and if anyone was brave enough to look closely enough, they would have seen floating with in the strands of hair, wisps of something that resembled the trapped and troubled souls of the damned! Her face was unusual for two reasons. Firstly, she wore the sort of eternal smile that had over the long hard years of her life, changed from youthful and happy to ancient and ghastly. Secondly, her skin had the hue of a violent inorganic orange, half basket ball, half traffic cone. Her heavily made up eyes peered out like black dots of darkness over the lens if an arc lamp and god forbid should anyone try to guess her age. The wrinkles in her face had been dragged tort and the flesh bunched and clipped behind head with a trusty metal clothes peg, just below her hair line. The effect was to give her a look of permanent surprise, mixed with mild annoyance.

She left the quayside and stepped onto the busy port road, the whores had not yet taken up their places along the road, but this did not stop one wag in a cart from pulling up next to her to ask how much! With emotion hard to show upon her rigid face, for a moment the man thought that he was about to get lucky, a clean and relatively disease free whore was a lucky find indeed on the port road. As she lowered her hand back to her side, the smoking remains of his legs, minus his torso toppled sideways to land in the footwell of his cart. Demonika placed her case on the empty cargo deck and climbed up into the driver's seat, kicking the still smoldering legs into the gutter below, where they were carried away enthusiastically by a family of overjoyed sentient rats.

The horse pulling the cart was ancient, its skin sagged under its belly like crepe paper, it was clearly lame in three of its five legs and to make matters even worse, the poor tired animal seemed to bow in the middle, making the cart all but impossible to pull at anything above an almost stationary crawl. Demonika raised her right hand once again and once more a flash of dark purple light arced from her fingers. The horse blinked in surprise. All of its aches just faded away, all three of its missing legs grew back and each hoof suddenly felt powerful and strong. To add to its feeling of vitality, the previously weakened back was suddenly strong and all of the muscles powerfully charged. He ached to run, it had been decades since he had last ran anywhere and the urge to run was almost over powering.

The cart was in similar condition as she prepared to leave the port and with one more flick of her hand, the cheap rotten chipboard repairs became complete solid oak planks, the wobbly wheels became finely tuned steel shod hoops and the rusty leaf springs pushed the axle hard into the road as they found the parts of them that had rotted away with the salty sea air.

Turning the horse and cart into the fast moving traffic, Demonika followed her nose, something was calling to her, a destiny that she could see, a future that she could almost smell. It was the odour of the Rusty Plough, the largest pub, in the largest city, in the largest country, on the largest landmass in the whole of the fairy kingdom. She could smell the centuries of spilt scrumpy; the decades of dropped crisps and the years of dropped cigarette ash. All of it had been not just walked into the carpets, but crushed under the feet by a myriad of people, beings of every alcohol loving species had walked and spilt and dropped their mess and under it all, the carpet had absorbed so much booze that it had developed a new form of alcoholism and had become in a strange esoteric way, capable of passing that feeling of sociable mild drunkenness to all who simply walked across it.

At the door of the pub, a tall and somewhat angry troll stood against the frame, smoking a vile smelling cigar. The smoke that rose from it was faintly puce in colour, glowing in pulsing light as it rose into the air. The smell was a mix of old boiled nappies, combined with burned cabbage and shredded tractor tyres. Whoever the creature was, it was clearly enjoying the smoke and took long deep drags on the cigar every few minutes. As Demonika approached the door, the troll stood up from where it leaned and looked her up and down before speaking. "Sorry love, no whores allowed in the venue."

The voice was the rich gravel of ice, sliding across ancient cold granite, hidden in frozen mountain passes. The creatures face was impassive, its cold, crystal eyeballs dark in the rocky sockets. Demonika smiled, her face took on the look of mildly surprised innocence. "Oh my dear being, you have me misunderstood. I am no lady of the night. I am instead a business woman, I wish to see the owner of this hostelry so that I may suggest a new and exciting business strategy to them."

The troll raised its arm and pointed at a rough painted sign next to the door.

Demonika smiled again. "I can assure you that I am no whore."

The troll drew on its cigar once again, holding its breath for a moment before releasing the acrid puce smoke. "Listen love, I would love to let you in, truly I would. But, my hands are tied." The troll showed her its hands and sure enough, a thick hemp rope bound them together at the wrist.

"I see."

The troll grinned kindly. "The boss here has certain standards, she don't mind thieves, murderers, muggers, bigamists or even humans who vote Tory. However, she don't like whores. She says that your kind make the place look untidy."

Demonika looked around the outside of the pub, the walls had once been painted white, but they were now stained by hundreds of years of urine, blood, missed punches and vomit. It was hard to imagine it looking much worse. "Well, I can help you there. You see, as I said, I am not a whore. But I aim to buy out the current owner of this establishment and then thoroughly clean this place up. Can you imagine it? The walls freshly painted, the bar stocked with fine international wines and ales? That is what I bring to this fabled and ancient city. My case here has some fine samples, if you would wish to see?"

Interested, the troll stepped forwards. "Alright then, show us what you got then."

Demonika's confusingly surprised smile was beaming as she lifted the case from the cart and held it sideways until a set of legs dropped from the corners. With the case turned into a table, she opened it with a snap and the troll peered inside. "Corrrr, you got proper troll ale. I have not had that in nearly seventy years."

She closed the case and touched the handle, which caused the legs to rise back into the body of the bag. "So, are you going to let me in?"

The troll smiled again. "Sorry love, no sales folk." It pointed to another sign below the one about whores.

SALESMEN CAN FUCK OFF

Demonika's face turned as passive as it could, she looked passively mildly surprised. "That says salesmen... yes?" The troll nodded. "I am a sales woman, you see?" The troll nodded again. "We are different. You know, men and women."

The troll looked at her thoughtfully for a moment before speaking. "Now look here, you know full well that the wording of the sign is neither here nor there. I am pointing out the spirit of the sign, not the actual wording of the sign. Philosophically, you can choose to be what ever gender you so desire, I am not here to judge you on that. To each their own and may it bring them happiness. However, it is slightly disingenuous of you to imply that the wording of the sign is somehow indicative of a female bias. We both clearly understand the principle of the sign, the intrinsic meaning of the sign, with out falling into the trap of stereotypical gender roles assigned at birth." Demonika nodded her head as the troll continued. "I am aware of the insidious bias of society towards the dominion of one particular gender over another, but at the same time, I am employed here to ensure that patrons inside are free to drink themselves insensible with out risk of getting home in the early hours having swapped all of their worldly goods for a three week time-share in Little Smirda, opposite the queens favorite public toilet! The signs says no salesmen. We can infer the meaning to be gender neutral, it means no sales people, in fact, no sales beings of any kind." The troll smiled. "Maybe I will have a word with the owner about updating the sign?"

Demonika took a deep breath and closed her eyes for a moment. Politically correct trolls were the thing she despised the most. There was, after all, nothing more annoying anywhere in the universe than getting stuck in a discussion with an intellectual and pedantic troll. Her only hope was to change tack. Find another approach. She reached into her case and removed a small letter, the envelope was addressed in the strange runic letters of the troll alphabet. "Well, given that you are not going to allow me entry, may I ask that you deliver this to the correct person?"

The troll took the small envelope in its large purple stained fingers. "Hey, this is to me. This is my Moo-Pa's handwriting."

Demonika gave the troll another of her strangely surprised smiles. "Well fancy that. I was asked to deliver it when I spoke to the owner, maybe you should read it now. I will wait here in case you have a reply."

The troll gently opened the envelope, inside the paper was lightly scented with the perfume of the winter rock lichens. Holding the delicate paper between infeasibly agile fingers, the troll began to read.

> My darling Helga,
>
> This woman is my friend Demonika, what ever you do, do not let her go anywhere with out a nice warm drink inside of her. She is terribly fragile.

Your Paa-Mo says that they hope
that you are not still smoking those
awful cigars, they stain your
fingers something terrible and you
know that they are not very good
for you!

You will be pleased to hear that
Little Gretchin is doing very well.
They have become a delivery
driver in Norfcorea and have
earned enough to buy a convertible
Dragon. You would love it if you
could see it.

Write soon my darling,

Love from

Moo-Pa

XXXXXXXX

Small tears of pure calcite leaked from the corners of the trolls eyes. "Awww, a letter from my Moo-Pa, thank you so much." The troll dabbed a large canvas hanky at the tears. "You had better go in and get a drink before you get cold."

The troll pushed open the door and Demonika stepped past it and into the gloom of the pub. The smell was not merely vile, but nasally offensive. The acid bite to the air would have stripped the enamel from her teeth, if Demonika had been capable of a true smile. The stale bite of ancient beer, the stench of foul toilets that had not been cleaned in centuries, the hound that served behind the bar, all of these things alone would have been enough to produce a terrible stench, but combined, the smells became a toxic weapon of globally significant proportions. As she stepped onto the foul rotten carpet, she felt the alcoholic haze begin to soak through into the very soul of her foot, seeping like a foul toxic damp, rising through the aged and indelicate flesh. The needle thin heel broke through the crust over the top of the carpet and she felt her back jar painfully as she became unbalanced for a brief moment until after an inch or so of downward travel, the heel hit solid ground once more.

Taking a cautious moment to pull her heel out of the floor, she took the several tottering steps to the bar and waited to be served. She reached into her case and took out a large legal looking, official envelope and slapped it hard on the bar. She straightened her back and gave off the unmissable pungent ooze of a lawyer in her appearance. This was bound to bring the manager down from her flat above the pub. With in minutes, a woman with straw coloured hair and teeth was stood at the end of the bar, a long white cigarette in her fingers, an orange glowing lit one poked out from between her teeth. She was a foot taller than Demonika, her face gnarled and haggard by decades of late night parties and early morning hangovers. Her saggy dress top was cut low revealing a deflated baggy cleavage that looked like two bags of dried leaves that had been left soaking in piss overnight before being sculpted into knotted comedy balloon breast. The smell confirmed that this had likely been the case. "What do you want?" She had the voice of a harpy, after a particularly hard lifetime of amphetamine addiction. Demonika gave the woman the best version she had of a friendly smile, it looked mildly surprised, mixed with painfully constipated.

"Ahh, hello. You must be the owner? I have here a legal document that contains roughly thirteen thousand complaints about this establishment. These complaints range from mild comments about the day time noise, to a few comments about late night disturbances, but most concerning of all, we have reports of under age drinking among your patrons."

The woman looked deeply suspicious of her new guest, her eyes narrowed, her brow knotted together and her face resembled a fallen dead branch laying across a lake of stained leather. "This pub has been here for nine hundred years. How far do these complaints go back?"

Demonika tried to look kindly. Her face merely looked surprisingly baffled. "Yes, I am aware that it has taken our office some considerable time to reply to some of these complaints, but as you know, we are terribly busy and even more so since King Bobney took his throne, we have been trying desperately to catch up. You know, get things going on the right track and everything."

"Well as it happens, I ain't the owner, I am just the landlord. I will get the owner here in a minute. Go and sit down, have a drink. He wont be long." The woman turned and vanished into the darkness behind the bar and the serving hound wandered over, jumped up so that it's front paws were on the bar and began to pour a small glass of something vaguely sweet smelling out into a delicate glass for Demonika. Once the beast was done, it pushed the glass across the bar to her with its nose and then in a whispery whine, its ears cocked one up and one down, a short growl, the meaning became instantly apparent to Demonika. "On the house."

Demonika took the drink and sat down in the far corner of the pub, away from any of the other patrons, some of whom were now eyeing her with the suspicious intent of criminals about to make good on an easy mugging. She placed the drink to her lips and sniffed the foul looking concoction, it was not poisoned as such, but with such a high alcohol content, it was still pretty lethal. Tipping the glass back she swallow the liquid in two gulps and waited for the pain of it hitting her stomach. After a few moments she was able to make her best impression of a smile once again. As she looked up to the bar, a new face appeared, he was somehow decadent, slimy in the way that only those who work in politics can be. She knew at once that he was the owner of the pub. "Ahhh, Mr Gold Flower, how very decent to meet you at last."

Goldflower stepped forwards and around the bar, he carried with him a small delicate glass of a fruity smelling wine, it was very clearly not something served in his pub. For a start it was not eating into the glass. "My manageress, Charity, informs me that you have come here with a list of complaints about our gentle establishment, is this right?"

Demonika attempted to beam a disarming smile at Goldflower. It was not a nice smile and he recoiled slightly. "Oh my Dear Goldflower, complaints are such strong words. I have come here to make you an offer! Nnnoo, not an offer, think of it as an appeal to your better nature. You are after all a thoroughly decent and upstanding gentleman in this community, many of the complaint letters state that almost fondly."

Pencil Goldflower was a vain man at best, having Demonika massage his ego with a few kind words soon had him smiling at her with the face of an imbecile, his eyes were those of a soft and gentle doe, when she is pumped full of anaesthetic, prior to being put down! "Why Miss… er, I did not get your name."

"You can call me Demonika sir, all of my close friends do."

"Why Miss Demonika, what a lovely name you have. You are clearly not from these parts."

she smiled again, her skin stretching across her cadaverous skull to the point that it was almost translucent and what was beneath was clearly horrifying. "Indeed, Mr Goldflower, indeed. I am from the far south of here. My father has a small estate beyond the rim of the world. A family business sort of thing, but I have come here to stand on my own two little feet for a while, until I am ready to take over the family concern once and for all."

Goldflower allowed his arm to stretch out an encircle the woman's shoulders. "Oh really Miss Demonika? Well well, you should allow me the honour of welcoming you properly to our happy little village. Tell me, how can I assist you here?"

Her smile turned sour, her eyes deader than any corpse he had ever seen. "I want your pub. You will be paid handsomely for this revolting little shit hole, but I want it now. All of it." She stared into his soul, his soul tried to stare back was too terrified of her and instead it soiled itself in the darkness of his subconscious. "So, if you will just sign these documents, then I can move in and that woman you have running the place can move out!"

Goldflower tried to put a struggle, his attempt was lame at best and pathetically worthless at worst. "But think of our patrons, they are fond of Charity, she is such a nice girl, they all like a bit of glamour in the place as they drink down their cheap muck."

Demonika gave him another ghastly smile. "I promise you Mr Goldflower, I will imprison Charity for all of the crimes she has committed against the patrons here. I will lock her up and throw away the key."

He looked at her as she spoke, she had the aura of a maniacal beast, if he looked hard enough he could swear that her shadow had horns and a tail. "But what will you do with the place one you have it? We have a huge amount of people who like to come here for a drink, away from the watchful eyes of those who would disapprove."

"Just sign the form for me please Mr

Goldflower, then I can build a wall around this place and I am going to force out the undesirables. This place will become a perfect little wine bar. I promise you that I am going to make this pub great again!"

Goldflower looked down at the page in front of him. It was a contract, that he actually stood to do quite well out of, although the small print which was almost unreadably tiny, said something about giving up his immortal soul. He looked at his name on the page, typed as it was in the lines of text.

'Mr Pencil Goldflower does agree to sell his pub to Miss Demonika Trumpett for the sum agreed.'

He smiled at her. "I am sorry, I don't have a pen."

Demonika slid a cheap plastic biro across the page to him. He flinched as he touched it, the ink was the colour of dried blood, the washed reddy brown of blood that has stood for too long in an unrefrigerated jar on a dusty shelf. He signed his name and as he did so, he felt a terrible cold wind charge through the pub. His fear had made him sign, so it was that with one small mark on a page, he had given the pub to what he could only think of as the Devil. At least he had got a fabulous amount of money for it though. But they both knew that the money would soon run dry, his well had been capped. A monster was now in charge of the watering hole.

Chapter two: Long live the King

The country of Norfcoria was a peaceful quiet place, a place of gentle meditating monks and diligent studious young people, who read as much as they could, just because they could. The country had a king, Jong Ill and he too was a quiet gentle man, who was also deeply beloved by the population, despite the friendly jokes about his appearance. He would often spend his days when he was not reading, out among his people, sharing in their lives and even helping out on the local yak farms.

"There is something honest about working with Yaks" he would say to his advisers, none of whom were particularly keen on getting yak shit on their robes of office. None the less, once the yaks were milked and housed once again for the night, the king would be encouraged to climb into his gilt carriage and ride in peace back to the palace. The royal coachman had got used to the old king and his agricultural leanings, which meant that the royal seat in the coach was often covered with a thick polythene bag to keep the mud and yak shit off of the plush scarlet velvet. The carpet had been lifted and replaced with a thick rubber mat that was easy to hose off when it got dirty.

When the king was not able to spend his hours happily among the people or his beloved Yaks, he would spend his days dealing with issues of state, which even his most dedicated of staff would admit that the king did not really enjoy. Jong Ill was a simple man at heart and he craved only most the simple pleasure from life, which is probably how he ended up with five wives and seven mistresses, all of whom loved him dearly.

The old king was a staunch supporter of the traditions of old Norfcoria, in particular the burning of Yak dung to heat their homes. It was cheap, came in plentiful supply and solved the problem of how to dispose of the tonnes and tonnes of Yak shit, which had been building up over summer. However, in recent times, the Medical Organisation of Norfcoria had issued public health warnings about such practices, stating that their homes had some of the worst indoor air pollution in the Kingdom, whilst also contributing to climate change. Respiratory ailments were on the rise, placing the Norfcoria Health Service under severe strain. King Jong Ill was not to be persuaded though – the old traditions were the best and he continued to bask in the ever-increasing sunshine, whilst regularly reaching for his blue inhaler.

So it was that at the grand age of forty nine, King Jong Ill died, his body all dried up like a shriveled pea pod and his lungs as rigid as a worn out pair of old leather boots that had spent three months at the bottom of a slurry pit, before being left to dry in the sun for a month. His only son, also the oldest of the king's three children was expected to take the throne and in the days leading up to his coronation Prince Jong the first, mourned for his father and studied the book of sacred duties that would teach him how to be a king. The book was two thousand pages thick and each page was written by hand, upon paper so fine, it was almost translucent. Over the centuries, the edges of the paper had been worried by moths, nibbled by rodents and had one alarming stain that no one wished to discuss, but was likely the result of an ancient prince getting over excited at the prospects of his ascension (so to speak) to the throne.

The prince's Aid Du Champ, was a man who looked like he was in his late seventies, he had served as the ambassador to the Fairy Kingdom right up until the arrival of King Bobney, where upon he had returned home to the royal court, away from international politics and had quietly hoped for a peaceful life of wandering around the royal palace, where he dreamed of dying in the arms of several spritely, but of legal age, young nymphs. Alas, his dreams were mostly unfulfilled and he spent his days helping the young prince with the legalities of running a nation. Many of the conversations they had were about the intricacies and interpretation of the law.

"Because is not really an answer though, is it?"

"It was answer enough for your father though, your majesty."

Prince Jong the first sighed gently and looked once at the ancient hand drawn script in front of him, his head sagged and his eyes heavy with the days reading, ached for the darkness of sleep. "So let me get this straight, the reason why the king of Norfcoria must have no less than three wives is… Because."

The old man shook his head once again. "It is the law, your majesty. You are bound by it just as your father was and his father before him and his father before him. I could go on."

The prince smiled thinly. "Indeed, you could. At length no doubt!"

Returning his eyes to the page, he continued

reading the ancient text and turned the page over once more. At this point in the book, the scribe had clearly grown bored of writing and had drawn a small picture of a young man with enormous testicles and he appeared to… The only words the prince could apply without appearing rather rude, was milking himself. He looked up once again at the aged and clearly tired Aid Du Champ and grinned. "Must I also carry out this royal duty?" He pointed to the picture, his face a mask of innocence.

The Aid Du Champ tried to remain dignified and hoped that his tone was not so patronising, that the soon to be king would have him executed. Although with the current evening as it was, death was almost a preferable outcome. "No sire, nor I must say have I heard that question before. Maybe you would like to continue to the next page, it is somewhat more agricultural in its outlook."

The young prince turned the page and found himself staring at a list of animals that it was necessary for the royal household to raise in order to have meat for royal feasts. He scanned down the list and noticed with some surprise that there were a number of things that he would not touch himself unless his life depended upon it and even then he was not sure.

"Why on earth do we need pickled wasps?"

The Aid Du Champ smiled once more, his old and grizzled face wore the smile like an aging performer wears the make-up of youth for a role they know that they cannot truly play. "Ah yes, you will see several dishes there that appear unappealing. The reason for these dishes is that they are traditional. It is traditional to feed them to ambassadors, royal guests from other kingdoms or politicians, just to see if they are stupid enough to eat them. It gives the king a guide as to how foolish a negotiator is likely to be."

The prince nodded his head respectfully. "That is, I must admit, rather clever and rather amusing. We must try it as soon as I am king."

The Aid Du Champ nodded his head regally. "Indeed your majesty, guests to the palace have not experienced that kind of thing before. I shall order it done as soon as your coronation is complete, after I have blessed the clouds and counted the sandy grains upon the beaches."

The prince looked up at the old man, his eyes became narrow slits of suspicion. "Are you teasing me?" He watched the man and saw that for a brief moment a genuine smile flickered at the corners of the man's mouth. "Maybe we should wait until we try that particular joke then."

The Aid Du Champ nodded his head in agreement. "That is likely most wise your majesty, you are already getting the hang of being a king. Only another thousand pages and then we can prepare you for your first royal court."

The book made for slow reading and the prince found that for some of the sections, his eyes glazed over and the reading was something that he was physically doing, but his mind was in neutral and he had no idea of what the passage actually said.

Finally he reached the last filled in pages of the book and it was here that he recognised the handwriting of his own father. He read the passage, the letters played out on the page in beautiful red calligraphy, the brush strokes across the page were as graceful and delicate as the brush strokes of a master portrait painter. He blinked twice and read the passage once again before looking up to his aged guide who appeared to have fallen asleep while stood up. The prince thought about slipping away quietly before the man stirred, but he suspected that such an action would be considered bad form and likely to get him into trouble before he even made it to king. So he coughed lightly, then again slightly louder before finally coughing with the forced hacking of a terminal yak dung smoker with only half a tobacco ruined lung left! The Aid Du Champ awoke with a start and almost fell backwards into the open fire that had been gently roasting away the pain in his arthritic knees. The prince asked his guide to clarify the point made by the old king with a simple question. "I did not need to read all off this old bollocks did I? If I had skipped to the end, I could have read father's note and we could have continued from there, isn't that right?"

The Aid Du Champ nodded sagely. "Indeed you could have done that, but I rather suspect that you would be a worse king for having done so. I rather imagine that is why your father added his note at the end, rather than the front."

The prince closed the book and gave the old man a sly look. The Aid Du Champ merely stared ahead silently, his face unreadable. "Did you guide my father this way too?"

The Aid Du Champ bowed his head slightly, the prince was concerned that he was about to nod off again when the man began to speak once more. "It was my honour to serve the court of your father, just as it is my honour to serve the court of yourself. Where possible I guided him to be wily and he was a sincere and studious man, who picked up the wisdom of ruling our great nation rather quickly."

The prince grinned slightly. "You mean that he was a devious old bastard?"

The old man chuckled slightly. "Some may have described your father that way, but it is not my place to pass such a comment."

Again his eyes stayed on the old man as he watched him for any sign that would reveal some flaw or chip in his defenses. Nothing appeared obvious. "No wonder that my father made you his main ambassador, I rather suspect that there is little that can slip past you. I rather hope that you can teach me as well as your taught my father, I suspect that there is much from you that I would wish to learn."

A genuine warm smiled crossed the face of the old man, before he got control of himself once more and his serene, if slightly constipated look returned. "It will be my honour to serve you, your majesty. May I suggest that we retire for the evening? You have a busy day ahead of you tomorrow and you will appreciate the rest if you take it now."

The prince nodded his head in acceptance. "You are right and I have been sat here reading this vile old book without a rest for what feels like days. A nice bath and a good night sleep are just what I need."

The Aid Du Champ nodded his head. "You have managed to read the entire book in just under fifty one hours your majesty. That is a new record and you only fell asleep twice. Indeed, you will make a fine king."

The two men stepped awkwardly from the reading room, the door was closed as they left and the Aid Du Champ locked the door with one large key. "There will be no need to open that door again until your own child is ready to take to the throne."

The prince grinned. "Unless I wish to add my own words or drawings to the royal book."

The Aid Du Champ smiled kindly. "I rather suspect that by the time that you are ready to make your mark upon the book, you will have learned enough to know that you don't really want to do so!" The Aid Du Champ smiled gently, "just as your father did in his later years."

Prince Jong stretched out his arms and leaned over backwards, easing some of the ache from his spine. "How many kings and queens have you been with as they read that book?"

Again the Aid Du Champ gave the prince a sincere and gentle smile. "Your majesty, you are my fifth. I gave your father his throne while he was barely out of boyhood, your grandfather was also a young man who lived for many years and there was your great grandmother. She was a magnificent woman with a mind as sharp as a needle, there were few indeed who got one over on her. My first would have been your great great grandmother. She was something of a tyrant I am afraid, but in her thirty summers as queen, she did not murder a single soul. Unfortunately she had several well-trained axe and sword men who were more than happy to do it for her!"

The prince looked shocked for a moment, his voice when it came was not the usual quiet that the Aid Du Champ was used to, instead it was a whispery hoarse sound, like that of a man dying of cigar poisoning. "Wow, I can have people murdered? For real? Actually murdered? Like killed?"

The Aid Du Champ shook his head sadly, regret filled his voice. "I rather wish that I had not mentioned that your majesty. That was a dark time in our history, we have other worries these days and murder is not a solution that you should consider. There have, it must be said, been some rulers in history who have considered the systematic murder of a population as a way to counter unemployment or lack of food, but these people tend to be of the sort of guiltless individuals who will happily pull out your spleen while you sit on the potty, just to see the look on your face."

"So no murdering then?" The prince sounded grudgingly disappointed.

"Do you really need me to answer that question your majesty?"

"What about if someone does something really evil? Can we murder them then?"

The Aid Du Champ raised his eye brows to the ceiling. "How does one judge an act of unbelievable evil? It is said that the current ruler of the fairy kingdom murdered a man on the night he took his throne, should we call the man who has brought peace and prosperity to that realm an evil being?"

"He does ruin a lot of sports equipment, that is quite evil." The Aid Du Champ tutted under his breath.

"I do hope that should you have the pleasure of meeting King Bobney, you will be somewhat more tactful. He is a little sensitive about his weight. However, crushing running machines and wearing out rowing machines hardly counts as evil."

"Tell that to the man who has to wash his shorts each day!"

The Aid Du Champ tried to ignore the sniggering prince. "I have the dignity of office Sire, I am not permitted to laugh at your joke. Also smut is not considered suitable for a man of your office either. Now I suggest that you go for your bath and then retire to your chambers for the night. Tomorrow brings you many new adventures."

He bowed low to the Prince and and waited for the man to walk away. After a few seconds he spoke again.

"Your majesty, I am not permitted to rise until you have left my presence. I would point out that the sciatica in my lower back is killing me."

"It has been a long day, I don't want you bowing to me any more, can we hug instead?" Startled, the Aid Du Champ stood bolt upright. His sciatic pain suddenly forgotten. As he stood as erect as a statue, the prince put his arms around the man's shoulders and held him a brief hug, which ended with him patting the Aid Du Champs back. "You did a good job today Cecil, thanks man."

The prince walked away and as the door closed behind him, leaving the Aid Du Champ alone in the hall, he muttered quietly to himself. "In all of my years, never has one of them hugged me. It is just not proper, he is going to be king tomorrow, he can't go round hugging people. What will people think?" A smile broke out across the man's face and as he wandered away to his own office, he muttered again under his breath. "He's a good kid though, he's going to make for an interesting king!"

The prince's private rooms were the usual sort of place for a late teen, pushing into an early twenties student. His bedroom wall was covered in the finest printed wall paper that money could buy. This had been covered with posters of rock bands, fast carts and famous swords men. There were also one or two pictures of fine ladies, who it appeared, revealed a little more of their under clothing than they probably should, but the prince was especially fond of those pictures and thus they stayed, although they had been coated with a film that made them wipe clean. Such a thing was never mentioned in the court, but the old king had laughed when he was informed of his son's nocturnal activities before adding with a wink to his chief of the military. "Remember that time after the chaos battle? We splashed the stuff everywhere!"

In his room though he had a small secret compartment and it was to this that he immediately reached for as he prepared for his bath. The secret panel slipped aside revealing the small space beneath the solid sentient oakwood wardrobe, taken from a tree long dead. Although not large, the space was just big enough to hold a magazine and nervously and while making sure that none of the palace staff were about, he took the magazine from its hiding place and retired to his bath. As he slid into the fragrant bubbles, he let out a soft sigh of contentment and once comfortable in the water, he opened his magazine at the start of the article he had been itching to read. "Oh my sweet beauty, I could gobble you up!" Silently, he turned the page of his magazine. "Oh my heavens, look at you!"

There came a gentle knock at the bathroom door and in an embarrassed chaotic shuffle as he tried to drop the magazine behind his bath out of the sight of whoever it was who had disturbed him, it slid out of his hands and landed face up on the floor five feet or so from the bath and somewhat too close to the door. The knock came again and slightly ashamed, he called out. "Enter, but don't look down" A young pretty maid entered the room and smiled at him. In her hand was a light pink bath brush and a bottle of perfumed hair oil.

"Your majesty, I have come to scrub your back and wash your hair." Inadvertently she looked down and caught sight of the magazine on the floor. Without thinking she exclaimed excitedly. "Oh your majesty, my grandmother is in that edition, she has the centre spread!"

The prince looked at her shyly, the girl was close to his age and she was remarkably pretty. Her large green eyes, her long silken black hair. The satin of her blouse, the shine of her boots. She was a goddess and for a moment the prince forgot his shyness. "I read that part of the magazine with great interest. I marveled at her talents."

The girl blushed slightly. "Should I tell my grandmother that she has a royal fan?"

For a moment, the young prince gave serious thought to offer, his mind was a turmoil of excitement. "Would she… you know, for me?"

The girl giggled. "Of course she would, you are going to be king tomorrow. How could she refuse. I am a little surprised that you liked her though."

"Oh I did, she was magnificent."

Again the girl giggled. "Well your majesty, you can imagine how we felt as youngsters when she fed us with those?"

"Oh indeed, you were lucky to have them, I have not seen finer."

The girl beamed her delight. "Your majesty, if you think that her buns are good, you should see her pastries."

For a moment the prince forgot himself and he almost stood up in the bath. "I would love to see her pastries."

Again the girl's face was full of delight and then with a mischievous smile she almost whispered. "I could bring you some in if you like? She has won awards for them in the city cake making contests."

Finally the prince remembered his manners. "It would not be seemly I am afraid for me to accept gifts from the people, I am here to serve our people, not take from them."

She smiled innocently. "If you don't tell, neither will I."

He gave her a wicked and winning smile. "It would be our little secret?"

"I promise your majesty to never tell another living soul." Her smile was as beautiful as the rest of her, he knew that he could trust her implicitly and he also knew that he had made a friend that he would always be able to rely upon. He held out his hand to her.

"Pinky swear?" She stepped closer to the bath and wrapped her own little finger about his.

"Pinky swear!" Her smile was genuine. "Now then your majesty, about that back scrub?"

He settled back in the bath and she stepped behind with her brush and looked down at his broad shoulders and slightly spotty back, his voice was a little shy. "I hope that you don't mind, but I get terrible blackheads on my back?"

"Your majesty, I am a highly trained beauty therapist and an expert with skin regimes, we will have that sorted in no time." She pushed him forwards slightly in his bath water, the bubbles maintaining his modesty. "We just need to exfoliate a little and then we need to find out what skin type you have. I am guessing that you are a greasy skin type?"

His thoughts went back to his years in school and awful spots that he had suffered with, the first time that he noticed the terrible smell produced from his teenage armpits before his nurse introduced him to the deodorant rock.

"I have a history of greasy skin, but dry on my forehead." He felt a little shy explaining it to the young woman as she scrubbed his skin with the brush. "I also get terrible itching on my scalp, can you do anything about that?"

* * * * *

The morning of the coronation was busy, servants ran around the palace, dropping flowers into every vase and candles into every candelabra until the palace glowed with the soft light in every dark corner and the scent on the air was like an old ladies knicker-drawer. The Aid Du Champ, dressed in his finest tights and bear skin jerkin marched along the main corridor to the prince's room and knocked loudly on the door. He had caught a couple of the previous kings in moments of an indelicate nature on the morning of their coronation as the rise to power had made them think that they could seduce the young women who worked in the palace. He was concerned that the prince was likely to be another of them and so when he burst into the bedroom he was somewhat startled to find the prince fully dressed and the young woman from the previous evening also immaculate in her uniform. In front of the prince was a small tray and upon it were several of the most elegant and succulent cakes that he had ever seen. They glistened with icing so pure it resembled the thin frost of a winters sunny morning. One of the cakes had a small candle in it that had been blown out. Set out in a rich deep blue, iced letters spelled out 'good luck with your coronation'. The maid and the prince looked up startled, as if they had been caught doing something deeply immoral and possibly likely to have her sent to a nunnery until she blossomed! Finally the prince spoke. "Cecil, how jolly nice to see you." The old man gaped at him, his mouth moving silently, fish like, unable to find words to express the unexpected nature of discovering such innocence. The prince spoke again. "Do come and have one of these Cecil. Sharon's grandmother made them and they are truly divine."

The Aid Du Champ crossed the room and eyed the young woman with suspicion. She took one of the prettier cakes and gently placed it in the old man's hand. "This one has dark chocolate chips and just a hint of chili. They are wonderful. Do try it."

The old man raised the sweet cake to his lips and tasted the smallest amount that he doubted could poison him. The cake melted against his tongue, the taste flooded across lips like waters through a broken dam. His eyes went wide and he took another nibble, dropping crumbs into his bear skin. "My dear girl, these are the finest cakes I have ever tasted. Your grandmother, she is a most gifted woman."

The prince nodded. "She made it as the guest

cake maker in this month's edition of cakes and pastries. She had the whole centre spread."

The Aid Du Champ eyed the young prince through narrow slitted eyes, but the girl quickly interjected. "Oh yes, I was telling his majesty about her only this morning."

The prince looked suddenly relieved and the Aid Du Champ made a decision to find out why after the days activities were over, but for the time being though, he had a coronation to deal with and a future king who was going to be late. "Your majesty, we must make haste to the coronation room, you must accept your crown."

The prince grinned. "First, I have a serious question that I must ask."

The Aid Du Champ looked confused, this was not how his day was supposed to go and he nodded simply. The prince indicated to the maid. "This is my friend Sharon. I want her to be a part of my main staff, she knows things that I think might be extremely useful. Can you make that happen?"

The old man looked at the two young people in front of him, he could see no sign of deviousness or mischief. "I suppose so, it is not uncommon for a new King to appoint an advisor for the less important matters of state."

The prince smiled so happily the Aid Du Champ wondered for a moment if he was simple in the head. "Come on then, lets get this crowning over with", the young man turned to

Sharon, "you are coming too!"

The Aid Du Champ flicked his eyes to the ceiling and then started off towards the door. The two young people followed him out and walked at a brisk pace to keep up with him.

The coronation room was filled with dignitaries and honoured guests, the rows of seats at the back of the room were packed with those people lucky enough to win a ticket in the lottery that had arranged them. As the Prince entered the room a mighty cheer sounded and with his friend at his side, he walked the length of the room and waited next to the throne as tradition demanded. He would only take to the throne when the Aid Du Champ asked him to do so. Sharon stood silently at his side, her face frozen with a still and polite smile. She prayed

337

that she did not look as nervous as she suddenly felt. For a moment she had to fight an impulse to pat down her uniform, but as the Aid Du Champ approached the throne and began his oration, she quickly felt the tension flow from her body.

"Prince Jong, we the people of Norfcoria would ask you to take to the throne and rule us fairly and with dignity. Will you do so?"

As tradition demanded the prince refused once by shaking his head and looking out of the window. The old man smiled a genuine grin of satisfaction, the prince was playing his part perfectly.

"Oh go on, please?"

"I don't want to, it's boring."

The lines were word perfect. He had absorbed them from the book as if he had written them himself. "Please your majesty. Be our king. No one else wants the job."

The prince looked thoughtful for a moment. The Aid Du Champ watched intently. "Can I have a glass of Yak milk first?"

The words were utterly perfect. The Aid Du Champ could not have been happier. "Bring the prince a glass of fragrant Yak milk."

A small glass of milk was presented to the

prince by one of the senior generals, Prince Jong took the glass and sipped it three times, just as tradition required, before replacing it upon the jewel encrusted golden tray.

"I want goats milk, not Yaks milk!" A second tray was presented and the prince took the chalice from the tray and sipped once. "Can I have some honey with it please?"

A drop of royal golden honey was allowed to drip from a royal golden spoon and into warm goats milk. The prince took a sip and then another. The Aid Du Champ waited and watched. Tradition demand that he then lift the chalice up high and drain it. The prince did so and having drained every last drop, ran his finger around the inside of the chalice and licked off the last of the honey. "now your majesty, will you be our King?"

Prince Jong climbed the three small steps and turned to face the room before sitting down gently. "Can you bring me another cushion, this one is too hard?" The extra plush velvet cushion was presented and the prince stood up for long enough for it to be slid under his bottom. "Alright, I will be your king."

The amassed crowd in the room cheered and the Aid Du Champ smiled, the new king had done his job perfectly!

Chapter 3:- The Mage's Chamber

Demonika stalked around the newly acquired pub, she had sacked the remaining staff and was making plans on who she could bring in to replace them. The first to go had been the politically correct troll that had acted as the doorman, who sent off with a boat ticket home. When she examined the kitchen, she discovered several generations of kettle goblins living below the fire grate and they grudgingly left after she threatened to spray them down with bleach and the fire hose.

The only aspect of the kitchen that she chose

not to touch was the small room where Wuffles kept his bed, hidden behind a shabby brown sack cloth curtain. The darkness within came with the delicate aroma of old dog, cheap kibble and lavender soap. Wrinkling up her nose, she decided to try in there another day and headed off to explore the rest of the building, the guest rooms, the communal bathroom and the large lavvy shed out the back. The smell of the lavvy shed had an exquisite bite to the nose that was something extra special, there were hints of boiled cabbage, intimations of flatulent sailors and down right proclamations of something awfully excremental! The floor was soaked in hundreds of years of drunken piss drips that had corroded a channel across the floor to the drain. The walls had probably never ever been painted, but if they had, the paint had long since peeled and this was probably due to the almost flammable toxic fumes from the drain. The hole in the ceiling was the only light in there, but if she squinted her eyes, there was a faint and disgusting phosphorescence around the urinal.

Back in the yard, a large stack of old beer and scrumpy barrels lined the rear fence and living in one of these was a small family of kittens and their mother. Demonika smiled, she loved kittens, she particularly enjoyed having them lightly fried in their own juices with some Elf sweat salt. She wandered back inside, Wuffles the dog was laid down by the hearth, gently cleaning his genitals with his tongue. Other than him, the pub was deserted and she had explored as much of the rotten shit hole that she wanted to. "We need to redecorate this place, it is vile. When was it last painted?"

Wuffles looked up from his goolies and gave her a look that intimated October, thirty years ago. "Really? Only thirty years? How has it got so disgusting in just thirty years? Wuffles moved his eyebrows. "Really? I thought that sort of thing only happened in brothels!" Wuffles wagged his tail twice and it thumped on the floor loudly. "I may be prepared to agree to that, but surely the mess could have been cleaned up?" Wuffles whined faintly and blinked. "They could have hired a cleaner surely?" This time Wuffles simply put his chin on his paws and growled slightly. "Well certainly not if that was all he was prepared to pay!" she laughed, "He deserved all he got."

Wuffles said nothing else, but he did stand up, pull on his apron and wander out to the kitchen. Picking up a large pan in his teeth, he prepared the stove and began to warm the oil ready to cook for Demonika. Demonika wandered out of the bar and climbed the stairs to Pencil Goldflower's private rooms, the door opened with a creak and inside she found the foetid remains of his mattress, soiled as it was with decades of onanism. The wardrobe had been emptied of all of Goldflower's clothes years before when he had moved out, but he had left behind several copies of the gentleman's magazine, Fairy Hole Dweller and several of them were also very heavily soiled. At the back of the wardrobe was a small panel that seemed somehow more solidly fixed to the wall than the rest of it. She tapped it and it sounded with the hollow thud of a secret door, but as with all secret doors, there had to be a secret way to open it. This was something that she would have to think about.

Under the bed was an old trunk and as she

pulled it out, something inside shifted with the movement and once clear of the bed frame, she pressed the catches and they popped open with a well oiled snap. As she lifted the lid, what she was presented with was a rather soiled turkey baster, several pairs of tight surgical gloves and a dozen small screw lid pots that could hold small amounts of fluid with out leaking. A puzzled look crossed her face, this was just another of the strange and unusual mysteries of the rusty plough.

A bark from below brought Demonika back to the real world, so she closed the case and wandered back down stairs to where Wuffles presented her with an absolutely perfect plateful of kitten vol au vents. Every detail was perfect, the delicate flake of the pastry was matched by the exquisitely gentle flavour of the fillings. The kitten liver pate was smooth and flecked with finely sliced herbs, yet she noticed almost immediately that there was absolutely no trace, no matter how small of garlic. With out having to tell him, Wuffles had known that garlic was one of the few substances that she could not touch, taste or insert. She picked up one of the fine pastries and took a small bite. The taste melted across her tongue, never before had she tasted food so well made. Every flavour was perfect, every herb was in just the right proportion, even the pastry, that usually most people of sound mind would agree tastes of very little really, was flavoured with gentle hints of butter and sea salt. For moments, Demonika could not focus on anything other the mild orgasm that her tongue was suddenly having, as it was washed with the flavours of Wuffles' cooking.

"Oh my word, this is truly exquisite!" She moaned with the intensity of a post coital moment, "Wuffles, where did you get these from? They are amazing". Wuffles wrinkled his brow and growled faintly. Demonika looked genuinely surprised. "Really?" She asked almost in disbelief. "But they were remarkable, I had no idea that you were such a talented Chef." Wuffles yawned, his eye brows knotted in taciturn silence.

From the corner of the room, a pair of small bright eyes watched from behind a vase of long dead dried flowers, the eyes were placed in an equally small bright face, which was attached at conception to a suitably sized head, which sat upon the unusually large for a fairy, shoulders of Norfcorean spy, Deevee Deplaor, known as Deeve to his friends in Winscome. He wrote down the details of his view, recorded the remarks and pretty soon had a good description of Wuffles' latest epicurean delight, ready for transmission to the King's kitchens.

Demonika placed the final morsel in her mouth, again the delicate flavours washed across her tongue, if her mouth were capable of multiple orgasms, she would be experiencing another moment of bliss. The final crumbs tumbled down her throat and as the flavours began to fade from her mouth, she trembled slightly, she needed a drink, but to take one would destroy the perfect balance that remained in her mouth and as desperate as she was to drink, she was equally desperate to keep that delicate balance present. Finally, she reached forwards and placed her hand upon a small bottle of beer. Looking up Wuffles frowned and tilted his ears forward slightly. "So which one should I have then to match the food?" Demonika answered tersely. Wuffles let out a slight groan, his ears tipped one forward and one back. She let out a sigh before replying, "I don't know Wuffles, I was never much of a cider drinker." Wuffles twitched both ears and murmured something like a short broken whimper. Demonika looked up at him with suspicion. "Well if you say so, but generally men who say the line trust me before a woman puts something in her mouth, have another motive for her doing so."

Again, Wuffles did not reply and Demonika twisted off the cap of the rough looking cider, pouring the thick liquid into a fairly clean glass from the collection on the bar. Following Wuffles' advice, she let the liquid settle, a thick sediment an inch or so deep formed in the bottom of the glass and still she waited. Finally, Wuffles let out a small squeak and she lifted the glass to her lips and took the smallest of sips. The liquid burst through her mouth, washing away the final taste of the food, but replacing it with a fresh clean taste of fresh apples, warm autumnal days and just the faintest hint of a winter blackberry. After a couple of seconds, the taste began to fade and she sipped again, but a larger amount. Wuffles looked up at her, his ears cocked, his eyebrows knotted. He winked one eye and laying his head on his paws once again, drifted off to sleep, his instructions given. Under any other circumstances, a dog giving her orders would result in the beast facing a short but horrifically painful remainder of the rest of its life. But Wuffles was an exceptional chef and his advice about the drink had been beyond reproach. He was truly a gifted bar man.

As she finished her drink, her mind played over the possibilities of what was behind the secret door upstairs. How could she open it and once open, would she need to close it more rapidly? As she thought, she tried to imagine all of the stuff she had seen in the room, the ugly wooden moldings that went around the ceiling, the bad paint and then finally the tarnished old chalice on the windowsill. It was completely out of place there, it was so out of place, that it could only be in the correct place for a hidden switch. A small movement of the chalice could be enough to open the lock, or there could even be a hidden button beneath it. She needed to investigate it further. The climb back up stairs was completed with the warm fuzzy feeling of a full stomach and the slight intoxication of a fine cider. The room felt different inside once she knew where to look for the hidden switch. Her hand brushed the chalice, it was firmly in place on the windowsill. Her eyes consumed every photon of light that had touched it as she stared at it in place, finally she closed her hand around it and with the small catch of an old cup stuck to the table with a ring of old spilled tea, she wrenched it upwards. Nothing happened.

Her temper flared, there was no reason for the filthy old thing to be there except to act as a switch for the hidden door. She turned the corroded and dusty old thing over in her hands and examined every blemish in the hope of finding an answer. Scratched into the bottom she found some ancient rough letters.

Holy Ale Cup

Property of J H Christ

AD33

With a violent fit of pique, she threw the cup over her shoulder and stamped around the room in frustration. Finally in fury she kicked out at the end of the bed, striking the large wooden leg with the sharp angled toe of her patent leather, high heeled shoe. The Bed moved somewhat more easily than she had expected and as she lost her balance, she slid against the wall and watched in fascinated horror as the bed swung on a hidden bearing, pulling a string from a crack in the floorboards, which in turn pulled a hook on the coat stand, which swiveled and turned a crank on the fire grate which produced a loud click from the hidden door. As the mechanism worked, her nose was greeted with the smell of old candle wax used to lubricate the secret joints and covert hinges. The door swung open and behind was a small room that appeared to have no rational way of being a part of the rest of the building. This was an ancient and dusty form of lost magic.

Demonika stood up, brushed the dust and soot from her pencil skirt and patted herself down. The room appeared to be in darkness, but there was no where obvious that she could take a candle from, so with a small sigh of resignation she decided to have a quick look and would return with a candle later. She stepped through the wardrobe and into the surprisingly well lit and airy study of a magician long ago deceased. In each corner of the room burned huge candles, held in an ornate and stylish candelabrum, the grate held back the flames of a large and healthy winter fire, the window was frosted with icy crystals on the outside, making it all but impossible to see out. One wall was covered from floor to ceiling in old leather bound tomes marked along their spines in letters of a language long ago forgotten. Another wall was festooned with strings of spell bottles held together with the dried cord made from the intestines of a cat. Finally and stood alone on an almost empty wall was a small cupboard, more of a display cabinet than actual secure storage shelf, but the illumination that showed what each jar contained within, emanated from within the actual jars themselves. She examined them closely and discovered that each jar had a small hand written label, the letters drawn in the finest inked italic script of a mage. The first label was turned so that she could read only one word. Caligula. The second read Stalin. The third read Pol Pot. There were jars upon jars, all glowing faintly, all holding the spiritual essence of a complete and utter bastard. The last jar was sealed with a heavy wax cap, tied with ribbon and marked with a skull and cross bones. The name label was just out of sight and as she turned it, she was horrified to discover that this was the worst of the worst, the one that all right thinking people truly feared. Bernard Manning! The thought of it made her shudder, she could release any of the others upon the world, but that one would remain locked away until the end of time itself.

She reached into the shelves and pulled out a

dusty jar, the glow from within was a dirty, sickly yellow, the jar itself was the smallest on display and when cradled in her warm hands, the flecks that glinted within seemed to speed up in their chaotic movements. She turned it over in her hands until she found the old and faded label, the text of which had been faded even more by a spilled liquid that had made the ink run. The words were simple. Adolf Hitler: Dictator.

The next jar that she pulled out was labelled just as simply, the writing was a small print in another person's hand writing. Elena Ceausescu: Dictator. The label was reasonably new, but at the same time it looked ancient and the dancing light within was a grotesque green, similar in colour to a rancid boil that has been infected for years.

She browsed the shelf a little more and pulled out a jar that was made from frosted glass, the light within was gold in colour, but not a nice gold. This was the tacky fake looking gold, of a mentally ill millionaire's private lift; or it could have been the gold used by a man who made his own golden bathroom and in which he enjoyed sitting upon a golden toilet, while brushing his teeth with a golden tooth brush, before having a nice long golden shower, every morning. The name plate was strange, made from a nasty dark red plastic self adhesive tape, with faded embossed letters pressed into it; that had been stuck to the glass at an almost, but not quite level angle. Idi Amin: Dictator.

Demonika gathered her glass vessels in her arms and made her way back towards the secret door and then back into the pub. The transition from the mage's office to the bedroom of the Rusty Plough made her feel faintly nauseous and the same was likely true for the glass bottles, especially since the green light filled one, suddenly developed a nasty vomitty pink hue too. Back in the bedroom, the glass jars were not so bright, but the colours were still visible, as she descended the stairs, she found Wuffles waiting for her at the bottom, his eyes hard, his tail very clearly doing the exact opposite of a wag. "Do you know what these are Wuffles?" She held one of the glass jars out towards him and he did not even sniff it. He shook his head and looked at her through eyes that had clearly seen too much. Demonika understood the meaning all too well. "They are only dangerous in the wrong hands. But in mine, they can do great mischief and be of even greater use." Wuffles whined slightly, one ear drooped over his face, the other held high. "Because, well can you imagine what I can achieve with these people as my slaves?" She answered, her voice losing some of her authority given the grilling she was receiving from the hound.

He kicked his front left paw in the air and snuffled slightly, his delicate whine was uncompromising, his intent nailed firmly to the ultimatum. Demonika stared at him, her eyes cruel dark slits of hate. "Well I don't need your help. Fine, you can leave. I will see you in the morning!" Wuffles stood and with his head drooped, padded out to the kitchen and disappeared through the dog flap, with a sudden and bizarre flash of dark purple light, that for a second caught Demonika off guard.

"Bugger me! Where the hell does that go to?" She placed the jars on the table and approached the dog flap as it swung gently to a close. She pushed it with her shoe tip, but there was no flash, so she pushed it harder and held it open for a second. Looking through it, she could see a light grey gravel path, made from fine stone chips. She was almost sure that it was not the correct view of the outside, but decided that she did not want to push through another mystery when she had plans for her afternoon. Firstly, she had to make contact with her new friends. Turning back to the jars, she noticed at once that the Adolf Hitler jar was trembling slightly as the other jars seemed to advance on it, despite remaining still. She scooped them up and went over to the small booth seats next to the empty fireplace and placed the jars on the table, before picking one up to examine more closely.

"Now then, I want all three of you to listen to me closely. I have a job for you and at the same time, this will give you corporeal form once again." She paused for a moment, "but, only if you do as I say, otherwise you will be lost forever on the currents of magic that flow through this place." The lights all pulsed excitedly. "Do you understand me so far?" All three jars pulsed in synchronized affirmations. "You must go from this place, once I release you and you must find a child, no more than three years of age. Once you have found that child, you must drive the soul from their body and only then you can take over their form and grow to adulthood once again." The jars pulsed with an intensity that was usually reserved for Pink Floyd concerts. "I cannot let you out here though, you must go into the human world, the place where you came from. Time is different there, you will grow faster in their world and very soon my friends, you must return to me so that we can rule this realm with fists of steel!"

She stood up and walked across the bar to the dog flap and bent low over the dirty and stained mat, that had for hundreds of years been used to wipe Wuffles' paws. She placed the jars down and selecting one of them, released the lid and shook the jar through the dog flap with the same action that a phobic shakes out a spider from a cup. The gaseous light within, took flight and vanished into the human world. She repeated the action with the final two jars and once her work was done, returned to her place next to the log fire that she summoned into life with a snap of her fingers. Resting her feet up on the ragged and stained fabric of the seating, she smiled to herself, the first part of her plan was coming together.

* * * * *

Wuffles stepped from the dog flap and stood peacefully in the garden of the Rusty Plough. The strange nature of quantum theory enabled the two worlds to share some physical attributes and one of those was a pub called the Rusty Plough. Where Demonika's version of the pub was dirty and run down, in the human world, the Rusty Plough was a clean, corporate wine bar with an excellent kitchen. Due to the forces of quantum pairing, a copy of Wuffles' best cookbook existed in both worlds and what ever he wrote in his version in his own world, would appear in the copy in the human world.

His fine delicate italics transformed into neat Times New Roman print. Where Wuffles had drawn a precise and accurate pencil line drawing in his own book, the copy had a photograph that appeared to be identical, even down to the dusty smudges on the crockery.

Turning back to the door of the pub, Wuffles used his nose to ease the door open and wander through into the building and to his girlfriend, Greta; the pedigree Afghan hound. There was nothing in anyway magical about Greta, she was a plain dog, in mind and body, but her coat shone and her eyes were soft, she was also more than agreeable to Wuffles' more physical needs and despite having been spayed three times, had given Wuffles over six sets of puppies. The owner of the bar had given up trying to control his dog, his vet had asked him several questions about Greta, but the evidence of her microchip proved that she was the same animal, despite the spayings and almost endless supply of puppies. The puppies themselves were nothing at all like their father, firstly, none of them shared his levels of intelligence, not even by a close mark. The nearest that any of them had come was one kindly moron and even by dog standards, he had been hopelessly thick. When he had finally been rehomed, his new owner discovered that if he threw a ball for the dog, it would run off at high speed, then forget why it was running and just keep going, which had caused several incidents of the dog running through traffic and even across thirty miles of Dartmoor during a summer trip! The only good aspect of his behavior was that he ran in an arrow straight route, which meant that his owners could chase him by car and then later catch him when he came over the hills towards where they had headed him off.

Wuffles did not mind in the least that his offspring were rehomed, sent away to distant farms or even given willingly to scientific companies for experiments. Had any one of them shown even a faint glimmer of intelligence, he would have stepped in, but the sad truth was that each one of them had been born several degrees thicker than even their mother, who even on her good days, spent most of her winter afternoons licking condensation off the sliding glass door that led into the pub garden. Still, she was amiable and a good lay when he was in the mood.

As he padded quietly through the pub looking for her, he looked around the familiar but different place. It mirrored the Rusty Plough of his home almost exactly in lay out, but where his place was dingy and dirty, this place was bright and sanitised with strong smelling antiseptic sprays. Next to the electric heater that had replaced the open grate fire, was the blanket that Greta would normally be found laying upon, but on this occasion there was instead a large cardboard box and from within came the sounds of whimpering and whining, the delicate sounds of puppies trying to feed and then forgetting what their mouths were for. He did not even bother to pop his head over the lip of the box, Greta would be busy and would not want him near her, so he turned around and wandered across the bar to the wall mounted music computer. Pulling his purse from the small hidden bag that he wore around his waist, he counted out two pound coins and carefully slid them into money slot. As the machine counted in the money, it displayed how many songs he could choose and as he keyed in the codes for his favourite songs, the first one started.

Laying down under the window, using just his

eyebrows and his ears he sang along sadly. "Only the lonely..." As the song faded out, it was replaced by another equally sad song as the King himself added to the gloom of the day. The owner of the wine bar wandered downstairs having heard the music. As he approached the Duke Box, he spied Wuffles and smiled sadly to himself and wandered out to the kitchen where he chose a small pork pie that had to be used by the end of the day. He put it on a small china plate, added a blob of pickle and a cheese cracker and returned to the bar, where he placed the plate on the floor in front of Wuffles. The hound looked up bleakly and an unspoken conversation of pain and loneliness crossed between them, as the barman gently scratched the dog between the ears. Finally standing up, the human checked the box of puppies and then wandered back up stairs, calling out to his wife. "Sheilah, Wuffles is back again and he looks really down. So I gave him a pork pie to cheer him up." Half way up the stairs his wife answered him and the barman called back indignantly. "Of course I put his favourite pickle on the side and I gave him a cheese biscuit. I know what he likes just as well as you do, you know."

Wuffles split the pie in half and gently dabbed the halves into the pickle before he flicked one and then the other up into the air and with manners unknown among dogs, gently chewed the food, letting the flavours wash through his mouth. As the final notes of Johnny Cash came to an end, Wuffles stood up and with a last glance at the whelping box, wandered back out to the garden and then back through the dog flap and into his own Rusty Plough back in Winscombe.

The glowing orbs of phasmic energy sped along the air currents, streaking through the matter of the buildings in the same way that light passes through water. The three of them arced across the town, each searching for that small spark in the air that would take them to their new host. The green smudge found her victim first and raided the bedroom of a small sleeping girl who had endured a truly difficult day of potty training and then administering some first rate pre-school bullying. The golden smudge of colour found his target next. An angelic looking junior psychopath who has spent the morning rubbing his own excrement into his Mother's new sofa before escaping to the garden to pull the wings off beetles and chew through worms. Finally the sickly yellow haze found a child to inhabit, a petulant three and a half year old that had already learned that the way to control Mummy was with a violent tantrum. He was exhausted after screaming through two supermarkets, five small local shops and he had even managed to cough up phlegm that he had even managed vomiting on an old man who had tried to give him a lolly.

His exasperated Mother had already swallowed three heavy tranquilizers by his bedtime and was considering her fourth along with a bottle of Jack when he finally went to sleep. With each possession, the vile urges of the children were subdued, the battle within their little bodies for control would keep them quiet for several days at the very least, the result of which was that two of the Mothers took their child to the Doctor suspecting illness and the third Mother downed three bottles of red wine and finally had her first good nights sleep since the birth.

Chapter 4:- Let's just eat...

The King of Norfcorea looked at the figures as they spread out on the large sheet in front of him. He cursed the man who insisted on printing the figures on the palace's finest linen bedding, but he had been told that this was the latest methods of accounting in the human world. Yet the King failed to see the advantage of spreading the sheet across such a vast area. If he needed to read what was in one of the small boxes of figures near the top, it was easy, but if he dragged the sheet across the table to read the lower boxes in the far corners, it was too easy to over shoot and then spend ages trying to trace his way back from the seemingly endless printed empty boxes. When he questioned the printer on why there were so many empty boxes and then why he did not simply make the boxes bigger the man looked nonplussed and assured him that the extra boxes could be used to input his own data. Having learned the hard way that the figures would require that he do the sums in his head, which often led to mistakes, he paid a wizard to perform some simple magic on the boxes and the figures would automatically perform what ever function was required of them. He had no idea how it worked, but work it did. The result was depressingly obvious.

The money that the Kingdom badly needed to

ensure that the economy kept going, was just not coming in. He had introduced a strict regime of austerity on the capital and the lords that served, but still money was short. His first business interest was in the construction of weapons, but as times grew more peaceful, the sales barely went anywhere. One of his advisers had mentioned that maybe by stirring up a small war in the provinces, they could sell weapons to the various lords in the outlying regions. He dismissed this plan for the utter foolishness that it was, after all, continuous war was barely a way for a civilized society to grow, it also consumed far more money than it generated through weapons sales. He sat with his manicured fingers stretched out into his hair and then the idea hit him, what was he best at? What was the best export that Norfcorea had to offer? It was of course, the nation's finest cooking.

He brushed the sheet aside and demanded that one of his aides ran off to his office and came back with several sheets of plain paper and his finest box of colouring pens. When the aide came back, his arms full, the King asked for his new friend to be called for. The aide looked perplexed for a moment and then the light of understanding broke through the gloom of his confusion. He dashed off to fetch the Kings newest aide and best friend, Sharon. After half an hour, she rushed into the room and almost shouting in panic, asked him what he wanted.

The aide turned purple with fake coughing and after a second, Sharon caught his meaning and bowed to the King demurely. The King looked up and saw her doing so. "Sharon love, you don't have to do that. You're my best mate." He turned his gaze to the aide who was silently apoplectic with fury. "From now on, bowing is only to be done in my presence," he raised his voice slightly to emphasize the word. "DURING official functions. The rest of the time, she comes and goes like she is my own sister, you got it?" The aide nodded once silently and the King called him over. "Now make yourself useful, colour this in, please?" He slid a large sheet of paper over to the man and handed him a number of pens and the pot of fine yellow ink. "I want that whole border done in yellow." He turned to Sharon, "I need your help and probably the help of your Granny too. Do you think that she will oblige?"

Sharon looked at the sheets of paper and the list of figures down one side of the columns drawn on on the page. The King's small but perfectly printed italics suddenly made sense to her and she gave him a huge grin. "Sire, that is brilliant! I am sure that Gran would be honoured to help." She read down one of the lists and smiling reached the end of the box of text. There was space in which more could be added and she could see the exact thing that needed to go there. "If we added something like, let's call it, House Special. We could chuck in all of the odd bits and off cuts into the dregs of the curry sauce and sell that off too, what do you think?"

The King looked at her with a look that was given only to leading scientists, when they discover how to produce free energy from cold test tubes. "That is possible?"

Her grin was infectious. "Not just possible, but profitable." She scanned the list of recipes and turned back to him. "You could do it to almost every dish there. Those idiots in Winscombe will swallow it all down like it is exotic fine food, rather than left overs and scraps."

His smile was beaming, his laugh was gentle and kind. "That my dear Sharon is why you are now one of my top advisers. Would you do me the honour of writing it in for me please?"

"Of course Sire, it would be my pleasure."

His face changed, a sudden sadness passed across his face, but only for a moment. "Please, call me Jong, I don't like my friends using official titles."

She smiled understandingly, "I will Jong, but only when we are alone. The same with old Fred there too?"

Fred the aide barely looked up from his colouring, his tongue poking out between his lips in concentration. "Eh what?"

"When it is just the three of us here like this, we use our first names, OK?" Sharon stated firmly.

Fred relaxed in his seat and continued his colouring, without even so much as looking up again he gave his answer quietly. "Yeah sure, whatever you want Sharon."

King Jong grinned wide and then happily continued with his own careful writing on the page of puddings. In silence the three of them worked away, occasionally passing the pages to each other for clarification or to add another recipe. It was only when the King noticed that Sharon had added a recipe to the list of starters that he thought sounded utterly disgusting, that he paused and questioned her further. "Eer, Sharon... Who would eat chicken feet in spicy sauce? It sounds utterly disgusting" Even Fred stopped colouring for a moment and looked up at her puzzled.

Sharon's grin was beautific, her voice syrup smooth. "It is simple, we tell people that they are a posh delicacy. The posh people will just yum them up, thinking that they are being clever, claws and all. We will make a killing. We usually have to pay to have the chicken feet disposed of, by doing it this way we can sell the filthy things to the rich idiots of Winscombe!"

The King looked unconvinced. "But what about the, you know..." he paused for a moment letting his silence speak for him, but Sharon just appeared mystified. "You know, the poo? Will we wash them? It sounds horrible to me, I doubt even our poorest beggars would eat them?"

Sharon pointed down the list and let her finger rest on a column she had labelled S-Cargo.

"But that is the beauty of it. We do the same with these too, tell them that they are a special delicacy and those idiots will yum them up, you just give them a posh sounding name and before you know it, what was once a waste product or a garden pest becomes a super exclusive meal for couples on their first romantic date. The guy will feel all clever telling his gullible date about these miraculous foods and before you know it, they are spooning disgusting lumps of gloop into each others gobs, while sharing loving smiles!"

Puzzled by the list of unfamiliar items that she had written on the menu, the King was forced to ask. "Sharon, just what on Earth is S-Cargo? It sounds like packing crates."

Her smile was the most evil thing he had ever seen, her eyes were darkened with pure mischief. "Simple, we gather all of the snails that are eating your flowers, the gross clams that block up the sewage outlets and all of the other slimy things that we hate, then slap them on that list there and tell them that only our richest people eat them. Simple economics, turn something of no value into a commodity of such high value that they would sell their own children to buy it. We could sell them fish eggs and tell them that they taste wonderful. Those idiots over there will not only buy the foul muck, but tell each other how good it tastes in magazine articles read by the overly rich."

Fred looked up from his colouring and for a moment sat in silence, the King and Sharon turned to him as he sat in silent thought. Finally, he spoke, his voice quiet. "How do we sell this muck to people, do we open shops here and sell it over the border or do we move there and send the money back here?"

The King thought for a moment, his face impassive and then his eyes shone as the idea struck home. "I have it, Sharon you will love this. They order from home and we deliver it to their doors. It wont matter if it is cold or even going off by the time they get it, they will have waited for so long, they will almost pay double just to avoid having to cook at home!"

Sharon beamed at him. "You are getting the hang of this aren't you. Tell them that by asking us to cook for them, they are saving time which they can use for other things. What they will actually do is pace up and down, fretting about their order until we arrive with their food. They pay twice what it is worth and we pop home with a pocket full of cash." She stopped suddenly, a glint in her eye that would have frightened an axe murderer. "We could even charge them a fee to, you know, actually deliver it!"

All three of them burst out laughing, the scheme was flawless, the money would start rolling in as soon as the posters arrived in Winscombe. After several hours of them sat around the table and after finishing a round of jam sandwiches for lunch, the menus were completed, each dish was numbered, each section contained a variety of meals, each more disgusting than the last. The curries developed went up in heat from mild, through hot, into volcanic and finally ended with incandescent. If the fool who ordered the sauce was able to eat it, he would likely have to keep his toilet paper locked in an ice bucket along with a pair of dragon skin gloves!

The printer collected the sheets of brightly coloured paper from the throne room himself, the King showed him how he wanted each sheet folded so that it resembled some kind of failed fan and then with a kind smile and a handshake, dismissed the man. Days later the printer returned to the King, his cart full of the beautifully printed menus and the King called Sharon and Fred to check them all through. They each chose at random, five menus and checked them over for mistakes and errors, but they were flawless. Feeling pleased with the scheme, the King ordered that the menus be sent to Winscombe immediately and then he sat back and waited for the cash to begin to roll in. True to Sharon's word, the orders did not gently flow in, rather they absolutely flooded every caterer that signed up with the King's scheme, with hundreds of orders. Powerful fairy delivery boys ran at speeds previously unknown, to addresses in Winscombe, to deliver foul smelling boxes of slightly cold food to lazy good for nothings, who despite having cupboards full of food, could not be bothered to cook their own dinner. Each menu printed made the Kingdom of Norfcorea thirty times the cost of the printing, the money rolled in and just as Sharon had said would happen, the chicken feet and garden snail supplies soon started to run low. To counter this, Sharon put the prices up and still demand was high. The fish eggs which were laid in their billions, but only during the spring sold at an almost cataclysmic profit, the apparent rarity of them made them so expensive that only the richest of Winscombe's idiotic populations could afford such 'delicacies'!

After six months, the merchants of Norfcorea were growing fat on the profitable markets of food delivery. The fairy delivery boys had introduced off their own backs, the idea that buyers should give them a small tip for the effort it took to complete a job that they were being paid handsomely to do and so even they made enough to live extravagant lives and even began to subcontract out the work to underpayed Winscombe people. The tax collected by the King's officials was so vast that schools were forced to come up with more and more ludicrous ways of spending the cash they were given. The King used huge sums of money to create new hospitals, with exotic new treatments that every person in Norfcorea was entitled too, entirely free of charge. Those people too sick or too old to work, were instead sent off to live out their lives in gentle rest homes on the warm south coast, where they spent their time painting pictures of the mountains or writing poems about the mountain rivers, all of which they sold at great cost to the people who could afford to pamper and indulge their no longer ailing relatives. The influx of wealth spread far and wide among the

Norfcorean people and life grew significantly better for every citizen.

After just one year on the throne, King Jong the First was not only greatly loved by his subjects, but he, Sharon and Fred had become national heroes. At a special ceremony in which a greatly amused Aide Du Champ placed a medal of honour on both Sharon and Fred, he eyed them with a new respect, in secret he had marvelled at their deviousness, admired their humour and greatly enjoyed their spite. But as with all economic booms, it could not last for ever.

After eighteen months and following a state

visit by King Bobney at which they ate the human delicacy of cheese burgers and French fries, King Jong the first sat with Fred and Sharon and looked glumly at the sheet spread out before him. The figures were high, but somewhere, something was not as it should have been. Something was eating quite literally into their profits. Even allowing for delivery fairy tips, late delivery refunds and out of court settlements for food poisoning or ingestion of toxic substances, the money was slumping in one area of Winscombe, the area around the Rusty Plough pub. They knew the reason, even Sharon had mentioned the cause in respectful whispered tones, for the cause of this slump was a chef so famous in his circle, so beloved by his people, that he had managed to maintain his business when many others had been forced to employ Norfcorean chefs or risk going out of business altogether. "How do we tempt Wuffles into joining us in out little venture?" The King's question hung like a bleak storm cloud in the air over the table at which sat Sharon, Fred and the Aide Du Champ. Combined with this desire to recruit Wuffles, was also the figures that spread out like a dark plague on the sheet, that told another terrible story. They were the figures for those delivery fairies caught trying to get back home to Norfcorea from the great city of Winscombe. The numbers had at first been very small, but as the money began to rush out of the city and into Norfcorea, Demonika Trumpet had, in her childlike, devilish ways, began targeting the delivery fairies and those held captured were imprisoned in special camps, that had conditions so bad that not even the British would consider a camping holiday there. To add further difficulty to the plight of the delivery fairies, Demonika Trumpet had told the people of Winscombe that she would build them a mighty wall to keep the work shy, the lazy and the revoltingly self serving, safely inside the city and away from the hard working people of Norfcorea.

The wall had from the very start been a complete and utter farce. Demonika had penned a vicious and threatening letter to King Jong the first in her own blood red script, informing him that she intended building the wall to keep his food deliveries out of Winscombe. To then add further insult on top of the remarks she had made about his people, she wrote that she fully expected him to pay for construction of the wall, all the way along the border between their two nations, given that he had stripped so much of the wealth out of Winscombe. The language of the letter had inflated her ego, made her look fanatical and even bordering on maniacal, but most of all, it made her look like she knew that her own arguments were completely and utterly foolish.

King Jong the First had dispatched a spy to report to him on the state of those Norfcoreans held captive in the camps dotted along the Winscombe border, at the base of the Norfcorean mountains. The spy had spent many hard days bribing guards with wads of Norfcorean cash and even cooking them grotesque meals made with inedibly hot curry sauces and giant horrific looking beetles, until at last he was able to enter one of the camps. What he saw horrified him, he could not believe that the people of Winscombe could debase another life form so thoroughly, but the humiliation and degrading torture endured by the camp inmates thoroughly shocked and sickened him. His escape back to the Kingdom of Norfcorea took with him the hopes and misery of those held behind the wire, forced into wearing bright orange jump suits and then coerced to endure many hours and hours of continuous, sickening Morris Dancing. The horror of it had made him wretch and feeling sickened and shocked, he fled back to the border, where after bribing a guard with a bowl of shredded crispy frog and eggy rice, he fled back up the mountain path to the Kingdom of King Jong the first.

The report sat open on the King's desk. He had read it with open mouthed horror and was still to share the contents with his team of advisers. Unusually, he had not said even a word of it to

Sharon, for fear of upsetting his best friend. So as the staff meeting fell quiet, he knew that he could delay it no more, he had no choice but to reveal the truth of what he had learned. Bracing himself in his chair for the awfulness he was about to share with his friends, he choked slightly, his reaction was so strong that Sharon saw his suffering and reached out her hand to hold his in comfort of her friend. "What is it Jong, what can be so bad?"

He reached to his desk, pulled the thick paper document from purple paper wallet and spread the pages on the desk in front of him. "Given that so many of our delivery fairies are not returning from Winscombe, I despatched my master spy to the great city to discover the truth of what has been happening to them. I have the report here and this does not make for easy reading." He paused, his breath came in hard gasps as he struggled to fight back the emotion. "I know what they have been doing to our people." He could hold back no more and an anguished sob forced its way from his chest.

The Aide Du Champ, an old man who had seen almost all of the depravity that sentient life could inflict on each other, seemed the least shaken and sat still in his chair unmoved. "Come Sire, how bad can it be? There are always casualties in war, even a cold war like this one. Our border with Winscombe has been turbulent for decades."

Sharon reached for one of the papers and instinctively, the King's hand fell across them to stop her from reading them. She resisted his move and picked at the paper, trying to drag it out from under his arm. "Come on Jong, I am a big girl now." Her eyes fell on the only two words that she could read under his arm and her face turned ashen in horror. "Oh my word, No!" Her voice was a harsh whisper, her blood felt like iced treacle in her veins. The horror of seeing those words together was enough to push even hardened generals to impulsive swearing, even after witnessing a terrible and bloody battle.

The King nodded his head and slowly lifted his arm from the papers and handed one sheet each to his advisers. Fred skim read the file until he reached the words and silently he put the paper down and closed his eyes; hiding, as well as he was able, the fact that he had been reduced to horrified weeping. The Aide Du Champ read the page carefully, he then read it again just to be sure, with the cold horror of an experienced old war horse. Finally he put the page face down on the table and removed his glasses and began rub his eyes as if suddenly that had grown tired from reading the awful text.

"This is accurate Sire?" The Aide Du Champ

asked quietly. The King Nodded his head before the Aide Du Champ could ask him again. "I am so very sorry that you have been forced to endure this knowledge alone Sire, you should not have to carry such vileness inside of you. That women is a monster and a war criminal. She knows what she is doing, this is systematic destruction of fairy folk, the cold blooded murder of our people."

Sharon finally spoke, her voice trembling and quiet. "No fairy should be made to endure even one second of morris dancing, let alone protracted painful hours of it. That is a cruelty never before seen on this world. Has she not learned from the human world the terrible social cost of Morris Dancing?" She almost spat the last two words from her mouth, as if they contained a taste so vulgar and revolting, she could barely deal with saying them.

Fred picked up his sheet and read it again before he spoke in unusually coarse terms. "Fuck me, that woman is a sicko. What kind of a beast does this? She cannot do this lightly, this is too barbaric to be anything other than coldly calculated."

The Aide Du Champ slid his glasses back onto his face and after letting out a sigh so slow and painful, it almost sounded like a death rattle; he chose his words carefully. "Sire, trusted friends of our King, I can only conclude that this woman aims to destroy our people. Morris Dancing has been outlawed in the fairy realm for nearly twelve thousand years, because of the terrible indiscriminate nature of its fallout. To find out that in this day and age, this woman is now using this universally outlawed method of torture against our people is not only a declaration of open warfare between our two states." He paused for gravitas, allowing his words to sink in among his listeners. The King's gentle face was inscrutable, not even Sharon could read his mask of state. The Aide Du Champ continued quietly, "It is utterly unforgivable. Given that these camps are also built in the Cotswolds, a place so miserable and damp and plagued with disease, it shows just how much contempt Demonika Trumpett has for our nation and our people. This is inhumane even by her standards, but we can do something about this. We have the weaponry now to deal with this barbarism first hand."

"I cannot condone any action that will lead us to war, we must negotiate with this monster to release my people. Only then if she refuses will we resort to war." The King's face was firm, but unreadable.

The Aide Du Champ glared angrily at the young King, as he gave thought to what he had just heard. He was fond of the young King, his idealism was all well and good, but with lives at stake, it was possibly misguided. He just had to find the way to break the news to him that negotiating was probably unlikely with out the backing of force. "Sire, we have recently acquired some high yield air burst custard munitions, these weapons could be deployed from the air, via high level dragon flights."

The King looked at the Aide Du Champ with a face that spoke of shame and horror and disgust for the words the man had just spoken. "Custard bombs are utterly illegal. I will not sign an order that allows their use. They guarantee destruction on both sides, the death toll will be catastrophic. Frankly I am shocked that you would go behind my back and buy these shameful devices."

The Aide Du Champ settled back in his seat. His face set for an angry battle of wills with the man who ruled the country. "Custard bombs of this special sort produce a high yield detonation, the spread is great, the half life is short and..."

Sharon cut him off, her words angry and harsh, unusual for someone more used to gentler speaking. "You cannot force King Jong to fight a war with Custard Bombs, how many innocent thousands will suffer? What you are talking about is not warfare, it is cold blooded murder!"

"And yet, she is doing just that to our people and we sit here doing nothing?" The Aid du Champ's voice had risen to a loud berating shout, but he remembered his place well enough not to direct his anger towards the King. He sat back down in his chair and quietly added, "these are clever tactical devices, with this brand new technology, we can guide the bombs directly onto our chosen targets. Collateral damage will be kept to an absolute minimum Sire, we have the ability to fly these devices over their targets with ease. Maybe you can send a warning shot, drop a weapon on them that shows our intent, but make it a low yield one that does not fully detonate?"

Fred looked up from his paper shaking his head. "A deliberate dud could be easily misconstrued as the failure to detonate a fully working device, which will probably be put down to a lack of our technical ability. This is a dangerous game you are proposing Sir."

Finally the King spoke, his manner was of a man who had to carry alone a difficult burden and he fully intended to continue to carry it alone. "Friends, I concede the point." He turned to the Aide Du Champ. "You will prepare a single low yield device and have it ready for deployment at one hours notice. It will be launched only upon my command only. Is this absolutely clear?"

The Aide Du Champ nodded thoughtfully.

"Your wisdom is clear Sire."

"Good, now I want a messenger to be sent to Winscombe and I want that vile woman to know that we have the key to her destruction waiting here; but we wish to negotiate with her, for the release of our people from her illegal and disgusting camps. We will not be bullied and we will not bow down to this orange skinned psychopath." The King turned to face Fred directly. "What I ask of you, I do with the full knowledge that it is a burden that no man should ever have to carry alone. Would you do me the honour of carrying this message personally Sir?"

Chapter 5:- The frightful view

Mrs Felicity Goldstein sat wringing her hands, her light blue floral dress was sensibly long in the leg and made of a fabric that was easily washed, which was important while raising a child like young Isaac. Unusually, Isaac had stopped the normal gurgles and pre-speech that babies usually have and had instead turned almost mute. His eyes took on an angry, almost pious stare that seemed to bore through her soul like a hot rivet through ice, as she cared for her spawn. Watching him change from infant to toddler to a fearsome four year old had been traumatic for her. She felt that he spent his days judging her every action or decision, his sneer of contempt for her, haunted her sleep. The Mother's support group of which Felicity was a member, had two other parents with equally terrifying children. Finally Felicity spoke, her voice was cracked and sad, with a dark hint of shame and and a shade of worry. "Isaac finally spoke. I don't know how he managed it because he has never uttered even a single word to us before. But his first word to me was a fully formed sentence." She sniffed back some tears, "only his words were awful, truly dreadful, I don't know where he could have heard such language. Jeremiah and I would never say such things, well we just wouldn't would we. After all, he lost relatives."

The small group shuffled uncomfortably in

their circle of seats, many of them had heard for themselves the terrible things that Isaac Goldstein said on the first day of infants school. Of the group, only Angela Thorn and Stacey Flaherty kept their heads low, their own children had also developed something of a reputation in their very first week of infants school. Angela Thorn and her Husband Martyn Walters had been called into the school when their son Freddie had been caught arranging a small harem of girls and then, when he was challenged over his behaviour, he had threatened to cut off the head of the teacher who had discovered him.

Felicity continued her mumbled horrified words. "Isaac's first words were…" She sniffed briefly, "I can't bring myself to repeat them, they were so awful." She sobbed and gently blew her nose into the white cotton hanky that she believed as a middle class parent, she should have with her at all times. " When we looked it up, it was a quote from Mein Kampf!" Her sobs came fast and uneven, her shoulders resembling a seizure as she tried to regain her cold austere stoicism.

"I know what you mean." Stacey Flaherty spoke quietly, her emotionless voice sounding flat, her eyes were bleak. "When we got the phone call from the school, it was because our Zephirine had done something awful to one of her class mates. She was sat in the head's office with the self righteous menace of a dictator and when the head asked her why she had done it she told him that…" Stacey too started to sniff slightly, as tears pricked at her washed out blue eyes. Her skin was greyish and appeared somehow bleached of natural colour, which clashed badly with her cerise satin top and shiny black culottes. "She screamed at us all that she would not answer any of our questions and that she had made it clear at the start that she would not recognise the court in which we were trying her!." Stacey dabbed at the tears on her cheeks. "When Ian tried to pick her up, to take her home, she bit him on the hand and started to scream that we were terrorists and members of the…" She stumbled for the word because it was not familiar to her even though the memory of it was permanently scorched into her brain, "Members of the Securitate!" In the seat next to her, Felicty reached out her hand and it was gratefully clasped by Stacey.

Angela Thorn was made of sterner stuff, but she was also clearly shaken by her son's words and actions. "Freddie was also strangely silent as an infant, but we put this down to him being more cerebral and not being allowed to watch television." She cast a derisive look at the other two weeping women. "We would only allow radio three to play in the house. When he came up to me, while Martyn was at work, and declared himself to be the hero of Africa. I naturally assumed that he had heard a play on the BBC." She paused for a moment. "Well you would, wouldn't you. It was only later that I found out that he had become friends with..." Her derision was as darkly obvious as a large black hole in a freshly paved driveway. "He had made friends with Isaac Goldstein at school, only it took a while for me to find out because it seems that when he is at school, the young Isaac prefers the name Adi, while his friend Freddie calls himself Idi." She gave Felicity a foul and angry stare. "One does wonder when our race will finally let those awful events of the nineteen forties rest in history?" Felicity let out another loud sob.

* * * * *

Demonika stalked the length of the bar in the Rusty Plough, the language of her curses would have turned the air a violent purple, if it were not already arcing with sickly blue bolts of magic. Wuffles had taken the afternoon off and was in the other Rusty Plough in Little Smirda, leaving Demonika to serve the afternoon rush with beers, cider and plates of pre-cooked pies. Her hair was misshapen from its usual elegant style and her eye make up was smudged, which gave the skin around her eyes the look of lizard scales. She could not have been more angry. Winscombe itself was under a military style lock down and she had tripled the hours that the Guard were forced to work. It was also costing a pretty penny feeding all of the Norcorean 'illegals' that they had caught and then held prisoner in the camps outside of the city. One of her few advisers allowed to speak had suggested just letting the prisoners go, so Demonika had given it a moment of thought and then had the man eviscerated over a bonfire. After that, no one argued with her. Since taking on the pub and the rule of Winscombe, she had developed the nasty habit of smoking Troll-fags and the smoke being vile and dangerous, she often chose to smoke them outside. She stepped from the pub doorway and sat on the small wall that surrounded the cart park. She sparked up her first evil smelling troll-fag and inhaled deeply the acrid purple smoke, which she held in her lungs for a few brief seconds of blissful peace.

It was then that she witnessed first hand the surreal crime that many of the cities elderly ladies had been reporting. Her eyes went wide, she choked on the troll-fag smoke and flicked the filthy thing to the floor in horror. For a second, maybe two, they locked eyes, even under his full head mask, she could gaze into his sad lost eyes, the eyes of a madman. He opened his coat and shook his pitiful manhood at her and then before he could close his coat, he fouled the pavement with a smouldering turd of gargantuan proportions. Demonika felt her jaw hang open as the man then scampered off into the crowd and vanished. Leaving behind the vile and strangely furious looking dropping. Try as she might, she could not stop gawping at the horrid thing as it sat there steaming on the sidewalk. It was only when a busy trader, who was shouting into a clearly very wonky mobile phone, slipped in the faecal surprise that she found that she was able to move again and she quickly coned off the remaining offensive faecal mound. Back inside the Rusty Plough she dialled the number of the City guard and hummed angrily until the phone was answered. "Winscombe City Police Guard, Sargent Thomas speaking, how can we help?" Demonika almost screeched down the phone, her piercing voice was like claws down a black board to the poor man and he quickly tried to

431

calm her down. "Is that you Mayor Trumpett? Has there been a murder? Please, calm yourself Madam and tell me all about it." He allowed her to screech for a few seconds more before cutting her off with his best official tone of male dominance. "Madam, if you do not calm down, I will be unable to help you and will have to terminate this call!"

As she shouted yet more angry and considerably more filthy insults down the rotten handset, Sargent Thomas could feel the manhood within him wilting. "Should I just come down to the Plough to discuss it with you Ma'am?"

Finally, she had got through to the cretin and before she put the phone down she ordered him to bring his finest forensic scientist with him. She then slammed the phone down for good measure and returned to her favourite seat by the fire, that she kept roaring even on the hottest of summer days. The drinkers complained, the stench of the carpet as it finally began to dry out after decades, if not centuries, of spilled drinks was enough to make even the most battle hardened swords men weep acidic tears of remorse. The door of the pub swung open and Sargent Thomas wandered into the bar and sat down at her table. "I now understand your anguish Ma'am. The scientist is as we speak, armed with a rather large shovel and is scraping up what remains of that vile excrescence." He flipped out his notepad and licked the tip of his pen, marking another line onto the thick black stain on his tongue. "Could you describe this individual to me please Ma'am?"

Demonika looked up, the image felt like it had been burned into her brain with a welding torch, the sight of it was likely to haunt her for several nights to come. If she slept at all, it was likely that she would struggle when the lights turned out. She looked the Sargent in the eyes and began, her voice husky and sad. "Firstly, he wore a long brown coat, but it was filthy and matted with what looked like cow..." she searched for a word that meant shit, but more polite. The word she chose was "Mess". The sergeant gave her his kindest pitying look and she continued. "He wore a head covering, a kind of weird looking mask, but made out of old sack cloth and that too was caked in cow… er… mess."

Thomas wrote the words carefully in his note book, speaking out the last few as he did so. "Cow… er... Mess." He looked up and smiled. "You are doing really well, these sorts of crimes can be terribly unpleasant to witness. What else can you tell me, was he a human man, a troll or maybe even a fairy?"

Demonika slammed back the shot that she had been nursing and continued with her description of the vile man. "He was human and male, although with the size of the thing it would be hard to say that he was successfully male." Thomas chuckled slightly and then remembering himself forced a serious look onto his face and waited for her to continue. "It was odd, it looked like he was wearing trousers, but it was just some trouser legs tied off above his knees. He was naked otherwise, but his body was coated with, well more like smeared with more cow mess." She felt more comfortable using the term now. "When he opened his coat at me, he was staring into my eyes, really intently. It was then that he let out the monster er… poo."

"Can you describe the colour of the trouser legs please Ms Trumpett?" Thomas asked kindly.

She thought for a moment before she finally answered. "Well, if I was pushed, I would probably say light brown, maybe even a dark mustard yellow. But it is hard because they were quite thickly coated in shite... Sorry I mean mess!" If she were capable of blushing, she probably would have. Instead, she looked away to give the appearance of being bashful about such coarse and common language.

Having collected all of the details that he could, Sargent Thomas stood up from the table and then pulled a small paper pamphlet from his pocket. "Crimes like this are never your fault, if you need some support, why not talk to these listening trolls? They are very good and will give you a hard, stony, but kindly shoulder to cry on." He dropped the pamphlet on the table and after giving her is best kindly smile, walked back outside and took a blissful breath of polluted city air. Winscombe often stank like hot drains filled with boiling sewage, but actually inside the Rusty Plough, the air was far worse and the fumes of rancid fermenting drains was almost pleasant after that.

* * * * *

Felicity dabbed at her tears. It had been three months since she had last been to a Mother's

Support, group meeting and when she arrived and sat down, she faced across from only two other members and the counsellor as they sat in a small circle of four. Angela Thorn had barely acknowledged her entrance, but Stacey Flaherty had given her a kind pat on the shoulder as she made three cups of strong tea laced with a double shot of gin for each of them. The first to speak was Angela, her cruel words cut through the air with a spite and venom that in other worlds would have killed, or at least maimed.

"So Freddie, or Idi as he now asks to be called even at home has now been in trouble with the Police." She sniffed curtly and forbade her self from the indulgence of tears. "When he was arrested for spray painting strange tags on the cars parked outside the supermarket, he shouted some rather strong words at the Police. Of course, I can only assume that he learned such words from his best friend Adi..." She stared pointedly at a weeping Felicity.

The Counsellor made a small note on her pad and spoke with the kind tone of the professionally trained listener. "Would you want to share what he said to the Police Angela?"

Angela cleared her throat and spat the words out. "He said and I am quoting verbatim him here from the Police report. 'I have to keep law and order and it means that I have to kill my enemies before they kill me'." Shocked, the counsellor wrote down the words and considered what she would have to say to the social worker she was meeting later that day. Angela continued though, her voice forced and despite the quiet calm, sounded angry. "It gets worse, while in questioning he said to the officer almost in jest this time and again I am quoting from the Police report. In any country there must be people who have to die. They are the sacrifices any nation has to make, to achieve law and order!"

Stacey added her own comment. "You are

lucky that Freddie speaks to you. Zephirine has put Ian and I into exile after we asked her to tidy her bedroom, she said how can one tell us something like this? How can one say something like this?" Stacey sipped her 'strong' tea and swallowed before continuing. "After that she has resolutely refused to speak to either of us for days now. The only words we hear from her are when her friends phone her on her mobile. It seems that her only friends though are Isaac Goldstein and Freddie Thorn-Walters." she then added smugly, "at least our darling daughter has not been brought home to us in a Police car!"

Felicity let out another loud sob of despair and

the counsellor passed her a paper tissue that she screwed up and sobbed into quietly. Finally as the room waited in silence she almost whispered her statement. "Hello, my name is Felicity Goldstein and I am parent of a problem child."

The rest of the group did the usual bored welcome and encouraged her to speak.

"This week we also had Isaac brought home to us by the Police. This time it was more serious and they confirmed that they are going to press charges, which means that Jeremiah and I now have to go to court. We have tried locking Isaac in his room, but he somehow escapes, even through the bars on his windows." She blew her nose politely into the paper tissue and tucked it into the pocket of her rough and dusty jeans. "It was after he had burned down those sheds on the public allotments, he said to the Police this." She pulled a piece of paper from her handbag and read out the typed words. "If you want to shine like the sun, first you have to burn like it!" She folded the paper and put it back in her handbag and dabbed at her nose with her own soft hanky that was now stained and soiled after months of weeping. She then pulled a child's school book from her bag and flicked through the pages until she came to a page of carefully written italics that looked more like the handwriting of a grown up, than the scrawling of a four year old. "Let me read out what he wrote in his English book, when he was asked to write a story about kindness." She took a deep breath and steeling her self for the revulsion that she was about to express. "The strongest must dominate and not mate with the weaker, which would signify the sacrifice of its own higher nature. Only the born weakling can look upon this principle as cruel, and if he does so it is merely because he is of feebler nature and narrower mind; for if such a law did not direct the process of evolution then the higher development of organic life would not be conceivable at all."

She closed the book, visibly shaken and

replaced it back in her handbag. The counsellor wrote down something in large coded letters and gave her a look of grave concern that was not entirely sympathetic, before closing her note pad and sitting up to bring a close to the session. Felicity and Stacey walked out together, but Angela strode out with the walk of a woman refusing to acknowledge how bad her life was. Of them all, the counsellor decided, Angela was the one she liked the least.

* * * * *

Demonika called the meeting to order by tapping the rim of her glass with the edge of her razor sharp steak knife. The other members of Winscombe City Government looked at her expectantly, her face was grim and her eyes gave them all a cold hard stare. Her hair was swept up in a large almost beehive style on top of her head and wrapped around it was a band of some kind that was clearly designed to hold the whole colossal mound stable. Applied with it was probably close to three cans of fragrant hair spray and the smell rising from her was eyewateringly sickly at best and down right toxic for those sat right next to her at the meeting table. "Right then you spineless sacks of shit, it is about time that we did something about that arsehole King Jong the First. He has flooded our city with terrible food while sucking money from our coffers. What do you propose?"

The group of officials mumbled quietly and no one spoke in anything other than a near silent whisper. It was clear to her that not one of them had a clue of what to do next. "Right, I propose that construction of the wall continues along our border, that should stop the little bastards from getting in. But we still need to deal with the King himself. Norfcorea had best not make any more foreign muck food for the City of Winscombe or they will be met with fire and fury the likes of which the world has never seen!"

Her rousing speech seemed to go down well, but when she looked at her notes, it was clear that she too had absolutely no idea what to do next either. Finally one of the officials stood up to speak. She was a woman in her late fifties with thin greying hair and wore a truly awful and horribly inappropriate pair of brown leather riding trousers with some swanky low heeled boots. She looked like an overly plump teenager, ravaged with the face of a hag. Her voice was shrill which Demonika found highly irritating, but the woman spoke clearly enough for the rest of the city government to hear. "What this city needs is strong and stable leadership. These terrorists will not win, our strong and stable leadership will prevent them from ever doing so." She sat down again and Demonika goggled at her in disbelief and surprise. Another of the ministers stood. "When my learned colleague says terrorists, I assume that she refers to the disgusting individual known only as the Flashing Poo-er?" The same woman stood up again and smiling nodded her head. "Indeed my learned friend. This terrorist has exposed himself to over six elderly women in the city and has then on each occasion left behind a stool of truly colossal proportions. Our scientists report that this individual cannot be eating enough fibre, leading to a strong case of constipation. So when he does release his vile emission onto the city streets, there are several days worth of waste material left behind and frankly it is a danger to all forms of traffic in the city."

Demonika hung her head in her hands and let out the sort of sigh that only the most desolate and alone can manage. Another of the ministers stood and spoke at length about the contents of the large bowel movement and this met with jeers.

The woman minister stood again and once more wittered on about the Flashing Poo-er's stool. "I can assure my friend that there are many complex reasons as to why this individual may have to rely upon the charity of food banks, but I feel that we need to promise the city a strong and stable Government who will give them a secure future." She sat down with a flourish that clearly meant that she was pleased with herself.

Demonika groaned with a miserable dread that the conversation was about to continue, so she brought it to an end with an angry shout. "Who gives a fuck about this fucking pervert, we have to sort out Norfcorea and that human louse, King fucking Jong the fucking first!"

The room fell silent, all eyes were on her and she almost exploded until after nearly three minutes of silence there came a knock at the large wooden door that sealed the ministerial chamber from the other rooms in the government building. The knock was low down on the door and given with the force that only a child could manage, but it was loud enough to cause every pair of eyes in the room to turn to the door as it was opened. Three small beaming faces looked into the room, finally finding the object of their quest. Demonika at last smiled, the evil in her eyes shone through all pretense and finally the side of her character that she had worked so hard to hide from the people of Winscombe, finally shone through.

"Ahhh, Adolf, Idi and Elana, how wonderful to see you all. Please do join us, for the sake of all that is unholy, do please join us?" Three chairs were pulled out from the table and three small faces appeared, none of them looked joyous to see the other ministers and in response, the ministers visibly shrank away from the awful children, sat whilst simultaneously scowling diabolically.

* * * * *

Angela finally broke down at the support group meeting. Her face was most ugly when it was crying, thought Stacey to herself, which gave her the chance to smirk across the room to Felicity who caught the full meaning of the look and with a movement barely noticeable, nodded her head in agreement. Weeping quietly, Angela spoke of her lost child with the words of a grieving parent missing an angelic if not saintly child, rather than the aggressive and abusive monster that her child had become. In her hand she clutched the note that had been left for her. Every parent in the group carried with them a similar note and each one of them had cried, but for one of them, it also came with a guilty feeling of relief.

"My Freddie, he ran away from home!" Angela wailed, her eyes black smudges of ruined eye-liner and tears. "He took off with those two brats and has gone to the fairy kingdom to fight in a holy war!"

The counsellor wrote the word Jihadi several times on her notepad and tried not to think about her own family and if they were likely to

455

be traveling on any form of public transport while she was sat in a meeting with those awful women. With Angela closed up with weeping, the counsellor invited Felicity to talk next because she seemed the least upset and the counsellor wondered if this was going to develop into survivor guilt and scribbled it down on her notepad.

"This is day three of Isaac being gone from our home and it feels so quiet without him. He liked to listen to the Nuremberg speeches of Hitler at high volume on Youtube, on his laptop in his room, which to be honest I found quite depressing. I came home from the corner shop last week and found him applauding as he watched Triumph of the Will and I have no idea where he learned to speak German so fluently. He was able to speak along with some of those speeches, he even had the gestures down perfectly. Luckily Jeremiah was up stairs with his headphones on." She looked angry for a second. "Maybe that is why the bastard had his headphones on?" She let out an angry exclamation. "I told him not to be so fucking spineless with the boy, it is a kill or be killed world I said." She paused for an angry moment to pass before continuing with her rage. "And I said, I can fight only for something that I love, love only what I respect and respect only what I at least know!"

The counsellor leaned back in her seat, shut her eyes and rubbed the bridge of her nose with her thumb and fingers. After a couple of seconds of blessed darkness, she opened her eyes and wrote the words fascistic outburst on her pad.

Stacey spoke next, her face was sanguine, her eyes without their usual haunted look. "Ian and I, well we just hope that Zephirine does not come back pregnant. Isn't that why kids usually run away? Given that she had told me that she loves her precious little Adi-Wadi. We will not be happy if she comes back with a baby!"

The counsellor almost sat up in shock and

wrote 'disturbing notions of sexuality in the children' on the pad before she tried to reassure the women sat with her. "You do know that humans do not generally reach that degree of sexual maturity until they are in their teens?"

Stacey looked at her with the same contempt that a bad teacher looks at a failing dyslexic with dyspraxia. "Well, kids grow up quick these days, don't they? I seen it on the telly, that Jeremy bloke with the shouting and the security guard fights."

The counsellor could stand it no more, "These children are barely five years old, god alone knows what could be happening to them right now and you selfish bitches have spent the entire time complaining about how hard your lives are now that you have children! Some of us would give up a kidney to be able to carry a fucking baby!" She slammed the cover of her note pad shut in anger. "These sessions are now fucking over, get out the fucking lot of you!" She stood up, grabbed her notepad and ran weeping from the room. The room was left silent for several seconds until Felicity commented on the actions of their therapist.

"What a cow, she don't know what it is like to have a child, who is also a Nazi sympathiser from birth." She pulled the tissues from her handbag and found one that was the least smudged with tears, bad make up and snot, to wipe her nose with. "Selfish bitch, she don't care about us and our feelings."

Chapter 6:- The past revealed.

"Sire?" The voice was cold, it was clearly the voice of the young man running towards King Jong the First and he very clearly carried bad news. The man jogged along the palace corridor and when he reached the King, bowed low, his eyes staying level with the King's hands, as custom stated was polite. "What it is Sir, what news causes you to run along this corridor to disturb me on this beautiful morning?"

The man was dressed in the subtle clothes of the Service of Secrets, his robes looked to be normal soft cottons and spider silk, but the hard edges showed signs of plate armour hidden beneath. His hair was cut unusually short, to prevent it being grabbed in a fight no doubt, but his eyes were red, his face streaked with tears. "King Jong the First, it is my duty to inform you of developments on our border with Somerset."

The King nodded at the man in agreement, but the man remained silent. The King stared at him and waited for him to speak again, but the silence remained until at last the King was forced to ask the man to speak.

"Thank you Sire, I bring news of the camps that hold our people hostage. The Morris Dancing, sire. It is now constant. The death toll is bordering on catastrophic." The King dropped his head sadly, his gaze falling to his own slippers and rolled up newspaper. "There is more Sire, the wall has been completed, our border is now heavily reinforced with blocks brought in from the human world, it is impenetrable to all of our weaponry. The only thing is, they have failed to construct the right foundations and in several places, the wall is already being propped up with scaffolding and dark magic."

The King looked longingly towards the small doorway to where he had been heading and for a moment considered heading there anyway, but he knew that such news would need to be shared with his advisers. It was entirely likely that the Aid du Champ already knew, but the others would need to be told that war was in all likelihood inevitable. Cursing his high fibre diet, King Jong the First dismissed the spy and turned back towards his offices and called out to waiting staff that the cabinet of ministers was to be assembled. He continued to stride with dark confidence towards his own office for a few fractions of a second more, but suddenly his leg stopped in mid-air, he pondered for a moment and then turned back towards the small door and walked with the graceless tight buttock walk of a man on a mission to complete the morning crossword before using the paper elsewhere and then washing his hands.

The Aid du Champ sat in his usual seat, Sharon sat opposite him and Fred was reading the paper whilst sat on the chair opposite the King's own velvet padded seat. They had been waiting for several minutes already and the air was charged as the Aid du Champ silently fumed and Sharon quietly cursed the name Trumpett. When the King walked in, both of the agitated people stilled their faces, but oblivious, Fred continued reading his horoscope, his face growing ever more concerned.

"Ahhh, Sire. How delightful that you choose to see us." The Aid du Champ was as charming as he was sarcastic and the King gave him a banal smile. "If it pleases Your Majesty, we have a great deal to discuss. I trust that you solved the morning crossword?"

The King nodded his reply to the Aid du Champ just as Fred looked up, rather startled, from his stars and exclaimed loudly, "Oh bollocks!" With all members of the cabinet sat down at the table, the King turned his face to Fred and with a smile indicated that he was to speak. "Sorry Your Highness, I mean Jong, it's just that my stars today say that I am about to enter into a period of difficulty in probably hostile environs, but not to worry because I have the trust of good friends."

King Jong smiled at him kindly, "Well volunteered Fred, I want you to lead our troops in the coming war against Winscombe." Fred's jaw dropped, his face a mixture of emotions crossing his aged and leathery skin. "However my friend, I do not want you going into this alone, I want you to have the very best of advice as you do so," the King paused for a moment. "So I want you to be accompanied for some of your journey by my closest friend and most cunning adversary in the games." He turned to Sharon, his face serious. "I know that I am asking you to go willingly into danger, but I have a far greater mission for you and one that is going to stretch all of your tactics and cunning. I want you to bring Wuffles to my palace, as a hostage if necessary. Can you do this?"

Sharon grinned at the King, his mind a white hot furnace of cunning and mischief. She knew that it would require a chef of excellent talent to attract the famous Wuffles to defect. Admittedly she might not know six ways of how to murder a man with just a tooth pick, but she did know how to tempt a being with wild tastes and an exotic palate. "Yes, I think that I can. Will I be alone or will I have a team with me?"

"Excuse me Sire, but we are on the brink of launching high yield custard missiles and you want this girl to kidnap a dog?" The Aid du Champ was incredulous, his eyes wild with suppressed fury. "What on earth good will that do? It's a fucking dog!"

The King smiled at his chief adviser, but it was not a warm or friendly smile, it was instead a devious and slightly evil smile. "Come now Terry, you must be aware of where the true power lies in Somerset? It is hardly with that Trumpett woman, there is someone behind her, guiding her actions. How else can she know what she knows? The rumours are that Demonika Trumpett is a former street prostitute who worked her way up to a position of power." The Aid du Champ winced slightly at the use of her name and every person at the table noticed it, but especially the King. "Terry, is there something that you have not told me about this woman? Something that all of us need to know?"

The Aid du Champ tried to shrink away into his chair, but he was barely able to move from the gaze of all three of the people watching him. Slowly his face flushed, his cheeks turning a deep burgundy. His voice was unusually quiet, his eyes cast down upon the table in shame. "The thing is Sire, I er..." He stumbled for words, aware of all the eyes of those sat at the table boring into him with the intensity of laser mining equipment.

"Oh spit it out man!" Chipped in Fred who was already worrying about his future as a military general.

"I used to be married to her Sire."

Sharon almost exploded with laughter and Fred stared at the old man with a look of concern, but the King was inscrutable and his face was impossible to read, it was a skill that he had learned about in Monarchy, the monthly magazine that came with a small part to build a model throne room and was the trade magazine for all ruling monarchs, oligarchs and patricians. They had even run a feature on him prior to his ascendancy to the throne, which they had sent to him afterwards as a free back issue. "I see."

"How can you be so silent now, Jong, have you considered that he could have been leaking secrets to her?" Sharon exclaimed angrily, but the King's quiet calm was almost as charming as his fine silk robes and she soon sat back down at the table, although both Fred and her continued to scowl angrily at the Aid du Champ.

"I ain't ever spoken to her since I left Sire, and that was before your father was born. When I was a pilot of the seas, I met her in one of the ports of the far east and before you knew it, we were wed. I have been paying her alimony ever since. It was only a few gold coins a year, but after all of these decades, it has probably started to add up. To be honest, I had completely forgotten about her."

"Until she came back into our lives Terry, until she came back." Fred almost spat across the table.

The King rested quietly in his chair, his face remaining unreadable. "So, what can we do to ensure that Wuffles is acquired by us? I would prefer the carrot as opposed to the stick if I am honest. An angry chef can lead to an early death."

Sharon nodded her head emphatically. "I would suggest that we deliver a box of our finest food, not this shit." She waved one of the menus in the air for a moment before dropping it back to the table. "He is a connoisseur, a food critic of the highest order. Have you read his restaurant reviews?" She dropped a selection of copied articles onto the table from her handbag. "He knows the true difference between death by chocolate and assault by cocoa I can tell you."

The King nodded sagely, this was another skill that he had learned from his magazine and he found that he could use it more and more often and thus avoid having to make any hard decisions at all. His gaze turned back to the young woman and she basked in his interest for a moment.

"If we can encourage him to sample some of our finest delicacies, maybe we can tempt him to leave the Rusty Plough. Once he has left, the magic in that place will leave with him. He must be encouraged to set up his new kitchen in the royal palace." The Aid du Champ was quietly pleased to have the topic turned away from his ex-wife for a moment, but he rather suspected that the new King was holding that piece of information for a time when it would be of greater use. He turned to Sharon and tried to give her the same sage look that the King had done, but from him it seemed merely to be slightly overly friendly and not in a good way. "Do you know a chef good enough to prepare a feast to encourage Wuffles away?"

Both the King and Sharon grinned and nodded their heads.

"Oh yes Terry, Sharon and I know just the woman. Don't we my dear friend?"

"Oh yes we do and we do not need a feast, merely a taste."

* * * * *

The road to the border with Somerset was windy and since the advent of fast food delivery, rather wide and hammered flat by the feet of a million delivery folk. Sharon and Fred trudged along it in the rain, covered with large umbrellas each, the walk was no less bleak as each gust tried to savagely mug the brollies from their grasps. Behind them strode the army of Northcorea, dressed in smart green uniforms, masks of fierce battle screams worn over their tired cold faces. Each soldier had sworn an oath of allegiance to the throne and once ordered into battle, they would rather die on the field of war, than return in defeat to their king. Behind the long column of troops came the supply carts, the spare camels and the one secure and iron clad cart that contained the delicacies to tempt Wuffles away to Norfcorea.

In places along the road, it had been shored up in order to repair erosion by the countless delivery folk and it was at these places that the rain gathered in large muddy puddles. Such obstacles were mere piffle to the powerful troops of King Jong the First, but for Sharon and Fred, both of whom were more delicate in their disposition, they presented a cold wet quagmire of misery that ended each day with sore feet and cold wrinkled toes. The march to the new great wall was supposed to take three days, the troops found this to be a dull and uninspiring dawdle and ached to run at the speed that the delivery folk started at. But it was not seemly for troops to run head first down mountain paths screaming with elation and terror, as most of the delivery folk had done for the past year.

At the base of the mountains, Fred ordered a scout party to head out across the plain to find somewhere safe to build their camp and with unrestrained joy at finally being able to move at speed, the Norfcorean soldiers whooped and yelped with joy as they sprinted into the distance and very quickly vanished from sight among the scrubland bushes. Snakes and scorpions hid deep in their burrows, tarantulas curled themselves up into silk wrapped balls and hid in the dark, all of them waiting for the Norfcoreans to pass by. The rumours had spread from the city, never trust a Norfcorean, they eat anything with legs and several things without! Despite the rumours being false, the animals hid none the less and it was only one small spider who had broken her leg who was found by a bored young soldier who was squatting down to enjoy the aroma of a particularly pretty flower. As she tried to scramble away, her tiny spider voice cried out in terror. "Please, don't eat me! I have a family."

Startled, the soldier stumbled backwards and fell onto his bottom in the dust. Recovering from his shock, he could see the small arachnid limping towards the cover of a large thorn bush and he dashed ahead of her and scooped her up in his hat, which caused her to scream in terror and try to hide under the brim. So sat like that the soldier and the spider stared at each other for half an hour until at last she spoke to him.

"Please don't eat me?"

"Why would I want to eat you? You are a spider!"

She looked at him confused, all eight of her eyes watching his face for signs of the truth. "You are from Norfcorea, you lot eat anything with legs and some things without! I don't want to be eaten." she began to cry and wept her tiny spider tears into the fabric of the soldiers hat.

"Err, excuse me. You do know that what you said is racist. don't you?" The spider looked up confused. "Just because I am Norfcorean, you people assume that we eat all sorts of horrible things. Do you know what I had for breakfast this morning?"

The spider untucked herself from the furthest part of the soldier's hat and looked him in the eyes. "Did you have fried snake and boiled silk worm omelettes? I heard that this is traditional food for you people."

"Well actually, I had seasoned rice, a cup of fruit juice and three slices of grilled goats cheese. Why on earth would I eat snake or spiders when I can have that?" He looked at the spider firmly in the face. "Anyway, why are you the one to judge, when you eat flies!" He smiled at her, his face was kind and noble and she knew that she could trust him. "What is your name little spider?"

"Shirley Braithwaite, what's yours?"

"Madam Braithwaite, I am proud to know you.

My name is Bus Zoan Wan, I am a trooper in the Royal Norfcorean Army." He looked at her closely, "You appear to be hurt, may I offer you some assistance?"

Shirley held out her fragile and painful broken limb, a large wasp stinger was poking through it, but thankfully the stinger had gone right through and had squirted the pressurised poison into the soil. The gland on the end though was still pulsing, ready to deliver another evil toxic shock wave of neurotoxin that would not just paralyse Shirley, but leave her in absolute agony. Bus Zoan Wan examined the wound and saw the seriousness of it immediately.

"Madam Braithwaite, if I pull that stinger from your leg, it may pump you full of a terrible poison, from which you would never recover. Am I right in thinking that you are able to regrow your leg if you lose it?"

She looked at the stinger and then at the earnest young face of the soldier. "I know what you are going to say. You have to remove the leg or I may die." She gazed at him and saw only compassion in his eyes. "Will you hold my palp while you do it? I don't want it to hurt."

"Of course Madam Braithwaite," He poured out a tiny droplet of military issue pain killer and offered her the dot of medicine on the end of his finger. "Drink this, it will help with the pain." She sucked up the fluid and felt almost at once the pain of her wound fade away until it was a nagging hurt, rather than a screaming agony. "Now brace yourself Madam."

His knife tip was clean and the cut quick. Before she could even yell out, he was applying a thick, blood-flow stopping grease to her wound. Finally he scooped her up in his hat once more and stood up. "Madam Braithwaite, you need to rest so that you can heal. Where would you like me to place you so that you are close to home."

If her face was capable of smiling, she would have done so. Instead she spoke carefully and as clearly as the pain medication allowed her. "Would you mind if I stayed with you? I feel like I have found a long-lost friend and I know that I will be safe with you." Her eyes searched his, "I can curl up in your pocket if that is OK?" He opened his shirt chest pocket and slowly and even slightly drunkenly, she slid into the warm dark place and before she could say world wide web, she was fast asleep and dreaming of it.

* * * * *

As the troops built the Norfcorean camp, Sharon and Fred pored over the maps that they had of the area, looking for the best place to burst through the wall. The scout party had found three places and each had their positives and their dangers, but one was clearly the better option because it was the most difficult and thus less guarded. To get through the border and into the outskirts of Winscombe, she would have to crawl through rolls of barbed wire, climb over several collapsed sections of Trumpett's wall and then get past a small encampment of Somerset soldiers. She grinned at Fred, dropped her cape and went off to her tent to change into her dark blue infiltration uniform.

Crawling through the barbed wire was difficult and occasionally painful for Sharon, despite the thick rubber knee pads and gloves which she wore to protect her from the wire barbs. The darkness of a moonless night made the journey slightly harder, but after a few hundred metres of hands and knees travel, she escaped into the mud and rubble of the collapsed wall and crept quietly into the dark. Ahead of her was the camp fire of the Famous Somerset Guard and sat around were four over-weight, under achieving squaddies, two of whom were horribly drunk. One of the soldiers was sat quietly reading and the final soldier who clearly a lot younger than the others kept asking if he should go on patrol. The leader of the squad, who was the most drunk of the drink soiled men almost shouted at the boy to sit down, shut up and keep his nose clean. Sharon crept past them with ease and within minutes, she was on the road to the centre of the city, hidden in the dark by her stealthy clothing and careful manner. Tucked under her arm was a small well wrapped box, the carefully baked delicacies that both her Grandmother and the King had prepared to tempt Wuffles away from the Rusty Plough.

After an hour of walking, the sun had started to

rise above the horizon and the sky had turned a livid cherry red that was as beautiful as it was horrifying. For moments she could have imagined that the sky was a huge furnace and she was walking towards the heart of it, but as the sun rose higher, the sky changed again and became somehow even more beautiful. As she wandered along the road, watching the heavenly show above her, a call from behind dragged her back to the real world. "I said ahoy there young lady, would you like a ride?" The strange cart pulled up next to her and the most startling aspect of it was that it had no horse pulling it. Instead, there was a large wooden wheel held in a mechanism that allowed it to twist in a frame and provide steering, but this was not the strangest aspect of the device. Rather, stood in the bottom of the wheel, covered in thick woolly hair, were two small figures and dangling in front of them from a stick was a clearly very bored looking frog. The cart driver tried again. "Are you heading to the city young lady, would you like a ride; save your feet?"

Sharon looked at him and blinked. She reached into her pocket and pulled out her Somerset phrase book, flicked through a couple of pages and read one of the carefully scripted lines that was designed to make her look like a lost tourist.

"Good morning, afternoon, evening, delete as appropriate. Can you tell where I can chip shop pleases?"

The cart driver smiled kindly. "You made it through the wall then, come with me my dear, I know just where you need to be." He patted the seat next to him and she climbed up onto the wooden cart. Once there, he pulled a strap across her lap which caused her to give him a look of dubious concern. "Don't worry love, this will stop you falling off." He pointed to a handle in front of her, "hold on love." He whistled and the two hairy beings in the large wheel almost ran up the inner wall of the wheel in front of them. As they did so, the wheel began to roll forwards and slowly they began to pick up speed until they were heading along the road at quite a pace. The two beings each ran frantically, reaching out their hands for the frog hanging in front of them from the middle of the hub; the noise they made was a frantic panting and grunting along with the occasional snarl. Sharon watched them fascinated and noticing this, the driver grinned as he steered the wheel along the rutted and dusty track. Twenty minutes later the cart shot past the sign that welcomed visitors to the city of Winscombe and the driver dragged hard on a large brake lever hung from the side of the cart. The lever in turn pulled a rod, that in turn pulled another lever that acted on a large rubber pad that rubbed hard against the outside of the large wheel. The smell that came from it was a mixture of burning rubber and animal urine and the creatures in the wheel began to whine and moan as their legs pushed hard against the slowing wheel. Finally they came to a stop and the creatures slumped exhausted against the floor of the wheel. The cart driver turned to face Sharon, but she had already dived from the cart and had vanished into the busy streets. He peered around him and found no sign of her, but let out a short sigh. "That's a shame, I was going to buy you breakfast at the Rusty Plough. Never mind." He whistled again and the two creatures in the wheel leapt back up and set off at a run on the wooden wheel, propelling the cart forwards into the dirty streets.

Sharon weaved through the crowds, shot

silently across walk ways and vanished into shadows without anyone noticing her. When she finally found a place to check her map, she discovered that more by luck than judgement, she had arrived at the back of the Rusty Plough, The large wooden gate that she leant against was damp with algae and rot, but as she pushed against it, it held firm. She was about to push it harder when it suddenly swung open and she came face to face with the sad dark eyes of a large and slender dog.

"Oh shit! Sorry, I nearly fell on you." She looked at the face, the long slender nose, the sharp vicious looking teeth, the small pink bum bag wrapped around the animal's waist. "You are a good boy, aren't you." She was about to pat him on the head when she noticed that his facial features had changed slightly and that his new expression said something rather different. Intuitively, without him saying a word, she knew that he had just insulted her.

"There was no need for that, I was not being patronising!" She stared at him hard, he stared back at her, his face once again spoke to her and astonished, she answered back. "What do you mean you have been waiting for me? I am not late?" He whined slightly and gave her another look. "OK, yes, I have the pastries with me, why can't we taste them here?" He whined a little more, added a dark growl and then gave a small, yelp-like bark. She watched him intently and the understanding flooded into her. "Ahhh, I had gathered that you are Wuffles and yes I am aware that Trumpett owns the pub, but she has no idea who I am." He whined again. "Really?" She asked in response, "I had no idea that she would go so far. All three of them you say?"

Wuffles barked once and led her out into the streets. When he realised that she was struggling to keep up he sat down and spoke to her again. His voice was gentle whines, small growls and then he pulled a lead out of his bum-bag and passed it to her. She took it from him puzzled and he explained again until she got what it was he wanted her to do. "Oh I see, you want me to clip this onto you so that you do not lose me. That way people will think that I am taking you for a walk." He whined again and growled slightly. She almost stepped backwards, "Of course I would not treat you like a thicko dog. I came here because of you, Mr Wuffles; you are a Maestro, an artisan, your reputation alone is what brought me here."

She clipped the lead onto his leather collar and he stood once again, leading her off into the streets before eventually arriving at a small wooded park. After a few minutes in which he kept checking that they were not being followed, he led Sharon to a small patch of bushes and dragged her through a thin section to a clear circle of fresh grass with a small red and white checkered blanket laid out in front of them. The sounds of the city were muffled, the air was surprisingly fragrant and once Sharon had unclipped him, he poured a small bowl of sparkling water for himself and settled down on his blanket. He looked at Sharon and his face said only two words. Impress me.

Chapter 7:- Half Baked Alaska

The Custard War was rapid and brutal! The armies of Somerset and Norfcorea clashed in a horrific cataclysmic battle across the muddy fields of the border. The sanctioned use of Custard Weapons left a nasty taste in the mouth of both leaders and the unfortunate troops returning home with terrible custard burns and sugar poisoning, their faces haunted by the atrocity of war, which made every one feel like the end of the world was coming. The news networks had reporters on the battle field and one of them was actually caught in an exchange of tactical custard weapons that left her with a nasty yellow tinge to her skin and terrible diabetes. As she reported from her battle scarred wheelchair, the losses on both sides were severe, but it was obvious that the army of Norfcorea was ultimately going to win the war. King Jong the First gave statements about how war was the sad result of facing down tyrants and dictators who had lost the urge to negotiate. Demonika gave conferences with reporters where she shouted insults about the Norfcorean King and its people, she accused him of despotism and irrationality. She made claims that Norfcorea was a rogue terrorist state ruled by a megalomaniac who murdered his own staff. While she made these claims, the press watched on in horrified fascination, unsure as to whether they were watching real events or some kind of artistic performance piece.

In the rare moments of peace when he was able to grab away from state affairs, King Jong the First of Norfcorea stood in his plain white kitchen with a quiet thoughtful Wuffles. Together they gazed at a deflating baked Alaska, Wuffles although unimpressed, through his gentle kind face showed more compassion and kindness than any human master chef would have done. The king spoke first, his voice harsh, his manner angered. "Bollocks, I really thought that I had it this time." He stamped one foot hard in anger. "I don't know why I bother to stay in the kitchen, I am an idiot!" He turned to Wuffles, "you could slap two pieces of bread on my head and call me an idiot sandwich!"

Wuffles yelped once, his eyebrows knotted in consternation, his tail wagged slowly once or twice. The King stared at him for a moment.

"Thank you Maestro, you are truly very kind, but I just can't get this right. How do you make it look so easy?"

Wuffles whined again, his ears drooped and he panted twice.

"I know, you told me yesterday that I should not be so hard on myself. The art of cooking is a journey of discovery about both the food and

495

one's self. You told me this yesterday and I have meditated about it as you suggested."

Again Wuffles let out a small yelp, shook his head and flicked his ears.

"Yes, I understand. I have been trying to focus on that as you instructed me. The art of food is only ever about love: The love of cooking itself and the love of the people we invite to our table."

Wuffles wagged his tail and using his nose, flicked the oven door shut just as Sharon came back in with a plate of biscuits from her Grandmother. "Maestro Wuffles, my Grandma has asked if you would agree to taste one of her biscuits and offer your opinion on how to make them better?"

Wuffles padded across the kitchen, followed by King Jong the First and carefully took one biscuit from the fine china plate in his teeth and then padded quietly across the kitchen to his fresh new basket in the warmest and quietest corner of the gleaming kitchen. The King also took a biscuit as Sharon offered him the plate. He sat down on the stool and began to nibble on the delicate baked cookie. The biscuit broke in his mouth with a snap, the flavour of the caramel was exquisite, the subtle under flavour of the ginger bit teasingly at his tongue. The rum soaked raisins added a smoky flavour of illicit sensual indulgence. He took another nibble and the experience only intensified. Wuffles came back to them and sat down, his face serious, his eyes seemed so deep and sad, he sat with the gentle grace of a master about to give forth wisdom that could change their lives forever. His face was like that of a wise and ancient sage and he spoke in ways that the two Norfcoreans found wondrous. His eyes said the most as he gave his verdict on the biscuit. "Your Grandmother's biscuit was most pleasing, the elegant flavours, the subtle shifts in texture as it crumbles. I can taste the joy in the baking, the love with which it was made. Those flavours are what are missing from most foods in this modern age." He looked thoughtful for a moment and then with his ears forwards, his nose down and a sharp single yelp added, "suggest to your Grandmother that maybe she would like to try a granite milled flour as opposed to a gritstone milled flour. The granite adds a sharpness that only a truly sensitive palate can detect and this comes across in the biscuit as an infinitely subtle hint of lemon zest, without the need of actual lemon."

Sharon wrote down the instruction, made notes on the essences that Wuffles had spoken of and then bowed low. "Thank you, Maestro." She left the kitchen with a skip, leaving the King alone with Wuffles once again. The king finished his own wonderful cookie and sat dejected on his stool. His mind was full of self-doubt, he had spent most of his childhood secretly cooking, his recipes were first rate and yet here he sat in misery because he was unable to prepare a simple baked Alaska. He felt something resting on his thigh and as he looked up, he felt the gaze of Wuffles boring into his soul from where he had laid his head on the Kings lap. The soft warm eyes spoke of such kindness, of such hope and understanding, the King nodded his head.

"I do not know how you have such patience in me Maestro, but I will try again under your guidance." Wuffles wandered over to the walk-in freezer, tugged the door open and took out yet another bowl of layered ice cream that they had prepared the day before. He pressed the bowl into the King's hands and together they headed over to the prep counter and set about with the cake base. Once the layer of ice cream was set upon the base, the King began once again to whip up his meringue. He looked to Wuffles for reassurance and nodded his head. "I am not sure that I have fifteen minutes of whipping in my arms."

Wuffles nodded sagely, with his face saying all that he needed the King to learn. "And that is why you failed."

The King nodded his understanding. If he was to complete this task, he must do so silently, saving his energy for when he needed it most, namely when the icing pipette was used to create the small rosettes of meringue. Finally finished and still silent, he pressed the creation into the oven and closed the door, whilst Wuffles stood back and watched quietly. He knew that the King now understood, he knew that the young man had done exactly what he had needed to do, but he also needed the King to see for himself, for only this lesson could prove to him the value of his perseverance.

* * * * *

At the battle field Fred stood with his most trusted general, Shy Ting Skaid. The Norfcorean soldier was missing an eye, a wound from his days spent duelling whilst at military university. He leaned heavily on his crutch, the implement that had replaced his right leg which he had lost while fighting water serpents in Norfcorea's mystical lakes. His left arm had been torn off by the very same dragon he had then slain at the battle of Horned Mountain. His right hand of only three fingers held down a map on the desk and his single foot (which had been replaced with a plastic one after he had fallen from a great height while playing Griffin Polo) was stuck firmly into the muddy ground. He was a veteran soldier, a man of great bravery and usually the first to give some reckless or otherwise impetuous stratagem a damn good thrashing until it worked. Fred had grown rather fond of the man, although watching him stagger across the muddy battle field had shown Fred that he was not alone in his idolisation of the man. The Norfcorean troops also loved him and it was a commonly held belief among the soldiery that those who were able to place a hand upon the man's crutch, would be imbibed with his incredible good fortune.

The Somerset guard had fled the battlefield, utterly routed by the Norfcoreans. The wounded and the dying were left where they fell, but the gentle Norfcorean medics could not bear to listen to the men suffer and insisted upon helping those who could be helped, and gently nursed those who could not. At first, the Somerset troops were fearful, they remembered well how they themselves had treated the Norfcorean prisoners of war, but the gentle kindness of the Norfcoreans and their excellent culinary skills won through and very soon they had the Somerset men healing and living quiet peaceful lives in their own prisoner camps, where they utterly rejected any attempts at escape and spent the evenings putting on camp and unusual drag shows for each other!

However, the use of propaganda by the Somerset generals made the troops terribly fearful of their Norfcorean enemy and word was passed quickly among the troops still fighting the Norfcoreans, that the dreaded enemy committed terrible and humiliating crimes against captured Somerset troops. Thus after every battle, as the Norfcoreans gave help and medicine, they were forced to endure the endless cries of men, terrified of cannibalism or worse still, Morris Dancing.

Fred looked at the Map as General Skaid pointed out how the lines had shifted. It was hard to understand when the General spoke, he was after all missing his tongue because it had been torn from his mouth by the bravest warrior of the ferocious Eagle Clawed Warrior People, but even they had finally fallen to the General's unstoppable personality and had gladly made peace with the man only days later. As he spoke, he sniffed, which was a ghastly sound since he had once, while relaxing on a Sunday morning at home, slipped while shaving and given himself a nosectomy!

* * * * *

Demonika Trumpett sat upon a throne of misery, built as it was from the bones of defeat, upon a plinth of humiliation. The pub was silent. When Wuffles had left, he had taken most of the magic and all of the quaintness with him, leaving behind just the dour odour, the filthy carpets and the terrible rat infestation, that he had always managed to keep under control in the kitchen. Miserable, she sat at her once favourite seat, close to the now cold fire place and sucked hard on her formerly enjoyed Troll Fags. The war was not going well at all, in fact her troops were losing badly and not even her special task force of evil had helped. Two of the three children that had come to her, bringing with them their military experience, leadership and rigorous brutality, had all but shut themselves away in the upper floors of the Pub. The third, the most vile and hated of them all, was ensconced in the basement, hidden behind thin wooden doors, blocked by a combination of heavy furniture, book cases and most of the cushions from the pub seating. Laying low behind the barricades, in a fort made from blankets draped over an old kitchen table was the reincarnation of an infamous dead Dictator. Around him were his supplies, stacked up just in case the worst should happen and the Norfcoreans lay siege to the city. He lifted the lid of one of the large boxes of toffees and took another from the tin, unwrapped it and popped it into his angry, down-turned mouth. With the wrapping paper, he simply dropped it to the floor, where it hit the top of a large pile of sweetie papers and rolled down the surprisingly large mound to the buried floor beneath. Stood opposite the little boy, staring across the vast distance of reality that the small untidy table failed to show, were two of the Somerset Army Generals. Both men were dressed in dark green, with large red hats full of pink fathered plumes, They stood lamp post straight and staring forwards as their military strategist chewed his way through yet another family box of toffees. After an hour they had finally given up on the hope that diabetic shock would cause the child to stop screaming and just be quietly sick, but somehow against all expectations, he had continued to consume quantities of sweets that would have dropped a donkey purely by the weight of them alone. His parents referred to him as Isaac, but to his army, he was known simply as Fuhrer.

The little boy slid from under his desk in a furious rage, then stamped across the floor, spat onto the carpet in contempt and finally turned to face the ashen faced men who had brought him the latest news from the front. "We are sorry Fuhrer, but the troops cannot be rallied any more. The Norfcoreans are just too aggressive, they are approaching the city now."

The little Fuhrer stamped his feet, bellowed wordless noises and then collapsed to the floor where he screamed, kicked and thrashed while his men blandly looked at the air above him. When they remained silent, he looked up at them and noticed that they were looking away and he fell silent. When they finally turned back to him, he continued with his tantrum, his hands thrashing on the floor of the cellar, his feet kicking in uncontrolled malevolence.

Upstairs from where Demonika sat was the closed room where Freddie Thorn-Walters was attempting to seduce a distraught and pitifully crying Zephirine Flaherty. He had already ordered the decapitation of several of his own generals whom he had accused of conspiracy and cowardice, but much to his disappointment his order had not been carried out. What it had in fact accomplished was that both children had been sent to their rooms by an angered and rather large Colonel who had finally had enough of their childish tantrums and poor behaviour, so had personally marched them both upstairs and then told them to behave and think about what they had done.

With her plan effectively failed, Demonika sat and brooded. The Norfcoreans were only a few miles from the city limits and her great wall had fallen with an unforeseen ease, caused more by its own bad design and poor foundations than by Norfcorean ingenuity. She gave thought to what it was that she had wanted to achieve in the first place and slowly realised that in truth she had not really had that much of a plan, she had just wanted to stir up some kind of trouble, spread disharmony and most of all, get the idiots around her hating each other as much as she hated them all. Sadly, that was the only part of the plan that had actually worked. Her three young protégées had fallen out with each other; within hours of reaching the city, the war had been so badly organised owing to their own petty arguments that many of the Somerset Guard had simply fled, rather than get caught in friendly fire as two generals fought for the same objective set out for them by the arguing two leaders.

The smoke from her Troll Fags had dyed her fingertips an alarming shade of purple, her face had the cracked and sullied skin of a wax work that had been frozen and then fallen over in the snow. Her make-up was dropping off in flakes and beneath the warm and youthful looking veneer was the grey and haggard skin of a tired and elderly woman. For a moment she gave thought to the possibility of a ham sandwich from the kitchen or maybe one of Wuffle's famous gourmet Gala Pies. Just the thought of the flavour rich filling of quails eggs, honey baked pulled pork, finest back bacon, fresh ground ginger, mace and fresh black pepper was enough to make her salivate. As she was about to call out to him, she remembered with painful regret, that Wuffles was gone. The kitchen was cold, the stove was rusty and lifeless. The pans were rusted and dirt encrusted, the dirty plates had built up in the sink until she found that she had used all one hundred and seventy five of them, after which she had resorted to using all of the side plates and then the pudding bowls. Slowly she began to weep and even more concerning to her, she began to wonder about leaving Winscombe altogether, creeping away silently in the dark. Her life was in chaos and she felt, not for the first time, more alone than she had for many, many years.

The door into the pub burst open, which made her jump with sudden fright. The wooden frame, rotted by decades of filth simply fell apart as the doors broke in half and the splintered remains scattered about the room. Stood in the open doorway was a Norfcorean soldier of great rank, his chest was covered in medals, his hat was topped with a large feather of the brightest blue and his plain wooden crutch had the ribbons of the Norfcorean infantry woven around its stays. He hobbled towards her and bowed low, holding the bow for a few seconds and then standing once again, a feat that she thought miraculous given that he was clearly only half the man that she should have been.

"Madam Mayor, my name is General Shy Ting Skaid of the Norfcorean infantry. Will you accept that the battle is now lost to you? Will you accept our terms for peace?"

Demonika stubbed out her filthy Troll fag and dropped the remains into the ashtray along with the other half smoked butts. She stood up and looked the General in the eye. "Have my troops surrendered to you?"

The General nodded his head with a controlled nobility that she found almost excruciating, especially given that his hat was barely balanced on his singled eared head. "They have Ma'am and we are now treating your wounded and feeding the hungry among your troops."

She sagged as she thought again of the food

that she missed, the flavours that had gone from the pub, along with Wuffles. "Then I have no choice but to sue for peace, what heavy toll will you demand of me and my people, what assets will you strip from this once proud nation?" Her face felt imperious as she spoke; she felt like the last vestige of nobility, giving way to a tyrant who would destroy her.

"The King wants only peace Ma'am, not your assets. A collaboration of our two great nations could see a new way forward, a third way, if you will." She was forced to acknowledge that in some hard to define way, this half worn away man had even managed to beat her in the nobility and human dignity stakes as he spoke with such courage and charm. By her own admission, she barely stood a chance. "Perhaps Madam Mayor, you would agree to meet with my superior Officer?"

She nodded once and the General stepped back towards the door and stood at attention. His body as straight as a cast iron beam in a vaulted roof. "Sir, The Mayor of Winscombe has agreed to discuss her terms with you, Sir."

An elderly and tired looking man in a poorly fitting set of battle field greens entered the pub and wandered slowly over to Demonika and held out his hand. "All right there, love, my name's Fred Bear Rug, I am one of the King's best mates." He grinned a disarming and surprisingly friendly smile at her as she shook his warm and soft leather feeling hand. "Come one then, let's get this mess all sorted out". He led her out of the pub towards a small cart that appeared to have no horse pulling it. At the controls sat a happy and jovial man who showed her to her seat and waited as Fred gently strapped her in. "Don't worry love, it is not to stop you running away, it is to stop you falling off!"

Once he was sure that she was safely secured, Fred jumped up onto the back of the cart and tapped the driver on the shoulder, "OK Eelom old chap, take us up the road a bit and let's meet the Royal party."

The driver whistled and the two hairy beings who were stood in the centre of the wheel let out excited squeals and grunts as the frog on a stick was jerked into bored wakefulness by a sharp tug. The journey was exhilarating and the speed almost terrifying as the cart shot up the road at almost twenty miles per hour. For a brief happy moment, Demonika almost forgot that she was heading to a serious meeting with the man who had defeated her armies in battle. But as the cart swayed perilously close to the outside edge of a high speed corner, she saw the tented village of the Norfcorian encampment ahead. On each side of the approach road, the men of the defeated Somerset Army sat around small camp fires, tucking greedily into Norfcorian food parcels. As Demonika stared at her humiliated troops, she became acutely aware that some of the men wore strange robes and seemed to be practising odd little dances while also trying to apply thick white face paint that made them look like young Norfcorean school girls! Bewildered she barely had time to question the thoughts in her head, but seeing her confused look, Fred took the time to explain how the men had been encouraged to express themselves in the arts, which included the finest opera that Norfcoria had to offer. "That, Madam, is the men learning to let go of their anger and their hate through the use of drama and song. The exact production is one of great joy among our people and tells the story of three Norfcorean school girls who sing together." Demonika shook her head in dismay and within seconds, the cart was careering towards a sliding stop with the driver pulling hard on the brake lever with all of his weight. Waiting outside of a large and fancy looking tent stood Sharon, the Aid du Champ and King Jong the First. All of them were dressed in fine robes of state and the King even appeared to be joking with his staff. When he saw Demonika approach his face became more serious, but the kind soft humour stayed in his eyes, even when the rest of his face looked more severe.

Fred helped Demonika from the cart and kept hold of her hand as she tottered through the mud in her huge heels, being finally presented to the King. His voice was as soft and graceful as a songbird on the first full day of summer. "Madam Mayor, after all of the harsh words and terrible injuries that our fighting has inflicted upon our peoples, may we please sit down in peace and enjoy a meal together as we discuss how to prevent this tragedy from happening ever again?"

"Your Highness, as much as I would love to sit with you and break bread, so to speak, you stand here in my country, not as a friend, but as an invader. My people and I are unable to resist you, so why the pretence of asking me if I will sit, when you can instead simply demand it of me?"

"Here we fucking go again!" The words were barely audible, the exasperated sigh of a man far too used to petty arguments and foul moods. For a moment not even the King could trace where the words had come from, he turned around and it was only when he found that the Aid du Champ had gone almost purple with embarrassment that he found the source.

"I beg your pardon?" The King stared at his

main political adviser, his eyes narrow slits of suspicion.

"I am most terribly sorry Sire, it was an entirely involuntary remark. It will not happen again, I promise you." The Aid du Champ looked as if he would welcome being swallowed whole by the Earth and then his eyes met the incredulous eyes of Demonika.

"Well blow me down a well! Terry, is that you?"

The Aid du Champ tried to hide behind the King, but King Jong pushed him forwards and towards his ex-wife.

"Well really, if I had known that it was you leading this army, I would never have surrendered when I did!"

The King coughed politely causing all people in attendance to turn their attention back to him. "Madam, please come this way. We may have a solution to the problems that our two great nations face."

Inside the tent, a large table was set up for fine dining, there were seats for all of the King's main advisers and a large grand chair for Demonika. She sat down and picked up the wine glass that had been filled for her and almost swallowed the contents in one go. A Norfcorean waiter filled her glass as she put it back down and gave her a look of mild disdain as she tried to reach for it again. From his own seat, the King addressed her. "Madam Mayor of Winscombe, leader of the whole of Somerset, it is with gratitude that I welcome you to this summit." He paused and allowed the waiter to fill his own glass. "I would like to introduce to you my advisers, some of whom you already know." He pointed to Sharon first, "this fine woman is my closest friend and also my finest adviser, her name is Sha Wren Ston. Next is my friend and adviser Fred Bare Rug and finally, although I understand that you already know my Aid du Champ, Terry Dak

Til." Demonika looked to each person as they were introduced and gave them a curt little smile. As the King fell silent and raised his glass to her, she lifted her own and he made the toast. "Madam Mayor, a toast to you and the growing peace between us." He took a sip of the sparkling wine and sat back down gracefully, his face unreadable and his dark eyes hidden in shadow. All the other faces at the table appeared to be watching Demonika, waiting for her to do something or to stand and say something. The Aid du Champ coughed at her quietly, the tiniest of throat clearings, whilst also nodding at her to stand up. She decided to wait and see what he would do, a smile of cunning forming upon her face.

Finally, after a few moments of embarrassed silence, the Aid du Champ stood up and raised his glass to her. "Demonika, it has been a very long time since we last spoke, the decades have likely turned into centuries." He peered at her for a moment, his glass hung in the air from his ancient frail hand. "You do appear to be as ravishingly beautiful in old age as you were in your youth."

Sharon almost choked on her drink and she glared angrily at the old man as he sat back down. She turned to Demonika and without false smile or hidden words addressed her clearly and quietly. "Look, this shit is all well and good, but basically, this war has fucked everything up. You know and we know that from here we either invade your nation or we march out and leave you, which looks bad on both of our parts." She paused for a moment and then with a glance to the King who remained utterly inscrutable, continued her quiet speech. "The King here proposes that we both bugger off back to our respective kingdoms and that we then have some sort of trade agreement." The King nodded his head briefly and Sharon continued. "Basically, we export our food into your place and you export those fantastic horseless carriages into Norfcorea. We sign a trade agreement and before you know, our nations are suddenly remarkably rich. Our food gets known around the Fairy realm, your carriages go global. Both of us have the markets sewn up. We can't bloody lose!"

Sharon sat back in her chair, triumphant. Her face almost as unreadable as the King's.

Demonika sat back in her chair, sipped at her drink and carefully thought about the proposition set before her. "Who pays to clean up the custard fields, that stuff will need shovelling out."

Sharon spoke again, her voice official sounding and firm. "Both nations cover the cost, weapons were fired by both sides."

Demonika considered again, "What about injured troops and their pensions?"

Again with a nod from the King, Sharon leaned forwards and spoke authoritatively. "Our hospitals are leaders in their fields. We will happily treat all veterans from both sides at no cost to your nation. Those carriages can be fashioned to act as ambulance carts to bring the injured to us."

There was one final hurdle to overcome and both the King and Demonika knew that it had to be mentioned. Placing her glass back on to the place mat she shifted in the chair and leaned forwards to address the King directly. "OK, say I agree to all of this stuff? What about Wuffles? If I agree, I get him back. Otherwise, no deal."

Sharon was about to speak, but the firm, yet delicate, voice of King Jong the First made her sit back in silence.

"Madam Mayor, in my time as King, I have met many of my subjects, I have spoken with delegations from all of the realms and have been given a royal blessing by King Bobney himself." He fell silent for a moment, allowing his words to sink in. "Yet I find that I have never met another soul who has the courage, the wisdom and the generosity of spirit as that of Wuffles." All heads around the table nodded in agreement and the King waited briefly, before speaking again, his voice quiet and well spoken. "Wuffles came to us of his own free will, we do not hold him in our palace against his will. He is free at any time that he chooses to go to where ever he so wishes. Wuffles has been given citizenship of Norfcorea as an act of friendship between him and us. I cannot and do not speak for him. As such Madam Mayor, you must direct your question to him yourself." The King looked up and signalled with a small nod to one of his staff. The young woman approached the King and stood silently by his side until he addressed her. "Please would you ask Wuffles to join us?" The young woman nodded once, bowed to the king and left the tent. For several minutes the tent contained silent thoughtful people and then the small doorway opened and the young woman entered again, followed by Wuffles. His fur had been brushed, his ears cleaned out and his nails clipped. A small bench had been brought to the table and covered with a soft pad and it was onto this that Wuffles delicately climbed up and sat down, equal to all who sat around him.

Chapter 8:- God, the Devil and the agoraphobic

The Rusty Plough in Little Smirda was silent, the Afghan hound puppies had long gone and Wuffles had not been back in weeks. With no patrons, the owner of the bar had shut the door and retired upstairs finishing off his favourite crime show box set on DVD. He was half way through an episode when he heard the music start in the bar, the tune was mournful as the delicate tones of Roy Orbison could be heard warbling through the floor. Wuffles was sat in front of the fire when the pub owner came downstairs carrying a fresh slice of Gala Pie. He placed the china plate on the floor in front of Wuffles and scratched him between ears, after which Wuffles bent low and began to nibble the food delicately, enjoying the subtle flavours of machine made food. Everyone likes junk food every now and again, he thought to himself.

"You alright Wuffles ol' mate?" The pub owner sat down on the plush looking but ultimately cheaply made seat. "Not see you for a few months. Looks like you have been well looked after though."

Wuffles finished his pie and looked up into the eyes of the pub owner. His expression was unusual for a dog and strangely the owner seemed to understand what it meant. Wuffles wagged his tail a few times and the meaning flooded through.

"No problem Wuffles, you want tap or sparkling?"

Wuffles whined slightly and tapped the floor with his front paw.

"Of course mate, never a problem for you. Coming right up." The owner wandered across to the bar and looked in the fridge for a bottle of sparkling water, and, finding what he wanted, cracked the top and poured the contents into a pudding bowl and took it over to where Wuffles was sat and placed the bowl on the floor. "Here you go mate."

Wuffles licked at the refreshing water, enjoying his fill before laying down once again. It was clear that he was waiting for something because once or twice he looked up at the wall mounted clock and let out a gentle sigh. After twenty minutes a quiet roar could just be heard in the distance. As the seconds passed, it grew louder, the unmistakeable steady thud of a motorcycle engine, the lazy v-twin type of American manufacture. The roar became a heavy thudding growl and it quickly became obvious that another bike was approaching with it. The Pub owner wandered across to the door and was about to slide the lock across and turn off the lights when Wuffles, seeing what he was doing, whined and flapped his tail on the floor twice. "Really? In here? OK, if you say so, but at the first sign of trouble I am phoning the law. It took me months to clean this place up after the last owner left, I don't want it ruined by a load of dirty bikers."

Wuffles barked and whined, his ears forwards and his teeth bared. The pub owner wandered behind the bar as he continued to chat. "Well Wuffles mate, I will hold you to that. Any mess and you clean it up." He laughed gently, "You know, I doubt any other pub in the country allows a dog to choose the patrons."

The pub door swung open and three large men wandered into the bar, each one clad in heavy black leather jackets, black leather jeans and black motorcycle boots. Each man wore a patch on the back of his jacket, a Howling coyote with a silver face and beneath that a club made of three crossed pistons. Across the bottom of their jackets was one large embroidered word. Winscombe. The three men walked up to the bar, each looking somehow terrifying, as if they were wearing the uniform of some dark underground militia. The leader spoke, his voice barely above a whisper, his tone darkly impressive.

"Oh good afternoon there, if I may, I would

like a glass of sweet sherry please? My comrade Jack would adore a white wine spritzer and our good friend Dave would like a diet cola, perhaps with a slice of lime in the top?"

The pub owner blinked in surprise and for a second was unable to speak. The two men stood behind their leader, looked around and choosing a table wandered across the room to sit down in a quiet corner away from the music player. Finally the owner was able to stammer out a few words, "err, certainly. Can I get you a menu, we are doing a special this week on bar sandwiches, made with local ham and beef?"

The Biker gazed at him, his face unreadable, the pub owner could not tell if the man was about to rob him or thank him, but the man's quiet reply was still surprising. "That is jolly decent of you old chap, unfortunately Dave and I are both vegetarian and Jack gets terrible heart burn if he eats bread, it's the gluten I'm afraid. How much do we owe you for the drinks?"

Wuffles wandered across the bar and after rooting in his purse, dropped three heavy gold coins on the bar and groaned slightly, while waggling his ears, the bar man translated. "He says that the drinks are on him."

The President of the bike club smiled gently, "hey man, you don't need to translate my brother's words for me, we speak the same language."

The barman wandered across to where Wuffles had placed his gold coins and swept the coins up in his hand and looked at them. They were from a place that he knew could not exist and in a currency that he could never spend. He grinned and walked out from behind the bar and over towards Wuffles.

"Hey Wuffles, you know the house rules, we use English pounds here. He tossed the coins to the dog who caught them easily. "Those things are worth more in their weight in pure gold than you have ever spent here, so the drinks are on the house, you know that. Go and join your mates, I will close up and leave you all to chat. I will be upstairs if you need me."

The barman stepped back behind the bar and left, back up the stairs to his crime box set and settled into his favourite chair, making it through two episodes before he fell asleep, snoring lightly and leaving a fleck of dribble in his neatly trimmed goatee beard. He awoke to the sudden sound of a motorcycle engine roaring into life and as he sat up, he heard a sound of something or someone climbing the private stairs that led to his flat above the pub.

The living room door slowly opened and from the near darkness of the hallway came the head and shoulders of Wuffles, tongue hanging peacefully from his mouth, tail slowly and happily wagging.

"Hey boy, you never been up here before, you want a bite to eat or something?"

Wuffles sat down and shook his head, his sad eyes and gentle face almost made it look like he was smiling.

"Well, you are always welcome, you know that, especially when the wife is away at her sister's, I like the company."

Wuffles whined slightly and flopped his ears forwards and then back again before closing his eyes and sighing. The pub owner watched with a growing sense of sadness.

"Oh man, I am sorry to hear it. But you have to follow your heart boy and you do what feels right." He paused for a moment and then asked the obvious question. "Why did you need to see those biker lads?"

Wuffles made a strange chuckling noise and drummed both of his paws on the floor in front of him, his ears darted back and forth and then he let out a slow growl. The pub owner sat back incredulous.

"Really?" He settled in his chair, his face full of wonder, "you mean to say that I had God and the Devil in my pub?" He paused for a moment, his face in deep concentration. "Oh hang on, what about the other one, the big one, with sergeant of arms on his patch, who was he?"

Wuffles groaned and whined a few times and then hid his eyes with his paws and growled! The pub owner laughed and slapped the arm of his chair.

"Really, he's an agoraphobic? Who would have

thought it?"

When Wuffles stood up again, he held his head tilted to one side, ears forwards and let out a soft groan. He walked forwards and rested his head on the man's lap and whined again, the man lifted his hand and for one last time gently scratched the old dog fondly between the ears.

"Well old boy, if you ever pass by these parts again, do please call in for a pie and a pint."

* * * * *

The Aid du Champ to the court of the Kingdom

of Norfcorea sat at a café table with his ex-wife and said nothing. Sat directly across from him, Demonika was equally silent, a silence with an almost violent intent against the noise about them. Finally she spoke. "Have you seen anything of our son?"

"No, not recently. I tried phoning him, but he got confused and flushed the phone down the toilet."

She laughed quietly, the real humour of it almost creasing her make up. "I went to visit him a couple of weeks ago and he got so excited, he crashed his moped into a slurry pit full of cow shit. It was not nice and it it took me three hours to clean him up."

It was the turn of the Aid du Champ to laugh.

"Did he really, why am I not surprised? Is he still hanging around with that bike club?"

Demonika nodded her head, "He is. I have something over the club vice president, so although they don't want him, they have no choice but to keep him. I did buy him a new moped though, a nice little pink one with pedals. He was very pleased with it. It matches his little safety helmet."

For a moment both of them were silent, a waiter delivered a tray of drinks to the table and laid out a steaming cup of tar-like black coffee for her and a dark gold pint of finest scrumpy cider for him. Demonika lifted her incredibly strong espresso coffee and sipped the acrid liquid within, with no sugar to sweeten the bite of the oil black liquid and no cream to mellow the taste, it was just as she liked it, strong and bitter. The silence returned, an awkward painful silence, the only thing it lacked was a loud ticking clock to signal the passing seconds of their shared misery. Finally, she broke inside and the words flooded from her."Look, I am sorry I left you, but I had little Guppy to care for and you were off invading foreign countries. I felt like a single mother, only without the perks of being single."

He sighed, his head dropped sadly. "Look, I know that I should have been a more attentive husband, but it was the bronze age, they were really getting into war back then, it was my job."

"You always put your work before your family though, didn't you? We were always second to that. You were away more than you were home. Poor little Guppy had no clue who you were right up until his seventieth birthday." She sipped from her cup again and placed it back on the saucer on the table.

"You make it sound like I was a terrible husband, I tried my best, but those were busy times." He paused sulkily, "How many times were you called away for some voodoo curse or some such thing?"

Her eyes flared with anger, her skin almost

turned incandescent, the most observant might even have noticed that her feet seemed to burst into flames for a few fractions of a second where they touched the ground. "I was the goddess of the witches, it was my fucking job too, but oh no, I was married to the god of fucking war and his job always came first. No matter how many witches had their prayers unanswered or how many lonely elderly ladies were burned at the stake because I was busy breast feeding our son. You had to be off waging war on some unfortunate bloody nation or other." She lifted her cup and slurped back the dregs of evil brew within and slammed the cup back down, sending the saucer slithering across the table. "And another thing, where were you during the great plague? I bet that you were balls deep in the disease goddess!"

"Well if it is infidelity you want to talk about, how come our son is half fucking human?" He lifted his pint and held it in the air for a few seconds and then put it back down, sloshing some of the golden liquid over the tabletop. "Funny when two Gods can create life together and it turns out to be half fucking human and to cap it all, I swear that he had goat genes in him too! What were you thinking woman?"

"Don't you start on poor little Guppy, I love that boy with all of my being. Anyway, I was lonely and you were gone for three whole centuries. It was one slip. How many innocent virgins did you bed on your travels?" His face went scarlet with shame and she continued. "After an eternity in this realm, I slipped once and have never been with anyone else since. I missed you so much. You used to come home, stinking of blood and guts and death and then I'd treat your wounds, wash your back in the bath and then you would present me with some gift from your spoils of war. I still have them all you know." She reached inside her blouse and pulled out a golden ring held on a long silver necklace chain. "I still have my ring, I could not bear to throw it away, even after all of these years."

He reached inside his tunic and pulled out a heavy chain that also held a thick golden wedding ring. "I kept mine too, throwing it away just felt wrong. That is why I never stopped the alimony."

She smiled, her face gentle and feminine. "I used your money to buy gifts for our son, I paid for the finest education, got him the best presents and made sure that he had the very best of Nannies when I was away on business. He wanted for nothing."

"Except brains!"

They both laughed and very slowly each

reached out a hand until with a flash of lightening from the heavens, they held hands, albeit briefly.

* * * * *

The King of Norfcorea stood in his kitchen, the baked Alaska he had prepared as a leaving dish for his friend was perfect. He lifted it from the oven and carried the dish through to the grand dining room. Sat waiting at the table were Sharon, Fred, Wuffles and the inventor of the horseless carriage. When they saw what the King had prepared they applauded loudly and Wuffles let out a gentle but strangely comforting howl. The king lifted the serving slice and cut slabs of achingly glorious pudding and placed a good sized portion on the fine china plates and passed them around. When each person at the table had a pudding, he lifted his glass and tapped the side gently with a dessert fork.

"Friends, we have much to celebrate and much to commiserate. Firstly our dear friend Wuffles has decided that he wishes to travel the realm and discover new and exciting dishes. It is an odyssey indeed and I wish that I could undertake your journey with you, but alas the duties of state prevent such travels, so we bid you a final farewell old friend and wish you many happy days ahead. Should you ever pass through our Kingdom again, you will be made as welcome as a member of the royal family." The people around the table applauded gently and Wuffles let out a soft bashful whine of happiness. The King continued his speech as soon as everyone was quiet again. "We also need to welcome our new friend Eelom, the inventor of the horseless carriage, a man who has done more for the relations between Norfcorea and the city of Winscombe than any other person alive." Again the guests around the table applauded loudly and Eelom waved them away with friendly laughter.

"But that is not all friends, we also have some news of a more personal nature to someone at this table." The King turned to Sharon and asked her to stand up, which she did while slowly blushing. "I understand that Sharon's wonderful boyfriend has finally popped the question!" Again there was more applause and Sharon almost folded in half, as she giggled happily. Even Wuffles who normally restrained his more natural actions, lovingly licked her hand and wagged his tail. "So Sharon," continued the King grandly, "Show us the rock he gave you?" She raised her hand and upon her finger was the most exquisite diamond ring, the gem stone although tastefully small, was also a delicate shade of faint pink, the band beneath it was made with normal gold entwined with fairy gold and the effect was stunningly beautiful.

The King raised his glass and led them in a toast, "To old friends, new friends and beloved friends, may you always find joy where ever you find yourselves."

They raised their glasses and drank and then sat down to the finest pudding the King had ever made.

* * * * *

The Rusty Plough in Winscome, the capital city of the country of Somerset had sat empty and deserted for months. A ragged 'for sale' sign had sat in the window until it finally fell down and read simply as Or Sale. With no punters spilling drink and with no people weeing in the corners, the carpet was finally able to dry out and when it did, it shrank back to reveal a beautiful polished floor mosaic of ancient and magical powers. Trapped within the picture was a cursed magician and the curse that trapped him, was to hold him there until pure sunlight fell across him once again. The Or Sale sign slipped in the window once more and simply read Ale, the sun shone across it and splashed across the mosaic with a glorious golden light that crept across the floor to the face of the cursed magician. Finally, as the rays released him, he leapt from the floor and choked as the dust left his clothing. He stared in relief around the rotten pub and then noticed what had become of his once beautiful home; he could have howled with anguish, but instead he flourished his wand and prepared his incantation. Everything would soon be back to how it was.

* * * * *

The Mothers of Troubled Children support group sat in a small circle. The therapist was new and she sat there with the professional calm of a certified psychopath. Felicity Goldstein was the first to speak.

"Little Isaac came home in a bit of a temper. He had somehow put on close to three stone in weight and we have had to send him to kids' fat camp. He has now however decided that he is no longer that awful man. Instead, he is now obsessed with Batman, which is, in some ways, far worse. Last week, he arrested old Mrs Portcullis after he accused her of shoplifting in the supermarket. It caused a terrible fuss."

Angela Thorn spoke next, her usual callous crispness was gone, her clothing had taken on a new look, a strange sort of adventure or travel suit with trousers that had more pockets than seemed actually usable. "It seems that while he was away, young Freddie has finally learned some manners. It also seems that he has become obsessed with adventurous military types and is even now excelling in the scouts. I am now the Akela of the local troop and he wants to be the next Baden Powell when he grows up! At least he has stopped claiming to be the saviour of Africa."

The final speaker was Stacey Faherty, her face was drawn, her eyes strangely dark, as if she were wearing an awful lot of eye-liner. "It appears that my darling Zepherine has discovered her dark side and has now become a Goth. She raves about ravens knocking on chamber doors and insists that I am not allowed to dress in modern colours anymore. I have to dress like I am attending a Victorian funeral, but it seems cruel not to indulge her a little. Well she looks so pretty sleeping in her custom coffin bed. Mind you, I caught her in the garden last week decapitating her dolls, which was a little unsettling, but at least she talks to us now and has stopped accusing us of being in the Securitate!"

The therapist made her notes in careful italics and noted that all three woman were probably close to emotional collapse, if not physical exhaustion. Finally she spoke, her accent heavy with a Viennese twang. "Well it is so gratifying to finally meet some mothers who have so much to discuss."

The End

The Wuffles Play List

Dearest Wuffles, the Hell Hound is a delicate soul. His enjoys art, poetry and music, but when he feels down, he goes to the Rusty Plough in Little Smirda and puts his favourite tracks into the Duke Box.

These are those tracks, so please, find them in your record collection, buy them on CD or just listen to them on line and think of Wuffles, as he wanders the never ending road of adventure.

Artist	Song
Roy Orbison	Only the lonely
Elvis Presley	Heartbreak Hotel
John Leyton	Johnny remember me
Ricky Valance	Tell Laura I love her
The Animals	House of the rising sun
Elvis Presley	Are you lonesome tonight
Percy Sledge	When a man loves a woman
Rolling Stones	Paint it black
The Shangri-Las	Leader of the pack
Johnny Cash	Hurt

About the Authors

Margaret Ingram

Margaret Ingram is a genius level engineer and writer, she is also the Head Honcho of the writer's club, the main teacher and inspiration to the other members. She may not believe it, but she is the glue that holds them all together.

Sally Ann Nixon

Sally Anne is a writer and inheritor of fine antiques, rescue cats and family furniture all of which need a lot of upkeep. Beloved among the group, she leads an eventful life, full of incidents that anyone sane would avoid. It does make good writing material though.

Jan Housby

Jan is a peaceful and ethereal young woman, with her heart and soul firmly in the land of fairy. A determined keeper of cats and ferrets, she can often be found in hedgerows fighting off little folk!

Geraldine Paige

Geraldine likes to write short children's stories and poems. She also enjoys Spanish dancing and singing with her local choir. She is devilishly good fun with a subtly naughty side to her.

Margaret McNerlin

Margaret has been writing poetry for quite a few years and literally fell head over heels for writing stories, as she fell down a flight of steps at her first visit to the writers club! She hopes to be able to continue with her writing for some time, in both her preferred genres, and she hopes you enjoy what she writes.

Jayne Hecate

Jayne is a simple misanthropic writer with an urge to tell dark and evil stories. When not writing, she can be found skulking in her office, listening to loud Black Metal or chasing villagers across the moors.

Carol Jadzia

Carol is an experienced Photographer, biker and put upon Spouse of Jayne Hecate. When not snapping pics of her Motorbike, Carol can be found whizzing along the major roads of Britain, marveling at how many idiots are allowed a driving license. She is also the photographer and provides our cover images.

Thanks

The club would like to thank all members, readers and kind souls who indulge us in our passion for writing by buying this book.

Thank you to all of the authors who have submitted their work to make up this book, which is probably a bit self serving, given that we do this so we can see our names in print in an actual book!

However, thanks must go as always, to our Glorious Leader, Head Honcho AKA Margaret, who writes us a lesson each month and with patience, kindness and occasional outbursts of extreme violence, teaches us to be better writers.

We would also like to thank Carol for providing the cover photographs once again. She very kindly gave us the pictures this time, so no further water boarding was required!

Jayne would like to thank Margaret for not killing her while they edited the damn book!

Margaret would like to thank Jayne for working for hours on the stupid thing!

Also Available

The First Compendium…

Available to Buy now in paperback and e-Book format from Amazon today.